SHOOTING STAR

SHOOTING STAR

CYNTHIA RIGGS

This Large Print edition is published by Wheeler Publishing, Waterville, Maine, USA and by BBC Audiobooks Ltd, Bath, England.
Wheeler Publishing is an imprint of The Gale Group.
Wheeler is a trademark and used herein under license.

The text of this Large Print edition is unabridged.
Other aspects of the book may vary from the original edition.
Set in 16 pt. Plantin.

LIBRARY OF CONGRESS CATALOGING-IN-PUBLICATION DATA

Riggs, Cynthia.
    Shooting star / by Cynthia Riggs.
      p. cm.
    "A Martha's Vineyard Mystery"—T.p. verso.
    ISBN-13: 978-1-59722-558-8 (hardcover : alk. paper)
    ISBN-10: 1-59722-558-4 (hardcover : alk. paper)
    1. Trumbull, Victoria (Fictitious character) — Fiction. 2. Women detectives — Massachusetts — Martha's Vineyard — Fiction. 3. Martha's Vineyard (Mass.) — Fiction. 4. Women poets — Fiction. 5. Older women — Fiction. 6. Actors — Crimes against — Fiction. 7. Large type books. I. Title.
    PS3618.I394S56 2007b
    813'.6—dc22   2007019902

BRITISH LIBRARY CATALOGUING-IN-PUBLICATION DATA AVAILABLE

Published in 2007 in the U.S. by arrangement with
St. Martin's Press, LLC.
Published in 2007 in the U.K. by arrangement with the author.

U.K. Hardcover: 978 1 405 64242 2 (Chivers Large Print)
U.K. Softcover: 978 1 405 64243 9 (Camden Large Print)

Printed in the United States of America on permanent paper
10 9 8 7 6 5 4 3 2 1

For
Dionis Coffin Riggs
poet
1898–1997

ACKNOWLEDGMENTS

Victoria Trumbull (or at least I, her amanuensis) has now completed the Tisbury Citizen Police Academy and has a certificate proving it. Many thanks to former Tisbury Police Chief Theodore (Ted) Saunier, who not only taught the rigorous and informative course, but who vetted my manuscript to make sure Victoria was using the right terminology and following correct procedures, and that the characters were handling guns properly.

As always, Jonathan Revere provided much of the inspiration behind the story, including the true account of his picking up hitchhikers at midnight while still in costume.

Dawn Haines is a real person, transmogrified into a snippy teenage actress, which she's not. At a fund-raiser for Vermont College's MFA scholarship program, Dawn won the grand opportunity of having her name immortalized along with Victoria's in addition to a weekend at the Cleaveland House bed-and-breakfast.

Thanks to the members of my two writers' groups, especially Jacqueline Sexton, Jeanne Hewett, and Shirley W. Mayhew, who insisted, despite my protests, that I change the names I'd started with. I did, and they were right. But all the following members worked to make the book better, including Rev. Bonna Whitten-Stovall (Southern Baptist), Rev. Judy Campbell (Unitarian-Universalist), Rev. Mary Jane O'Conner-Ropp (Methodist), and Rabbi Carla Theodore, all of whom made sure I wrote a straight line. And to writers Wendy Hathaway, Carolyn O'Daly, Ernie Weiss, Nelson W. Potter, Ethel Sherman, Charles Blank, Sally Williams, Barbara and Jack Moment, Barbara Linton (who attended the police academy with me, including a field trip one sleeting February night when she was on crutches), Gerry Jackman Dean, Ann Hammond, and others who've made suggestions that I listened to.

Thanks to Alvida and Ralph Jones and to Ann and Bill Fielder, who've gone over every one of my manuscripts.

A special thanks to Arlene Silva, who triggered this outpouring of words. She must feel like the Sorcerer's Apprentice, unable to stop the flow.

A final thanks to Islanders, West Tisbury villagers in particular, for providing me with characters and ideas — none based on actual people and events, of course. Someone once claimed that I'm killing off everyone on the Island I'm mad at, but that's simply not true.

*A Play in Three Acts Presented by
the Island Players*
FRANKENSTEIN UNBOUND
*A stage adaptation
by Victoria Trumbull
of*
Frankenstein, *or,* The Modern Prometheus
by Mary Shelley

**Cast members
in order of their appearance**

Robert Walton,
   the Arctic explorer . . . . . *Bob Scott*
Victor Frankenstein,
   the monster's creator . . . *Dearborn Hill*
The Monster . . . . . *Howland Atherton*
Henry Clerval, Victor's
   boyhood friend . . . . . *Bruce Duncan*
Monsieur De Lacey, the monster's
   adopted father . . . . . *Gerard Cohen*
Felix De Lacey,
   M. De Lacey's son . . . . . *Jeff Brown*
Agatha De Lacey,
   M. De Lacey's daughter . . *Toni Ferreira*
Safie, M. De Lacey's
   adopted daughter . . . . *TBA*
Elizabeth Lavenza,
   Victor's bride . . . . . . *Dawn Haines*
Alphonse Frankenstein,
   Victor's father . . . . *TBA*

11

William Frankenstein, Victor's
five-year-old brother   . *Teddy Vanderhoop*
Justine Moritz, the Frankensteins'
housekeeper . . . . *Peg Storm*

Understudies

Victor Frankenstein . . . . . *Billy Amaral*
The Monster . . . . *Roderick Hill*
Elizabeth Lavenza . . . . *TBA*

Ruth Byron, Founder of the Island Players
Dearborn Hill, Artistic Director

CHAPTER 1

Act One ended when Justine was hanged.

Victoria Trumbull, the ninety-two-year-old poet and playwright, sat in an aisle seat near the front of the theater watching the dress rehearsal of her adaptation of *Frankenstein.* For this occasion she wore her best suit, dark green plaid, and a blouse with a soft bow at the neck. She sat tall and held her head high. Her eagle-beak nose jutted out between deep-set, hooded eyes.

Dearborn Hill, artistic director for the Island Players, a large man with theatrically rumpled white hair, climbed up the steps to the stage.

"That wraps up Act One, people. Peg and Teddy have to leave early, so I'll go over the notes now for their parts." He checked his watch. "The rest of you take a forty-five-minute break. I want you back here at eight-thirty."

"Isn't Peg staying for the full rehearsal?"

13

called out a girl's voice from behind Victoria in the auditorium.

Dearborn Hill shaded his eyes against the footlights and looked out over the dark seats. "I can't see you, Dawn, but no, she won't be staying." He strode to stage left and back again, slapping a rolled-up copy of Victoria's script against his thigh. "For those of you new to acting," he gestured at the dim figures in the auditorium, "a professional production would not break during dress rehearsal. The cast would remain backstage."

"Professional!?!" Dawn again, a touch of insolence in her voice.

Dearborn went on, ignoring her. "Before you leave, I have an announcement. Some of you may already have heard that Teddy Vanderhoop has been offered a juvenile lead in a new television series." He took a few steps, turned, and looked out at his unseen audience. "His mother is in California now, negotiating with the producers. Until her return, Teddy is staying with Peg, whose part is over, of course, when Justine is hanged." Dearborn allowed himself a small smile.

"Mr. Hill?"

"Yes, Dawn?"

"His mom will miss opening night tomorrow."

14

Dearborn frowned and turned to Teddy Vanderhoop, a slight, redheaded eight-year-old, who had come out from the wings to stand next to Peg on stage. "An actor's life, right, young man?"

Teddy looked down at his feet and dug the toes of his untied high-top sneakers into the floorboards.

Dearborn held up his hands. "That's all, folks."

Victoria heard sounds of lifted seats, low conversation, and shuffling feet before the theater was quiet again.

Teddy was acting the part of five-year-old William Frankenstein, the first victim of the monster created by his big brother, Victor. Peg Storm was playing Justine, the Frankenstein family's housekeeper.

Dearborn strode over to the wings and returned with a bentwood chair. He straddled it, his arms folded over the back, the play script in hand.

Teddy waited uncertainly.

"You may step down, Teddy," said Dearborn.

As he came down the steps from the stage, Teddy glanced around. Victoria waved her copy of the play at him and moved over one seat so he could sit next to her.

"I hate that man," Teddy whispered.

15

"He can be difficult," Victoria agreed. "But he's quite a good director."

Onstage, Dearborn pointed his rolled-up script at Peg. "More emotion, Justine. Sorrow over little William's death. When you're on trial, show surprise, misery. Confidence that you'll be exonerated." He stood up. "Graceful suffering in the face of injustice. Even your name is a play on the word justice."

"Yeah," Teddy muttered to Victoria.

"Hush!" said Victoria.

Dearborn Hill pushed his chair to one side and opened the script. "Take it from where Justine says, 'God knows how entirely I am innocent.' I'll read the other parts."

Peg had never acted in a play before. Teddy's mother, who loved the theater, had urged her to try out for the role of Justine, and here she was now, on stage. Acting.

Partway through the rehearsal, Dearborn stopped and flicked his hand on the script. "More emotion, Justine." He put the script under his arm, clasped his hands, and looked up to where the judge would be sitting. " 'I commit my cause to the justice of my judges.' Avert your eyes." He opened the script and read, gesturing with his hand toward the judge's bench, " 'I pledge my salvation on my innocence.' " He looked

16

over at Peg. "This is, of course, an overly sentimental line, but Mrs. Trumbull has captured the feeling of the late 1700s in her script. And, I believe, she's taken much of the dialogue directly from Mary Shelley's book." He looked out into the dark auditorium. "Isn't that right, Mrs. Trumbull?"

"That's right," said Victoria.

Teddy made a gurgling noise.

Dearborn turned back to Peg. "Once more."

Peg took a deep breath and went over her lines again.

"Excellent," said Dearborn, after she'd finished. He turned to face the dark theater. "Are you still there, Mrs. Trumbull?"

"Yes," said Victoria. "Third row aisle."

"I may ask you to tweak Justine's lines before tomorrow."

"Isn't it a bit late for that?"

"Some of these archaic passages simply don't play well. We'll make adjustments throughout the run."

Teddy glanced up at Victoria and she smiled.

Dearborn turned back to Peg. "Be here with Teddy an hour before curtain tomorrow night."

"I'm awfully nervous. I'm sure I'll go up on my lines." Peg's smile brightened her somber, made-up face.

"You sound like a professional," Dearborn said. "No need to rehearse a curtain call. At the end of the play, come out with the De Lacey family. Hold Monsieur De Lacey's hand. Remember, the audience believes he's blind."

"Aren't you supposed to tell me to break a leg?"

Dearborn chuckled. "Break a leg, my dear." He turned back to the auditorium. "You out there, Teddy?"

"Yes, sir."

"I'm counting on you to make sure Ms. Storm shows up on time. You're the professional, remember."

From somewhere behind Victoria came a sound that was a combination laugh, snort, and grunt.

Dearborn shaded his eyes. "Someone out there? You, Dawn?"

Victoria turned, but couldn't see anyone in the darkness. Dearborn shrugged and strode off the stage.

Peg and Teddy walked up the hill from the theater. Low sun shone through the trees that lined Franklin Street where she'd parked. At this time of year, early July, sunset wouldn't be for another half-hour.

"I think you're a wonderful actor, Teddy."
Peg put her arm around the boy and hugged
him. "You're the absolute best."

Teddy grinned. He'd wiped off the black-
ing that the makeup woman had used to
cover his big front teeth, and they glistened
in the low evening light.

"I wish I could stay to the end. It's not
like I have school or anything. I mean, it's
summer."

"Tomorrow's opening night. You have to
stay for curtain call. *And* the party after-
wards."

"The party! Promise?"

"Cross my heart and hope to die. While
you were taking off your makeup, I ordered
a pizza from Louis's."

"Awesome," said Teddy. "Large? Pep-
peroni?"

Peg nodded.

"I hate Mr. Hill."

"Teddy!"

"Well, I do. He's a phony. And I hate Mr.
Duncan, too. He likes you a lot, doesn't he?"

"I'm afraid so."

"But you don't like him?"

"Pizza," said Peg.

At Louis's, Peg paid for the pizza and
handed the large flat box to Teddy. The
warm spicy smell filled the car.

Peg's house was next to Teddy's on Job's Neck. The house had been in her family for more than a century, but she'd almost lost it when she and Lennie were divorced after only four years of marriage. She'd bought him out.

The house was on the edge of a bluff overlooking Lagoon Pond and the harbor. A steep wooden stairway ended at a small dock where she used to keep her catboat. Lennie now owned her catboat. She'd see him occasionally, sailing her catboat past her house. For spite.

"Your mom should be calling soon." Peg checked her watch. "Are you excited about moving to California?"

"I guess."

"What does your father think about the move?"

"He told my mother she'd be sorry."

"Oh," said Peg.

"He told her he was going to make *sure* she was sorry. He wants half the money I earn because he's my father. That's what my mother says."

Peg knew more than she wanted to know about divorce. She changed the subject abruptly by pointing to a flock of mallards in the shallow water beyond Maciel Marine. A small skiff rounded Job's Neck and disappeared from view. They could hear the murmur of the outboard motor. Low sun backlighted tall grasses growing in the marsh on the right side of the road.

Peg turned onto the sand road that led to the point. "I'll miss you when you move to California, Teddy. And your mother. You've been good friends."

"Me, too. Can I pick up my bike?"

"Sure. I'll drop you off at your house and while you're riding back to mine, I'll bring in our costumes and the pizza."

"I want to get my comic books, too."

"I'll see you in about ten minutes, then. Don't be too long. Your mother's supposed to call."

"And the pizza will get cold."

Peg parked in her driveway by the side gate and got out with the costumes, leaving the pizza on the front seat. She pushed against the gate and it swung open. That was odd. She was sure she'd latched it to keep Sandy in. She went to the kitchen door, the entrance everyone used, and noticed the door was ajar. Someone hadn't shut it firmly. Like most Islanders, she never locked up. Neighbors walked in and left dishes of food or books they thought she might like, and she did the same. But neighbors usually shut doors and gates when they left.

Where was Sandy? She expected her scruffy mutt to rush out and greet her, barking and wriggling with excitement.

Peg shifted the costumes to one arm and pushed her way in. "Hello, anyone here?" she called out. "Sandy? Here, Sandy!"

When he didn't respond, Peg was sure she knew what had happened. Someone had not latched the door, and Sandy had slipped out through the gate. She'd hear from the Lears, who lived across the road. They were not dog people.

Evening light was fading fast. Through the window over the sink she could see the glow of sunset on the clouds, pink turning to violet. The kitchen was already in shadow. Peg reached for the light switch and flicked it on.

"Damn," she muttered. "Another bulb burned out. Unless the power's off." She looked out through the window and saw lighted windows farther down the point. "I hope it's not a blown fuse."

She felt for the drawer where she kept flashlights, still holding the bulky costumes in one arm. A floorboard creaked in the dining room.

"Hello," she called out. "Is that you, Teddy?"

No one answered. Old houses creaked all by themselves. She shrugged off her feeling of unease. A neighbor had stopped in and the house was resettling.

But where was Sandy? Perhaps the Lears had called the animal control officer. That meant she'd have to pay another fine because Sandy was running loose.

The play had her nerves on edge, the play, with its dark setting, its monster manufactured from spare human parts. And four deaths. Dearborn Hill insisted that Mary Shelley's book was misunderstood. None of the old movie or play adaptations had done the book justice. None was as faithful as Victoria Trumbull's adaptation. Peg supposed he was right, but still . . .

She switched on her flashlight and, by its weak light, went into the dining room, intending to lay the costumes on the table. If the dining room light worked, she would replace the burned-out bulb in the kitchen. She hoped she wouldn't have to go down the steep cellar steps in the dark to change a fuse.

Another board creaked. An old house muttering. When she was a child she loved to lie in bed and listen to this same old house adjust itself to the coolness of night.

She pressed the old-fashioned light button with its mother-of-pearl center. Nothing. What a time for the fuse to blow, when she felt so unsettled, and with Teddy staying over . . .

What was the matter with her? Then she realized what it was. Tomorrow was opening night. For the first time in her life she would face an audience, and she was terrified. How silly. Teddy, eight years old, wasn't the least bit afraid of going on stage. And here she was, thirty-two, and scared to death.

She was about to set the costumes on the table and trek down the steps and across the musty, cobwebby, brick-floored cellar to the fuse box, when she heard footsteps.

"Hello?" she said, now alarmed. "Who is it?"

Suddenly, a light flashed in her face, dazzling her. She shaded her eyes with the hand that still held her own flashlight and tried to see beyond the brightness.

"Who is it?" She laughed nervously.

No answer. The light beam traveled to the room behind her.

"What do you want? Who are you?"

"Where's the boy?" asked a muffled voice.

"The boy?"

"The boy. Teddy. Where is he?"

Was the speaker male or female? Was it someone she knew or not? She couldn't tell.

"He — he's not here."

"Where is he?"

"I — I don't know."

"I want the boy."

"Who are you?"

She sensed movement and ducked instinctively. A gloved hand slapped her on the side of her face.

Peg screamed, dropped the costumes on the floor, and backed away. The intruder was barely visible in the dim light, a shape in dark clothing. Before she could scream again, a hand covered her face. Peg tried to shake her head free of the thick woolen glove. She couldn't breathe. In the background, she heard bicycle tires on the crushed shell of her drive.

"Where's the boy?" The hand moved enough for her to answer.

Instead, she screamed out, "Run, Teddy! Run!" before the glove covered her mouth and nose again.

CHAPTER 2

Two teenaged girls, Tracy and Karen, left Island Java, the coffeehouse in Vineyard Haven, around midnight and stopped partway up the unlighted hill that led out of town. The night was cool for early July, and so clear the two could see the Milky Way above them.

Karen, the taller of the two, pointed to a slow-moving bright streak near the horizon. "Look! A satellite!"

Tracy, the shorter, dark-haired girl, watched the light die out. "A meteor," she said. "An earthgrazer."

"Wow!"

"My Dad always gets us kids up in the middle of a night in August to watch the Perseid meteor shower. He says the meteors come from the tail of a comet."

"Awesome!" said Karen.

Dew had settled on leaves and blades of grass, and as they brushed past hedges in front of closed stores, drops splattered on the brick sidewalk.

They stopped walking, and Tracy held her thumb out. "I feel funny doing this, you know?"

"Roddie said hitchhiking is safe on Martha's Vineyard, that thumbing cuts down on traffic," said Karen.

Tracy peered down the dark hill. "There's not exactly what you'd call, like, a lot of traffic right now. My parents would kill me if they knew I was thumbing rides."

Karen held her hair out of her eyes. "I see a car now."

Tracy looked toward the vehicle. "It's a police car. Going the wrong direction, anyway."

"Well, my parents would kill *me* if they knew I was picking up boys in coffee shops," said Karen.

"He was kind of cute."

"He would be if he took off, like, thirty pounds?"

"That's mean." Tracy turned as headlights flashed into view at the bottom of the hill. "Here comes a car. Smile."

The vehicle, an old, white station wagon, pulled up to the curb. Tracy opened the door on the passenger side. The dome light went on. She leaned down.

"Hi," said the driver. "Where are you going?"

Tracy backed away, put her hands over her mouth and screamed.

"It's okay," said the driver. "I'm in a play."

"What's the matter?" asked Karen. "What is it?"

The driver leaned over the passenger seat and grinned. "It's okay, really," he said again.

Karen, too, stared at the driver, and backed into Tracy. Both girls turned and raced down the dark hill toward the lights and safety of Main Street.

Howland Atherton had expected the police siren. When he heard it and saw the flashing blue lights in his rearview mirror, he sighed and pulled over to the side of the road. He rolled down the window and was searching for his registration in the glove compartment as the police car pulled in behind him. It took a few minutes before the officer got out. Probably checking the license plate. Howland watched in the mirror. The cop hiked up his gun belt, threw back his shoulders, and sucked in his incipient gut. Howland recognized him. Tim Eldredge, one of the state troopers.

Eldredge reached the open window on the

28

driver's side, bent down to speak to Howland, got as far as "Evening, sir. May I see . . ." when he, too, backed off. He straightened up, stumbled, and almost fell.

"Holy shit!" he mumbled. "What are you?"

Ordinarily, Howland would have gotten out of the car, but he thought about the boots he was wearing. The four-inch lifts made him close to six-foot-six, so he remained in the car.

"Atherton, Tim. It's Howland Atherton. I'm coming from dress rehearsal at the playhouse."

The officer moved toward the car, his hand on the butt of his gun. "Could I see your license, sir. And registration."

Howland handed them to the cop, who looked from Howland's picture on the license to Howland, the actor. "Dracula?" he said finally.

Howland sighed again. "Frankenstein's monster."

"A hysterical girl called nine-one-one."

"I figured," said Howland.

"Excuse me, Mr. Atherton, sir, but why in hell did you stop for them? I mean, knowing that you look like that."

"I forgot," said Howland.

"It's pretty realistic, you know, all that

blood and the stitches on your face. No wonder you scared the shit out of them." The cop examined Howland critically. "Bolts coming out of your head. Fangs. Look at those claws, will you. Did you shave off your hair?"

"Bathing cap." Howland tugged it off to show his matted, silver curls.

"I don't think I can cite you for anything. I know where you live if I need you." Eldredge saluted. "My advice, Mr. Atherton, is don't stop for any more hitchhikers tonight."

Howland headed for home again. He'd had nothing to eat since lunch, and his dogs hadn't been fed since early morning. He thought of the cold London broil in his refrigerator. A baked potato. A salad. His mouth watered. His stomach growled.

He had gotten as far as the big, split oak tree at the end of North Road when he heard the police siren again.

Again, he pulled over onto the grassy verge. This time he got out of the car.

Eldredge, who was five-foot-seven, shone the flashlight up into the distorted face, at the stitches, the blood, then down the torn clothing to the clumsy, hairy boots. "The full effect is something else, I gotta tell you."

Howland clawed at the rubbery, blood-soaked makeup, which started to come off his face in dirty, flesh-colored globs.

"If you don't mind, Mr. Atherton, sir, you better leave the makeup on for now." The trooper paused. "I'm afraid, sir, I'll have to ask you to come with me to the police station."

"You arresting me?" muttered Howland. "You got probable cause?"

"All that blood, sir."

"Blood? This isn't blood." Howland stopped pulling at the gory makeup. "What's the trouble, Tim? Can't you locate the girls?"

"No, sir, we can't. But it's something else."

"Not at liberty to tell me, I suppose?"

The trooper coughed softly. "You're in law enforcement, Mr. Atherton. You understand."

Howland leaned a hairy paw on the roof of his car. "I need to get home to feed my dogs."

"I'll call the animal control officer. Joanie will take care of them." Eldredge paused. "This is embarrassing, sir, but according to the rules, I'm supposed to put the cuffs on you."

"What!" said Howland, standing up straight.

"I gotta go by the book, Mr. Atherton.

Hands behind your back, please."

"Wait a goddamn minute," said Howland. "You can't do that."

"Sir, you don't want to be charged with resisting arrest."

"This is outrageous," Howland blurted out. "You know me."

"Yes, sir. DEA. But I've got orders."

Howland muttered something about rights and lawyers and Miranda, all the protests he, himself, had heard from others many times before. Then he turned sullenly, hands behind his back. He looked over his shoulder. "What the hell is going on?"

Eldredge snapped handcuffs on, then led Howland to the open door of the police car. "Sorry about this, Mr. Atherton, sir."

Howland sidled into the back seat and settled himself at an angle so he wouldn't have to lean against his shackled hands. "Not the girls, right?"

"You know I can't tell you, sir."

"Did something happen at the play-house?"

The trooper eyed Howland in the mirror and reached for the radio mike. "I'll call Joanie about your dogs."

"Thanks," Howland muttered.

After the trooper made arrangements with the animal control officer, he rekeyed the radio mike. "I picked up the suspect at the down-Island end of North Road."

Howland leaned forward. "Suspect?"

"Sierra fourteen to eight-six-zero," said the voice on the radio. "Ten-fifteen. One male."

"Jail!" said Howland.

"Ten-four." Eldredge hung up the mike and turned onto State Road heading into West Tisbury. He reached for the button that activated the siren.

Not a car had gone by in either direction.

"For God's sake," Howland growled. "Goddamned cops and robbers. Got to fight your way through traffic, Eldredge?"

Tim Eldredge looked again in the rear-view mirror and withdrew his hand from the button. The headlights, on high beam, reflected off the occasional road sign and the reflective tape on telephone poles. The arboretum and the agricultural hall were dark. Howland could smell new-mown hay in Whiting's pasture as they drove past.

The radio crackled and Eldredge lifted the mike.

"What's your location, Tim?"

"I'm on Deadman's Curve. Passing the cemetery."

"You going by Mrs. Trumbull's?"

"That's a ten-four."

"Pick her up, too, will you?"

"What!" Howland sputtered. "Victoria Trumbull is ninety-two, for God's sake. What in hell do you think she's perpetrated?"

Eldredge released the mike key and grinned at Howland in the mirror. "Mrs. Trumbull? I wouldn't put anything past her." He pressed the key again and spoke into the mike. "Does she know I'm stopping by?"

"She's aware that we need her help."

"Ten-four," said Eldredge, and hung up the mike.

"Putting cuffs on her, too, I suppose," said Howland, shifting to find a less uncomfortable position.

Tim grinned again. "I only have the one pair with me."

"Very funny," said Howland.

"We're not arresting her," said Tim. "She's coming in as a courtesy." The trooper turned left at Brandy Brow, paused at the stop sign, and looked both ways. No cars.

"You know, of course, Eldredge, *normal police procedure,*" said Howland, emphasizing the words, "would not allow for arrestees and any other person to be transported together."

"Yes, sir," said Eldredge. "Mrs. Trumbull

34

is a deputy police officer. We'll put her in front."

They passed the old mill and millpond. The still surface reflected stars. At the far end of the pond, Howland could see the pair of resident swans, ghostlike in the starlit night.

They passed the tiny, shingled West Tisbury police station, the only light showing in this part of the village.

Eldredge slowed at New Lane and turned into Victoria Trumbull's driveway. In the starlight, Howland could make out the shadowy roofs that cascaded from the tall main house to the two-story kitchen wing to the one-story summer cookroom and, finally, to the attached woodshed.

Before he'd known Victoria, Howland used to pass the rambling old house set back from the road and partly hidden by an anemic-looking horse chestnut tree and a spooky dark cedar laced with trumpet vine. He would imagine the ghosts that must inhabit the centuries-old Trumbull house, with its weathered shingles and mottled dark trim. On windy days he could see loose shutters swinging back and forth, banging against the house. Probably squealing on their hinges.

Once Howland got to know Victoria, she

had disabused him of his ghosts. We don't harbor any ghosts in this house, she'd snapped. Look for your ghosts someplace else.

Eldredge pulled up in front of the kitchen door. The lights were on. Victoria, shrunk somewhat from her once stately five-foot-ten, was still imposing. She came to the door, McCavity, her marmalade cat, twisting himself around her feet. She stooped down and scratched his head, then started down the stone steps.

Eldredge stood at the bottom. "Evening, Mrs. Trumbull."

Victoria held the railing firmly with one hand, her cloth bag and lilac-wood walking stick with the other.

In the light from the kitchen, Howland could see on her wrinkled face the shadow of her large nose. Victoria paused. "I'd better turn off the lights."

"I'll get them, Mrs. Trumbull, ma'am," said Eldredge.

"Thank you," said Victoria. "And what is your name?" she asked when the trooper returned.

"Tim Eldredge, ma'am."

"You're George's boy, aren't you?"

"No, ma'am. I'm his nephew."

"You look just like your grandfather," Victoria said as she moved toward the police car.

"Thank you, ma'am." Eldredge held the passenger door open for her.

Victoria peered into the back seat. "Still in costume, Howland?"

"And shackles."

"Why, for heaven's sake?"

"Probable cause." Howland smiled, exposing fangs. "I'm covered with blood."

Eldredge went around to the driver's side, got in, and started out toward the main road.

"Did they tell you why they're picking us up?" Howland asked.

"All they said was that a problem of some kind had cropped up, and they've asked the play's cast and crew to meet with them at the jail." Victoria smoothed the skirt of the suit she had been wearing at the playhouse earlier that evening.

"Where's your granddaughter?" Howland asked.

"Elizabeth is asleep. No point in waking her up. Have you had anything to eat?"

"I planned to eat supper with my dogs when I got home."

The trooper stopped at the end of Victoria's drive and said over his shoulder, "Joanie will take care of Mr. Atherton's dogs tonight and tomorrow morning, if necessary, Mrs. Trumbull. She said she'll walk them."

"We won't be kept that long, will we?" Victoria asked.

"Hard to know," said Eldredge. "Food's pretty good at the jail past couple of months. You know the French chef you picked up on drug charges last month, Mr. Atherton? Red Callaghan?"

"*French* chef?" asked Victoria. *"Callaghan?"*

"He cooks French," said Eldredge. "Used to work at Le Grenier in Vineyard Haven."

"He's in for eighteen months," Howland added.

"Right." Eldredge patted his stomach.

CHAPTER 3

The county jail, in Edgartown, was a nineteenth-century white clapboard house on Main Street at the end of the Edgartown-West Tisbury Road. Most visitors to the Island never realized the building was a jail. A month earlier, the picket fence out front had been covered with pink roses. A few blossoms still hung on.

Two couples were walking up the center of the dark and deserted Main Street, singing. Tomorrow, the street would be jammed with cars, and the brick sidewalks crowded with summer people wearing whale-print slacks, flower-print dresses, and bright sunburns.

Eldredge pulled into the parking area behind the building and helped Victoria out. Howland slid awkwardly along the seat toward the door.

From the back, the building looked more like a jail and less like a whaling captain's house. High, barred windows in the blocky extension overlooked the chain link fence that surrounded the parking area. Inside the fence, a security light shone on a vegetable garden backed by raspberry canes.

The trooper took Victoria to the front office and then escorted Howland up the creaky, wooden stairs to a small room with a battered table and chair.

"Sergeant Smalley wants to see you, Mr. Atherton. He should be along pretty soon." With that, the trooper waited until Howland was seated in the chair, and shut the door behind him.

John Smalley, the state police sergeant, didn't show up for another hour.

In the meantime, Howland was miserably uncomfortable. He wiggled his fingers behind his back to keep his hands from going numb. He was tired and hungry. His drying makeup itched, and he had no way of scratching. Every time he started to nod off, the handcuffs cut his circulation, and he'd jerk awake with his hands throbbing painfully. No one had come in to question him. No one had come by with food or water or an explanation. He'd spent the long hour cursing all law enforcement officers, including his own perfectly decent boss in Washington. The bare room had nothing to relieve the monotony of waiting. No posters, no notices, not even graffiti.

That was the last time that goddamned artistic director would ever talk him into performing in a play. Frankenstein's monster, indeed. The part should have gone to Dearborn Hill's nephew, after all. Roderick wouldn't have needed makeup. Hill was a goddamned pompous, officious bastard. Full of himself. Howland brightened slightly when he thought that perhaps, just perhaps, Dearborn Hill's dead and mutilated body had been found at the playhouse. Murder was the only excuse Howland could imagine for his handcuffs. There'd be plenty of suspects.

If Dearborn Hill was dead, Howland smiled to himself, he would not have to go on stage tomorrow night.

Finally, someone unlocked the door and Sergeant Smalley entered. The state police officer glanced at Howland with interest. Now that his makeup had dried and wrinkled, Howland supposed he looked even creepier than when Eldredge had first picked him up. The globs he had begun to pull off earlier dangled from his face on rubbery strands.

Howland had met John Smalley before. He was a tall, dignified man with close-cropped gray hair. Now, in the middle of the night, he wore neatly pressed tan slacks and a blue blazer over an open-necked white shirt. He was freshly shaved. Howland caught the clean scent of witch hazel.

Howland felt disagreeably filthy.

"Morning, Mr. Atherton. I'm sorry about the handcuffs. I'll get them off immediately." The sergeant unhooked a ring of keys from his belt. "There was absolutely no need for that. Trooper Eldredge was being overly conscientious. There you go." He tossed the cuffs onto the table. "Don't you know it's dangerous to stop for hitchhikers?"

"Yeah, yeah." Howland stood and stretched his arms over his head and opened and closed his fingers. "Why the state cops? Someone murdered?"

"Not yet, as far as I know." Smalley rapped his knuckles on the table. "Teddy Vanderhoop, the boy playing the part of young William Frankenstein, is missing, and the Tisbury police asked the state police to help."

"Peg Storm took him home with her."

"He's not there. Neither is Peg Storm. She plays the housekeeper, right?"

Howland nodded.

Smalley paced to the end of the table and turned back to Howland. "Doesn't the housekeeper appear in the second act? Why take Teddy home so early?"

"Justine is hanged at the end of Act One, so Peg's part is finished. Usually she stays for notes at the end, but Teddy is staying with her while his mother is in California."

"What's she doing in California?"

"Negotiating with a studio and looking for a place to live. Teddy's been offered a starring role in a new TV series."

"What about the kid's father?" Smalley pulled out a chair and sat down, looking up at Howland, who was still standing.

"They're getting a divorce."

"Oh?"

"She's from LA originally. He's from the Island."

"Tough on the kid," said Smalley.

Howland straightened his fingers and curled them again, then sat at the table across from Smalley. "Why was Eldredge so eager to put me in handcuffs?"

"He goes by the book. Two people missing, one a young boy. Foul play is a possibility." Smalley studied the drying makeup. "That getup of yours is a good way to camouflage foul play."

Howland held his hairy, clawed, blood-soaked hands out in front of him. "Why the jail?"

43

"It's available, has room, and is secure. Plus, we have a fine French chef, thanks to you."

"How's he working out?"

"For the first time in history, cops and courthouse employees are volunteering to supervise mealtimes at the jail." He shifted to face Howland. "You know the cast pretty well by now. What about Peg Storm. Is it Mrs. Storm?"

"She's divorced. Uses her maiden name, and goes by 'Ms.' "

"Likely to be any problem there?"

"Good god, no. Not Peg. Teddy's mother is supposed to be gone a week or so." Howland's face itched. "What time is it?"

Smalley pushed back the sleeve of his blazer and looked at his watch. "Almost quarter to four."

"Mind if I clean up?"

"Not yet. The higher-ups in the state have sent a forensic scientist over from Falmouth to check the stuff on your face."

Howland grunted. "The stuff on my face is stage blood. The monster gets shot in the last act."

Smalley grinned again, exposing large, crooked teeth. "That's not the way the book ends. Frankenstein dies, not the monster. The monster goes capering off across the

44

ice floes."

Howland frowned and flakes of makeup dropped off. "How come you know so much about the book? Most people have only seen movie versions."

"In college I did a senior paper on *Frankenstein, or, The Modern Prometheus.* By Mary Shelley."

"*Frankenstein*? For a criminal justice degree?"

"English." Smalley was still grinning. "Criminal justice came later. Who did the stage adaptation?"

"Victoria Trumbull."

"Ah, of course. That's why she was brought in tonight. Difficult to stage, I should think."

"According to her, the original ending was too complicated."

Smalley grinned. "You mean, where the monster goes off to the North Pole to collect his funeral pile and 'exult in the agony of the torturing flames'? I've always wondered where he intended to get the fuel."

Howland grunted.

"By the way, the entire cast, stage crew, and Mrs. Trumbull are downstairs. So is West Tisbury's police chief."

"What's Casey doing here?"

"As you know, Mrs. Trumbull is the chief's

deputy."

At that, Howland laughed. "You heard how that came about, didn't you?"

"Never did."

"Victoria lost her driver's license after she backed into the Meals on Wheels van," said Howland. "Casey felt sorry for her and offered Victoria a ride any time she needed to go someplace. So Casey acquired an ancient sidekick."

"Pretty sharp sidekick, I'd say," said Smalley.

"Casey's learned a lot from her. Victoria knows everyone on the Island, who they're related to, who they're not speaking to, where the skeletons are buried." Howland shifted position. "I hope they thought to give Victoria something to eat."

"They're having a regular tea party downstairs, listening to Mrs. Trumbull's stories." Smalley stood up and headed to the door. "Let's get out of this depressing room. We've got coffee and raspberry pastries downstairs. Chef Callaghan is cooking breakfast for the whole gang, including the residents."

Howland massaged his wrists as they went downstairs. "The forensic guy won't have much to work on if he doesn't hurry."

"She," said Smalley. "Dr. McAlistair,

M.D., Ph.D. She should be here by now. She was coming over on the morning paper boat. Gets in to Oak Bluffs around three-thirty."

"I can hardly wait to meet her."

"She's only been with the department a few months. She comes from Washington. Naval Intelligence. Turn left at the foot of the stairs."

"Thought we were heading for breakfast."

"Before we join the others, you're going to the lab."

Howland looked over his shoulder. "Since when did the jail get a lab?"

"About an hour ago. It's the sheriff's toilet."

"Great," said Howland.

"Through his office." Smalley slapped his hand on a doorframe as they passed. "You have any idea how old Teddy is?"

"Eight years old."

"Not easy to play a five-year-old when you're eight."

"Teddy's a pro," said Howland. "When he meets the monster in the woods, you believe he *is* one scared little kid."

"What's he going to play in the TV series?"

"A kid his own age. Don't know much about it beyond that."

The lights were off in the sheriff's office,

and Smalley switched them on.

"How did you learn they were missing so soon?" Howland asked.

"Teddy's mother called Peg's house from LA around eight-thirty our time, when she expected Teddy and Peg to get back from the play. She tried to reach Peg for the next couple of hours. Got increasingly worried." Smalley leaned against the doorframe. Howland perched on the corner of the sheriff's desk. "Around midnight our time," Smalley continued, "she called the Tisbury police, said she was afraid her husband might have kidnapped the boy. The Tisbury cops went to Ms. Storm's house. The power was off. Doors unlocked. They had a quick look around by flashlight. Costumes dropped on the dining room floor. Tisbury asked for our assistance."

"Has anyone contacted Teddy's father?"

"No answer at his house."

"How thoroughly did the Tisbury cops search Peg's house?"

"Just the first floor. State troopers are going back with a search warrant." Smalley checked his watch. "They're probably waking up the magistrate to sign the warrant now, as we speak."

"What about Peg's car?"

"Her car was in her driveway, a cold pizza

in a box on the front seat. The lights were on next door at Teddy's house."

"People don't simply disappear in the middle of the night on this Island."

Smalley shrugged. "Those two have. A thirty-two-year-old woman and an eight-year-old boy. Did she run off with him for some reason? If so, why not take her car?"

"Probably went to a late movie, or out for pizza."

"Not with a pizza in her car."

"Night fishing, then," said Howland. "You're going to feel foolish when they show up this morning with a couple of twelve-pound bluefish they caught surfcasting last night."

Smalley ran his hand over the back of his neck. "I hope so," he mumbled. "I hope so."

CHAPTER 4

The large, old-fashioned bathroom behind the jailer's office had a claw-foot tub on which someone had laid a sheet of plywood covered with white butcher paper. On the paper were a binocular microscope, several brown bottles, paper evidence bags, a box of latex gloves, a couple of glass petri dishes, and a few instruments.

A woman Howland had never seen before sat on the commode lid with a folding table in front of her, typing on a laptop. She was in her mid-fifties, with streaky blond hair pulled away from her face and held back with clips.

Smalley said, "Howland Atherton, meet Dr. McAlistair."

The woman removed her half-frame glasses and looked up. "Good heavens!"

"They insisted I leave the makeup on until you examined the stuff on my face."

"Quite right." She had a faintly British accent. "Sorry you had to wait so long. We had to get a warrant to take a sample." She made a wry face and offered her hand.

Howland held up his hairy claws. "You don't want to shake."

"Right." She stood up and came out from behind the table. She was slender and at least six feet tall, only a couple of inches shorter than Howland's usual height, and was wearing a starched white lab coat that came down to her knees. "Let's get that stuff off your face and hands. Must be uncomfortable." She looked down at his feet. "And take those things off. Do you have shoes with you?"

"They're in my car."

"You might want to get them."

"The car is eleven miles from here," said Smalley, who was standing by the door. "We'll see that he gets back to it when we've finished up."

Dr. McAlistair pointed to a metal stool. "Sit down, Mr. Atherton, and I'll relieve you of the makeup and booties." As she eased off his awkward furry footgear, she murmured, "I wear bunny slippers, myself."

Howland peered at her from beneath his overhanging brows. She was smiling.

"I'll see you in the dining room," said Smalley and left.

For the next half-hour, Dr. McAlistair scraped and bagged and labeled the stuff she removed from Howland's face and hands. Howland was content to sit quietly. When all of the makeup was off, she handed him a jar of cold cream and a box of tissues.

Howland scrubbed his face for several minutes and ran his fingers through his hair.

Dr. McAlistair examined him critically. "Quite an improvement."

"Yes, indeed," said Howland, wadding up the last of the tissues and tossing them into the wastebasket.

"You know where the dining room is?"

Howland nodded.

She put her glasses back on and returned to her seat and the laptop. "I'll join you in a bit."

Gray morning light filtered through the dusty barred windows of the sheriff's office as Howland headed to the dining room. He was still wearing the baggy black trousers and jacket of the monster, but the makeup was finally off. He felt light. He carried his costume boots, and his bare feet squeaked on the linoleum. A robin chirruped in the patch of raspberry canes behind the parking area. He was hungry and thirsty, but he was free of the glop he'd had on since seven last night. It must be close to five now. Ten hours.

He thought about the missing boy, a nice kid, bright, quirky sense of humor, a redhead with a toothy grin. A talented actor. The makeup people had blacked out those new front teeth of Teddy's to turn him into a kindergartner instead of the second grader he was, and he'd been entirely professional.

As Howland turned toward the dining room, he thought with some regret that Dearborn Hill, with his pompous talk, had not been a murder victim after all. Victoria Trumbull defended Dearborn's directing, but Howland knew how she felt about his push for a professional, as opposed to amateur, theater here.

He reached the dining room, opened the door, and looked around. Narrow folding tables had been pushed together to form one wide table. Two dozen people were seated around it, conversing quietly. State Trooper Tim Eldredge, on one side of Smalley, was holding his hand over his mouth, stifling a yawn. Howland glanced away. He felt himself yawning, too.

Conversation stopped briefly when he came in.

"Still in costume, Howland?" said Dearborn Hill, who sat next to Roderick, his nephew. They had turned toward the door when Howland entered. Dearborn's arms were folded across his chest, and he was leaning back in his chair.

Roderick Hill, the understudy for the monster, looked Howland up and down carefully. Howland set his boots on the floor next to him. "Care to try them on?"

After a few greetings, people went back to whatever they'd been doing — talking, reading, crossword puzzles, dozing.

The room was the size of a large family dining room, bare except for two tables and a stack of plastic chairs. At one end was a pass-through from the kitchen. Howland could smell coffee and bacon. Something sizzled. Fried potatoes, maybe. The cook, Chef Callaghan, moved back and forth, clattering pots and pans.

Howland stopped at the pass-through. "Callaghan," he called.

The cook looked up and sauntered over. He was in his forties, older than most of the kids Howland picked up on drug charges. His shaven head glistened. A lush auburn mustache drooped down on either side of his mouth. He wiped his hands on his apron and offered one to Howland. "Whaddya say, copper."

Howland shook hands.

Callaghan leaned out across the sill and examined Howland's costume. "Where'd the blood come from?"

"I'm in a play," said Howland.

The chef grinned. "Sure."

"Appreciate your cooking for us," added Howland.

"What I do."

"You look like hell," Howland said. "You get outside enough?"

Callaghan shrugged. "I weed the garden. Pick vegetables." He grinned again. "Tend a small crop I got going in the raspberry patch."

"I hope not," said Howland. "You've been here a month?"

"Twenty-seven days, twelve hours."

"You want to put in for trash pickup along the state road? If you're interested, I'll vouch for you."

"Maybe." And Callaghan turned away.

"Talk to the sheriff," Howland said to his back, and, feeling unsettled, he moved on to where the cast had assembled around the table.

Smalley greeted him. "Have a seat, Mr. Atherton. You know everyone here, I believe." He nodded around the table at cast members, stagehands, technical crew, summer theater interns, and a few unfamiliar faces. "Callaghan's cooking breakfast for us all, including the usual guests, who'll eat theirs in the TV room."

Victoria, seated across from Dearborn at the opposite end of the table, frowned. She had scolded Howland once for leaning back in a chair the way the director was leaning in the jailhouse chair.

When she saw Howland, Victoria lifted a knobby hand in greeting, and he joined her and West Tisbury's police chief, Mary Kathleen O'Neill, who sat on Victoria's right.

"Morning, Casey," said Howland.

The chief examined Howland's blood-soaked jacket and trousers. "Some outfit," she said.

"You should have seen me before." In addition to cleaning off the thick makeup, Howland had removed his hairy mitts and bridgework fangs before he'd left Dr. McAlistair.

Victoria passed the pastries and he helped himself.

The high school student who played Frankenstein's bride stood by the coffee-maker at the side of the room. "Coffee, Mr. Atherton?" She tossed her long, dark braid over one shoulder.

"Please, Dawn."

"What do you take in it?"

"Everything. Double cream, double sugar."

He bit into the flaky pastry. Raspberry juice dribbled down his face and he mopped it with a paper napkin.

Dawn set the coffee in front of him and took her seat next to Tim Eldredge. Howland watched with amusement as she turned large brown eyes on Tim, who was too exhausted to notice. The table was littered with the detritus of hours of waiting — papers and books, coffee cups, crumpled paper napkins, crumbs. Underlying the aroma of bacon and coffee was the odor of tired and nervous people.

Sergeant Smalley, looking crisp and fresh in his blazer and white shirt, and Tim Eldredge, looking shopworn in his crumpled uniform and shadow of a beard, were seated between Dawn and one of the stagehands. Bruce Duncan, who played Frankenstein's boyhood friend, sat on Dawn's left. He was mild looking and balding, in his early thirties, wearing a black sweatshirt with crimson letters that read "VETA" in capital letters, with "Vineyarders for the Ethical Treatment of Animals" below, in smaller letters.

Smalley rapped on the table. "Now that Frankenstein's monster is here we can finish up." He turned to Howland. "Mr. Atherton, I've already taken individuals aside and asked them to tell me anything they know that might help us find Teddy Vanderhoop and Peg Storm."

Bruce Duncan slicked a loose strand of hair over the top of his head and folded his hands on the tabletop. "Peg has a dog. Sandy, I believe. Have you found Sandy?"

Smalley coughed politely. "I'm sure we will, Mr. Duncan." He looked down at his notes. "As I said earlier, I called you out in the middle of the night because the first few hours after a child is reported missing are critical. You were the last people, as far as we know, to have seen Teddy and Ms. Storm."

Howland glanced around the table. Dearborn Hill, still leaning back in his chair, was making soft smacking sounds with his lips. He wore a black V-neck sweater over a black turtleneck shirt. Victoria looked down at her hands. Chief O'Neill, in uniform, on Victoria's right, was doodling on a piece of scrap paper. Bruce Duncan was cleaning his fingernails nervously with a nail clipper. Dawn Haines was drawing something in a large spiral-bound sketchpad. Occasionally, she'd brush stray wisps of hair from her forehead with the back of her hand.

"I questioned most of you, individually, before Mr. Atherton got here," Smalley said. "Who is missing, besides Teddy and Peg Storm?"

Howland bit into his pastry and wiped his mouth.

Dawn said, still sketching, "Billy Amaral."

Smalley looked up from his notes. "What part does Billy Amaral play?"

"The understudy for Frankenstein. *Victor* Frankenstein, my, like, creepy bridegroom." Dawn reached her hand to the back of her neck and flipped her braid over her shoulder so it hung down the front of her dark green T-shirt.

Dearborn Hill leaned forward and addressed Smalley. "*I* play Victor Frankenstein."

Smalley studied the artistic director. "Frankenstein was quite a young man, early twenties, I believe."

Dearborn Hill smiled. "An audience will believe whatever an accomplished actor wants them to believe."

Dawn looked up from her sketching. "Billy left early, after the second act."

"How many acts are there?" Smalley asked. "Two?"

"Three," said Victoria.

"I had specifically asked Billy to be present

59

for notes and curtain call rehearsal," said Dearborn. "He's understudying the most important role in the play, and he needs to work on his timing." He glanced from one actor to another. "I certainly don't expect anything to happen to me, but it's a matter of professionalism." He placed his hand on his breast. "This is a classic example of why our theater must go Equity."

Victoria scowled. "We don't need an Equity theater. We like to see our friends and neighbors on stage."

"Mrs. Trumbull . . ." Dearborn said.

Victoria continued, "Who wants to see third-rate paid actors from New York?"

"Mrs. Trumbull," said Dearborn, with studied patience, "your so-called 'third-rate actors' are professionals. A professional director can depend upon trained professionals. A professional director can never depend upon amateurs."

Smalley rapped on the table. "Anyone else missing?"

"Ruth Byron," said Dawn Haines, glancing up at Victoria, then down again at her sketch.

"Remind me who Ruth Byron is," requested Smalley.

"Ruth Byron is my wife's sister," Dearborn said.

"Was she at the rehearsal?"

"Yes," said Victoria.

"No," said Dearborn at the same moment.

"She was in the back of the theater," said Dawn.

Victoria added, "She founded the Island Players as a community venture for people who like to see their friends and neighbors act."

Dearborn smiled. "You're repeating yourself, Mrs. Trumbull."

Smalley turned to him. "Your wife's sister?"

"Yes. My wife is Rebecca Byron Hill."

"The people missing, then," Smalley went on, "are Teddy, who plays the part of William Frankenstein, and Peg, who plays the part of Justine Moritz, the housekeeper accused of murdering little William." He looked up. "Also missing are Billy Amaral, the understudy for Frankenstein . . ."

"*Victor* Frankenstein," said Victoria.

". . . and Ruth Byron, founder of the theater. Anyone else?"

Still sketching, Dawn said, "The two kids who play Monsieur De Lacey's son and daughter."

"The monster's adopted family," Victoria explained to Smalley.

"Yes, Mrs. Trumbull. I remember. Thank

you." He turned to Trooper Eldredge. "Have you tried to locate those two, Tim?"

"Their parents didn't know where they were, sir."

"Shacked up in a tent on Tisbury Great Pond," said Dawn.

Smalley turned to Eldredge. "Have someone find them and bring them in, will you?"

"They're at the head of Town Cove," said Dawn. "In *my* tent."

"Right." Eldredge got up and headed toward the door.

Smalley continued. "I know most of you. Stagehands, makeup people, stage manager," he nodded at a woman dressed in black, "lighting, sound, most of the cast, interns." He nodded at Roderick, who sat on Dearborn Hill's right. "And you are . . . ?"

Even sitting down, Roderick, who was in his early twenties, was several inches taller than anyone else at the table. "I am Roderick Hill. The understudy for Frankenstein's monster."

"Yes, of course," said Smalley, shifting his notes on the table. "Yes. Thank you. I do know who you are."

A state trooper entered the room, boots squeaking on the linoleum. Smalley looked up. The trooper stopped next to him, bent down, and whispered something.

"Get Tim Eldredge back here, right away," Smalley told the trooper. He turned to the people at the table. "You'll have to excuse me. All of you, please wait." He glanced toward the kitchen pass-through, where Chef Callaghan was setting laden-down stainless steel serving dishes. "Breakfast is ready."

Howland helped Victoria to her feet.

"Wonder what the trooper wanted?" she said. "Do you suppose they've found Teddy?"

"Didn't look like good news," said Howland. He sniffed the welcome aroma of coffee and bacon. "Let's get in line. I understand Chief O'Neill is here because her deputy was picked up as a suspect."

Victoria smiled. Despite a night without sleep, her hooded, dark eyes were bright on either side of her great nose. She reached into the cloth bag hanging on the back of her chair and brought out her blue baseball cap, which she held for Howland to see. He recognized the hat. Gold stitching in a bold curve across the front read "West Tisbury Police, Deputy."

CHAPTER 5

Victoria spotted Dr. McAlistair as soon as the forensic scientist entered the dining room, a few minutes after Smalley left. The tall woman in a tailored suit, tan slacks, and jacket with a brown and white striped blouse wasn't dressed like an Islander. The doctor glanced around the bare room, at the pushed-together tables, the grimy off-white walls, and the worn linoleum floor. By now, twenty or so people were lined up at the kitchen window. Victoria beckoned to her to join them in line.

Howland introduced them.

Victoria smiled. "You came over on the morning paper boat?"

"It was more like the middle of the night, Mrs. Trumbull. Much too early."

"Are you from England?"

"My parents are British, actually. Do I understand you're not only the playwright, but a police deputy?"

Victoria smoothed her tousled hair and smiled. "I've been some help to Chief O'Neill." She lifted a tray off a stack next to the counter, took a heavy white plate and utensils, and helped herself to bacon and scrambled eggs.

The cook was standing by the window when they reached it. He gave Howland a salute that was just this side of insolent.

Victoria looked questioningly at Howland, who was carrying her tray to the table.

Howland shrugged. "Chef Callaghan would rather not be in jail. As the drug enforcement agent who nabbed him, I'm responsible for his being here."

"Everyone will be sorry when his sentence is served."

"Everyone but Callaghan. He's serving eighteen months."

"A year-and-a-half is a long time. He's not from the Island, is he?"

"Rhode Island. Providence."

For a while, the only sound was the scraping of utensils on plates. Then conversation picked up. Why had the trooper come for Sergeant Smalley? Had they found Teddy? And Peg?

Dearborn's nephew, Roderick, had gone back to the window for a second helping. Like the stage manager, he was dressed entirely in black — a long-sleeved turtleneck shirt that bagged at the neck, loose trousers, and black running shoes. Victoria noticed that he was limping. He returned and sat hunched over his plate, forking food into his mouth.

"Obnoxious kid," said Howland. "Runs in the family."

"Roderick is a poet, Howland."

Howland smiled.

"He's really quite good," Victoria said. "He often reads his work at Island Java."

"Even poets can be obnoxious."

"Roderick has given me several of his poems to critique. I was quite touched."

"Victoria . . ." Howland didn't complete his thought.

Dearborn, knife in his right hand, fork in his left, was gesturing at Roderick, who nodded in reponse.

Dawn Haines had pushed her sketchpad to one side and watched Dearborn and his nephew.

This was the first time Victoria had seen the two close together. Roderick and Dearborn had a strong family resemblance. Both were heavy-set with high foreheads and protruding lips. Both had thick wavy hair, Dearborn's white and nicely styled, Roderick's light brown, slicked back and worn in a ponytail. Roderick, even seated, was much taller than his uncle and outweighed him by a considerable amount.

After they finished breakfast, Dr. McAlistair wiped the surface of the table in front of her and spread out some papers she'd taken from her briefcase.

"We needn't wait for Sergeant Smalley to give you the results of the preliminary tests, Mr. Atherton. Stage blood and makeup, as you said. I'll send the samples to the lab in Sudbury, of course, but I see no reason to examine them further unless something else develops."

"I hope we find Teddy soon," said Victoria.

The sheriff opened the door into the dining room. Conversation around the table hushed as Sergeant Smalley and Trooper Eldredge returned to their seats. Smalley's expression was unreadable.

"Bad news," said Howland.

"Teddy . . . ?" Victoria asked Smalley.

"We haven't found the boy yet, Mrs. Trumbull. We're still trying to locate him." Smalley looked down at the notebook he'd placed on the table. "However, we've found Ms. Storm."

Bruce Duncan, the animal rights activist, stood and ran his hands up and down the front of his black sweatshirt.

Dawn Haines set her fork on her plate.

Smalley looked down at his notes. "We found her body."

The strand of hair Bruce Duncan had smoothed across the top of his scalp flopped down to one side as he shook his head.

"Sit down, Mr. Duncan, if you will, please," said Smalley.

Duncan continued to stand. "First William is killed. Then Justine." He slapped his chest. "Henry Clerval . . . me . . . Frankenstein's friend . . . I'm next!"

"Splendid, Mr. Duncan!" Dearborn Hill nodded vigorously. "Exactly the kind of emotion I hope you can project on stage."

"Riiight," said Dawn.

"Please, Mr. Duncan." Smalley rapped his knuckles on the table. "We expect to find the boy alive."

Bruce Duncan sat and smoothed the errant strand of hair back on top of his head.

Smalley went on. "Obviously, I can't go into details. We obtained a search warrant and went through Ms. Storm's house. She was found at the foot of the cellar stairs."

Duncan stood again. "Hanged? Like in the play?"

"At the foot of the cellar stairs," Smalley repeated.

"For heaven's sake, sit down, Bruce," Victoria said.

Casey leaned toward her. "Who's he?"

"Bruce Duncan. He works at Precious Pets," said Victoria.

Conversation started up, with a nervous edge.

Smalley rapped on the table again. "At this point, our priority is to find the boy. I need to know every detail you can tell me about Teddy and Ms. Storm." The cast and crew studied one another. "A crime scene team is at Ms. Storm's house now. Does anyone know the name of her ex-husband?"

"I believe it's Leonard," said an elderly man who'd been quiet until now. "She called him Lennie."

"Your name again, sir?" said Smalley.

"Gerard Cohen. I play the blind man who befriends the monster."

"Thank you, Mr. Cohen. Do you know where Leonard lives?"

"He lives on-Island, I understand, but I don't know where."

Smalley turned to Eldredge. "See if you can locate Leonard Storm, Tim. I'll need to talk to him."

Dawn looked up. "Storm was Peg's maiden name."

"What is her former husband's name?" Smalley asked.

"Vincent," said Gerard Cohen. "Leonard Vincent."

"See if you can find him, Tim."

"Yes, sir," said Tim, and left the room.

"In the meantime, I'll go over what's happened during the past five or six hours." Smalley glanced around at the gathering. "Teddy's mother, Mrs. Vanderhoop, called the Tisbury police around midnight to report that she hadn't been able to reach her son, who was staying with Peg Storm. Shortly after she called, the state police got a nine-one-one call from two girls who were hitchhiking from Vineyard Haven to West Tisbury."

Roderick Hill, who'd been whispering to his uncle, sat up suddenly. "Two girls?"

Smalley nodded. "They claimed a monster had stopped to pick them up. We located and identified the driver to our satisfaction. We have not yet located the girls who called."

"Were they using a cellular phone?" Victoria asked.

Smalley nodded. "That's one problem, Mrs. Trumbull. A cell phone call to nine-one-one originating here on the Island gets routed through Framingham, State Police Headquarters. We know the cell phone number, but can't pin down the location of the caller." He drummed his fingers on the table. "Reception on the Island is notoriously poor. When we call the number, we get the 'out of service' message. We'll keep trying, of course. Yes, Dawn?"

"Does Peg's death have anything to do with the girls?"

Smalley shifted papers in front of him. "As yet, we have no reason to believe their call is related to either Peg's death or to Teddy's disappearance."

Tim returned, holding a slip of paper. "I have Vincent's address, Sergeant. Want me to bring him here to the jail?"

"Yes." Smalley looked at his watch. "We'll be here another hour, at least." After Tim left, Smalley riffled through his notes and continued. "The Tisbury police made a cursory check of Ms. Storm's house, found neither Teddy nor Ms. Storm, and called the state police. We obtained a search warrant and that's when we found Ms. Storm's body."

Dawn Haines moved her sketchpad in front of her. "She cared about this play and all of us acting in it. She was the only person treating Teddy like a grown-up. Except for Mrs. Trumbull. Everybody else acted like he was, like, a baby."

Smalley cleared his throat. "We're trying

to locate Teddy's father."

Dawn looked up again. "You know where he lives?"

Smalley glanced at his notes. "In Oak Bluffs near the lobster hatchery. Is that right?"

"That's where his house is."

"Roughly five miles from his wife and son," Smalley murmured and wrote something in his notebook.

Victoria said, "It's only a half-mile by boat."

"Teddy is an Equity player," said Dearborn Hill. "His mother usually sits through rehearsal until little William is killed, then they go home together."

Smalley nodded. "Was it generally known that Mrs. Vanderhoop was going to California?"

"Certainly. Mrs. Vanderhoop told me of Teddy's good fortune, and I informed everyone in the cast." Dearborn Hill swept his arm around the table. "She asked me to excuse Ms. Storm from rehearsal early to get Teddy home by bedtime. I told you, didn't I, that Teddy is Equity?"

"You did," said Victoria.

CHAPTER 6

"Would you explain, Mr. Hill, what 'Equity' is all about?" Smalley asked. "Does it have any bearing on this situation?"

"I'd be delighted," said Dearborn, adjusting himself in his seat. "Equity is, essentially, a theatrical union. A director, such as I, prefers to work with Equity players because we can depend upon their learning their lines, showing up for rehearsals, and performing on stage." He sat back. "Amateur players undercut the professionalism of theater."

Dawn Haines snickered. She had started to sketch again.

"Acting is a serious business, my dear, not to be laughed at." Dearborn scowled at Dawn. "Vacationers on Martha's Vineyard these days are people of discrimination . . ."

Victoria interrupted. "Have you contacted Ruth Byron?"

"Ruth Byron?"

"The playhouse founder."

Smalley scribbled a note.

"She hasn't been around for some time," Dearborn said.

"Actually, she's here most of the time," said Dawn. "Just not when Mr. Hill is around."

"Ruth inherited the theater building from her aunt," Victoria said.

Dearborn leaned back again. "Ruth and her sister, my wife, disagree about their aunt's legacy." He folded his arms across his chest. "Ruth and I have our own legitimate disagreement over artistic matters. No bearing on little William Frankenstein."

"His name is Teddy Vanderhoop," said Dawn.

"What are you drawing?" muttered Bruce Duncan.

Dawn tilted her head and held up her sketch. "Mrs. Trumbull. Is that okay with you?"

Bruce looked at the drawing, then turned away.

"Pretty good likeness," said Tim Eldredge, leaning forward.

"Ruth Byron hired Mr. Hill as artistic director on a trial basis," said Gerard Cohen. "He's an excellent director."

Dearborn Hill bowed his head in Cohen's

direction.

"Thank you, Mr. Cohen," said Smalley. "Does anyone know Teddy's father's first name?"

"Jefferson Vanderhoop the Fourth," said Dawn.

"We'll need to bring Mr. Vanderhoop here."

"He's rented his house for the summer," said Dawn.

Smalley sighed. "Do you know where he is, Ms. Haines?"

"On his boat. On a mooring in Lagoon Pond."

"Anything else you can tell me?"

Dawn shook her head.

Smalley murmured, "Vineyard Haven harbormaster."

"His boat is, like, on the Oak Bluffs side."

Smalley took a breath. "Oak Bluffs harbormaster. Is there anything else you can tell me, Ms. Haines, before I send Trooper Eldredge off again?"

She shrugged.

Smalley returned to his notes. "Did Ms. Storm have any close friends? Male or female?"

Dearborn Hill cleared his throat. "She and I went to dinner once or twice to discuss her role."

Smalley frowned. "Any other friends?"

"I was as close to her as anyone," Gerard Cohen said. His heavy horn-rimmed glasses had slipped down his nose. "She lived next door to the Vanderhoops on Job's Neck, across the road from me. Mrs. Vanderhoop encouraged me to get involved in the theater after my wife died. Right after Peg's divorce."

"Any other friends?"

"None that I know of. She kept to herself."

"Did she have a job?"

"She was a photographer. Weddings, family gatherings, that sort of thing. Not steady employment," said Cohen.

Tim Eldredge returned and Dawn stopped sketching long enough to look up at him.

Smalley checked his watch. "Did you locate Mr. Vincent?"

"No, sir. The address I had for a Leonard Vincent is a T-shirt shop near the ferry."

Smalley looked around the table. "Anyone happen to know if Mr. Vincent owns the T-shirt shop? Dawn?"

Shrugs. Blank looks.

"Anyone here *know* Mr. Vincent?"

Gerard Cohen spoke up. "I knew him only slightly. My wife was ill for several years, so I didn't get around much. The Vincents were divorced the year she died."

76

"Any idea what Mr. Vincent does for a living, Mr. Cohen?"

"Afraid not. He made quite a lot of money when he sold his half of Peg's house back to her."

"Don't leave yet, Tim. I need to talk to you." Smalley stood up. "I won't keep the rest of you. It's been a long night. Don't go off Island without letting us know where we can reach you." He tugged his wallet out of his back pocket, withdrew business cards, and passed them out. "At least until we locate the boy." He yawned, starting off a chain reaction of yawns around the table. "Tim, ask the sheriff to let us out. I'll take Mr. Atherton back to his car."

"I'll give Howland a ride in the police car," said Casey.

Dearborn Hill cleared his throat. "We still have unfinished business, Sergeant."

"What is that, Mr. Hill?"

"Tonight is opening night for the play."

"Good heavens, Dearborn!" said Victoria. "You don't intend to go ahead with the play under these circumstances."

"Ms. Storm's death is a tragedy, one we must respect." Dearborn's voice was low and mellow. "The greatest honor we can pay Ms. Storm is to treat her as the professional she hoped to become. The play must go on."

"The play most certainly must *not* go on," Victoria said. "We've got to find Teddy."

"I have an understudy in mind for Teddy," Dearborn said. "Our stage manager can step into the role of Justine." He glanced at the woman in black. "You know her part, Nora?"

The stage manager nodded.

Victoria flushed. "That's outrageous."

"It's professional theater, Mrs. Trumbull. We are guaranteed a full house tonight."

"Because an actor is dead? How callous." Victoria looked around the table. "Do any of you intend to go on stage tonight?"

"Count me out," said Dawn.

Howland nodded at Roderick Hill, his understudy. "You're welcome to the monster's role." He pulled a handkerchief out of his pocket and unfolded it. "Here are your fangs." He set the false teeth on the table in front of Roderick. "And your claws."

"I can't handle it," said Bruce Duncan, his elbows on the table, his forehead resting on his clasped hands.

"I was close to Peg," said Gerard Cohen. "I'd rather not go on tonight. Sorry, Dearborn."

"I know Henry Clerval's lines," said Bob

Scott, a slight man with dirt-stained jeans and a shaggy beard. Scott opened and closed the play as the Arctic explorer. "Bruce and I don't ever appear on stage at the same time."

Dearborn studied Scott. "I hope you'll trim your beard, as I asked you to before."

Scott grinned. "The ladies like it rough the way it is."

Dearborn turned away without further comment. "Thank you, my friends. Those of you who intend to go on stage tonight, be at the playhouse at three. We'll run through the play again, double time. That will give you a few hours of rest." He rose from his seat. "I'll notify the radio station that the play will go on, despite the tragic death of a key actress. Then I must round up actors to fill in for those of you unable to perform."

Dr. McAlistair gathered up papers and put them in her attaché case. "Sergeant, I have more work to do here, but I'm exhausted. Can someone book a hotel room for me?"

"I'm not sure we can find a vacancy this time of year on such short notice, but I'll have someone check."

"I have a spare bedroom," Victoria said. "If you don't mind sharing a bath."

"If it's not too much trouble, Mrs. Trumbull?"

"She's got a great old house. It's haunted," said Howland, not looking at Victoria.

Jefferson Vanderhoop the Fourth was bent over the engine of his forty-foot lobster boat, which was moored in Lagoon Pond, when the Oak Bluffs harbormaster's launch pulled alongside. A short, stocky, dark-skinned man was at the wheel. When he spoke, his cigarette stuck to his lower lip like a growth of some kind. A cap with NYPD in faded gold stitching was pulled down over thick black eyebrows. He left the controls, dropped a fender between the two boats, and looped a line over a cleat on the lobster boat.

A small wooden skiff tethered behind Vanderhoop's boat bobbed in the wake of the launch.

The launch passenger, a weary-looking guy wearing a day-old beard, a rumpled state trooper's uniform, and leather boots coated with dust, stood up and made his way unsteadily forward from the stern.

A flock of gulls took off into the wind, circled overhead, then settled back on the water.

Vanderhoop straightened up and wiped

oily hands on a rag. He grinned at the harbormaster, who'd stepped on board the fishing boat. "What d'ya say, Domingo?"

"How you doing, Jefferson. You know trooper Tim Eldredge?"

Eldredge started to scramble awkwardly onto the deck of the larger boat.

"Hey!" said Vanderhoop, glancing at Eldredge's boots. "No hard soles on my boat."

Tim dropped back onto the launch, undid his boot laces, tugged off his boots, exposing holes in both socks where his big toes stuck out, and made his way slowly to Vanderhoop's boat.

Vanderhoop scowled at him. "Not been around boats much? You live here long?"

Tim nodded. "Born here."

"What brings you to my boat?" Vanderhoop asked the harbormaster.

Domingo leaned against the pilothouse, crossed one leg over the other, and pointed his cigarette at Tim. "His show."

"State police business?" asked Vanderhoop.

"Yes, sir. Need to ask you a few questions."

"What's up?" Vanderhoop looked from Tim to Domingo.

Domingo put his hands in the pockets of his khaki trousers and shrugged.

Tim took a plastic card out of his shirt pocket and began reading out loud. "You have the right to remain silent. Anything you say . . ."

"Miranda?" cried Vanderhoop, standing up straight. "Why in hell are you reading Miranda to me?"

Tim kept reading and finished, ". . . will be provided for you at government expense."

"What kind of asshole are you, anyway?" said Vanderhoop.

Tim put the card back in his pocket and pulled out a notebook. "Would you mind telling me where you were last night, Mr. Vanderhoop?"

"What's this about?" Vanderhoop gave his hands another wipe and tossed his rag onto the engine block. Stripped to the waist and barefoot, he stood about six-foot-three and probably weighed two hundred thirty pounds. The small amount of excess fat he carried formed a slight bulge over the belt of his jeans. His dark hair curled below his ears and he was clean-shaven.

"Sorry, sir. I'm not at liberty to give out information at this point in time."

"I suppose my soon-to-be ex-wife filed a complaint?"

"No, sir. This is strictly informal. Answers

to a few questions. We can do it here on your boat, or, if you'd prefer, we can go back to the police barracks."

Vanderhoop leaned over the side of his boat and spat into the water. "Where was I last night?" He pointed down at his deck. "Right here."

"Can anyone verify that, sir?"

"I doubt it."

"Mind if I look around?"

Vanderhoop set large, callused hands on his hips. "What?"

"I'd like to look around your boat, sir."

"You got a search warrant or something?"

"I can get one, if necessary," said Tim.

Domingo grinned and turned away.

Tim continued. "I was hoping you'd cooperate."

Vanderhoop's face flushed. "What is this, anyway?"

Tim shook his head.

Domingo dragged on his cigarette. Ash fell off and dropped on the deck.

Vanderhoop glanced at the ash on his clean deck. "Got nothing to hide. Be my guest." He waved a hand at the pilothouse. "Don't mess up my stuff."

The wheel and controls of the boat were sheltered by the overhang of the pilothouse. Eldredge went down three steps into a tidy cabin. On his left was a spotless galley with stove, small sink, and ice chest. On the right, on a folded-down table, a chart was opened to Nantucket Sound. Forward of the galley an L-shaped bench and table on a telescoping leg formed a reading and eating nook. Eldredge studied everything that could hide a small boy. He squeezed through a narrow door. A small bathroom opened to the left. A showerhead on a hose hung above the toilet. A V-shaped berth tucked into the bow was made up with blankets and pillows, where Vanderhoop — or someone — obviously slept. A battery-operated reading lamp and a dozen poetry books sat on a shelf above the bunk.

Eldredge lifted one side of the mattress. Underneath was a two-by-three-foot piece of plywood with a ring for a handle. He tugged it up and looked down into a storage locker. The locker seemed to be full of rope. An anchor. Chain.

No boy. Definitely no boy.

Eldredge retraced his steps to the stern.

"Satisfied?" Vanderhoop grumbled.

Tim looked down at his notes. "When was the last time you saw your son?"

At that, Vanderhoop clenched his large hands into fists. "That bitch take my kid? I'll wring her neck."

Tim repeated his question. "When did you last see Teddy?"

"A week ago, maybe."

"Where was that, sir?"

"Right here." He pointed to the deck. "I motored over to the point. *She* dropped Teddy off, and we went out in the boat."

"Where is your son now, sir?"

"With his goddamned fucking bitch mother."

"Where, sir?"

"How am I supposed to know, goddamn it? She wanted to take the kid to California. I wanted the kid to stay right here." And again he stabbed his finger at the deck of his boat. "My kid wanted to stay right here, too."

Tim switched direction. "Can you tell me anything about Peg Storm, sir?"

"Peg?" Vanderhoop looked surprised. "Sure. Quiet. Next-door neighbor. Family lived on the point, three, four generations. No kids. Divorced. A small mutt named Sandy." He shrugged.

"Do you know her former husband, sir? You were neighbors, weren't you?"

Vanderhoop shook his head. "Lennie Vincent. Didn't have much to do with him. Nothing social. Never cared much for him."

"Why was that, sir?"

"Why I didn't care for him? He's a sleaze."

"Was he argumentative? Rude?"

"Nothing like that. Just didn't like the guy."

"Did you know anything about the play your son and Ms. Storm were in?"

Vanderhoop's face reddened. "I don't know where this is leading, Eldredge, but I'll tell you this. My kid was a nice, normal kid. Liked the water. Teddy and me, we got along good. Until my wife took it into her head the kid should be an actor. What *she* wanted. Be a movie star. She didn't make it, so she's going to turn my kid . . ." He pounded his chest. ". . . into some freaking actor."

Domingo finished a last drag on his cigarette and flicked it into the water. He lifted his cap and scratched his head.

Vanderhoop's expression went from angry to surly. "She take my kid? Did she?" he repeated, stepping toward Eldredge.

Tim Eldredge lowered his notebook. "Your son is missing."

Vanderhoop pounded a fist into the palm of his hand. "She does whatever she goddamned wants. Teddy's my kid, too. I got rights. She better not snatch my kid. I'll kill her first."

Domingo cleared his throat.

Vanderhoop turned on him. "You can quote me on that, goddamn it, Domingo. She takes my kid, I'll kill the bitch."

CHAPTER 7

It was still early when Casey and her deputy, Victoria, Howland, and Dr. McAlistair left the jail, but the temperature was already in the seventies. Main Street's sidewalks were crowded with shoppers. People strolled across the street between cars that were inching toward the harbor parking lot. An in-line skater whizzed past, almost slamming into a woman in shorts and sandals getting out of the passenger side of a parked car.

"What's the best way around this mess, Victoria?" Casey asked before they got into the Bronco. "You know the back streets of Edgartown better than I ever will."

Victoria had been born in a house on Main Street, a block from the jail. The buildings in Edgartown that had been ramshackle in her childhood were spruced up now, and the street was paved with asphalt and lined with brick sidewalks. Victoria had trouble believing the rents summer people were willing to pay to vacation in houses that had been derelict in her youth.

The slow flow of traffic had stopped. "Turn left, away from Main Street," Victoria said. "I'll show you the way as we go."

Casey negotiated the narrow one-way streets in the center of town, past white clapboard houses until they reached the straight road to West Tisbury.

Raggedy blue chicory and bright tawny lilies grew wild by the side of the road. The scent of sweet fern and pine drifted in through the open windows of the vehicle.

Casey yawned. "My day off. Look at that gorgeous sky. Perfect beach day." She yawned again. "I've gotta grab a nap before I take Patrick and his buddies to the beach."

"Patrick is the chief's son," Howland explained to Alison. "He's about Teddy's age."

"Ah," said Alison. Victoria, watching her from the front seat, saw her turn from Howland to stare out the window.

"Patrick is nine, a year older than Teddy," said Casey. "Teddy's mother must be worried sick."

"Yes," Alison murmured.

"According to Smalley, she's on a flight

back to the Island now," Howland explained.

"I can't even imagine how she feels. If anything ever happened to Patrick I'd go crazy."

"Yes," said Alison again.

Victoria examined the sky. "Better go to the beach soon. We're likely to have thunderstorms later." She indicated a row of low clouds, faint on the horizon to the northwest, mostly hidden by low scrub oak and pine.

Alison leaned over the front seat. "Is there a beach within walking distance of your house, Mrs. Trumbull?"

Victoria nodded. "About three miles from me."

"Maybe for you, Victoria." Howland grinned. "I'll stop by in an hour or so, Alison, and take you to my beach. How much time do you need to spend on Island?"

"I'm not sure. Ordinarily, in the case of a death under unusual circumstances, the undertaker transports the body to Boston for autopsy. But since I'm already here, and Ms. Storm's body is still here, and Teddy is still missing, the state police probably will want me to stay."

They passed a farm, where rows of sweet corn, beans, and tomatoes ripened in the

July sun, and entered the state forest. Silvery snags of red pine towered above dusky green scrub oak.

"I expected the Island to be more built up," Alison said.

Howland grunted. "It's built up, all right. Our population swells from thirteen thousand in winter to a hundred fifty thousand now."

"What do you do with them all?"

"Shopping," said Victoria.

They dipped down into a swale and up the other side, and there, on the left, was Victoria's gray-shingled house, set back from the road and almost hidden by trees. Casey pulled into the drive and stopped. Howland, still barefoot and still in his stained costume, walked gingerly around the larger sharp chunks of crushed oyster shell that paved the driveway and held out his hand for Alison, who stepped down from the high vehicle.

Victoria slid out of her seat. Her dressy plaid suit was wrinkled, the once-perky bow at the neck of her blouse drooped, her stockings bagged around her knees and ankles. Even with the hole cut out of her shoe, her sore toe throbbed.

Her granddaughter, Elizabeth, burst out of the door. "Gram, where have you been?"

"At the jail."

"What were you doing there?"

Victoria didn't answer directly. "This is Dr. McAlistair, Elizabeth. She'll be staying with us tonight, possibly longer."

Elizabeth, who was as tall as Alison, almost as lean, and about twenty years her junior, held out her hand.

"I didn't expect to be away this long," Victoria explained. "Dr. McAlistair is a forensic scientist from Falmouth."

"Why the jail? Forensic scientist? What's happening?"

"I'll let you guys explain," said Casey. "I'm taking Howland back to his car."

Elizabeth examined Howland's costume, from the stained black shirt and trousers to his feet. "Blood? Barefoot?"

"Don't ask." Howland got into the front seat of the police vehicle and Casey drove off.

"I hope someone's going to tell me what's happening."

"Before I do any explaining, I want a bath," said Victoria.

Elizabeth threw up her hands in frustration.

After Alison was settled in her room, after Victoria emerged from her bath in her worn corduroy trousers and turtleneck, Elizabeth finally learned about Peg's death and Teddy's disappearance.

"Peg had a dog, didn't she?" asked Elizabeth, as they ate their lunch.

Victoria set down her sandwich. "No one found the dog."

A half-hour later, a state police car pulled up in front of Victoria's, and Sergeant Smalley knocked on the kitchen door. Alison answered. She had changed into a bathing suit and long-sleeved cotton shirt that gave the impression she was wearing nothing under it. Both bathing suit and shirt were borrowed from Elizabeth. Smalley glanced quickly at her long legs, which she had deliberately not covered for Howland's benefit, and when Smalley looked up guiltily, she smiled. After her legs, her smile was her best feature.

Smalley cleared his throat. "Sorry to barge in on you like this, Dr. McAlistair. As you know, we found Ms. Stone at the foot of her cellar stairs. But I'm not comfortable with the idea of a fall killing her. I'd like you to examine the body."

"She's at the mortuary now?"

"Yes, ma'am. Rose Haven, the funeral home. Since you're on Island, we'd like you to do a preliminary exam."

"Quite right. Give me a few minutes to change."

While Alison was upstairs, Victoria worked on her weekly column for *The Island Enquirer.* She stopped, her fingers poised above the typewriter keys. Smalley was in the kitchen, pacing back and forth.

"I'm not comfortable, either, with the idea that Peg fell to her death," Victoria said. "I can't understand why she would shut the door at the top of the cellar stairs behind her."

He turned. "You're absolutely right, Mrs. Trumbull."

"She had a dog. Perhaps she wanted to keep her dog from following her? But her cellar stairs are steep and shutting the door would be awkward."

"Could be why she fell." Smalley looked up and smiled as Alison appeared, dressed in Elizabeth's jeans and T-shirt. She carried the attaché case she'd brought with her.

"I don't know how long we'll be, Mrs. Trumbull," Alison said. "Not more than two hours, I should think."

"I'll call Howland to cancel your beach date."

"Thank you."

There was no answer at Howland's. He showed up at Victoria's a few minutes later, and Victoria glanced up from her typewriter. "Alison's gone to Rose Haven with Sergeant Smalley. You've been outranked."

"By Sergeant Smalley? Not likely."

"May I use something about the autopsy in my column? I have space I need to fill."

"Afraid not, Victoria." Howland started toward the door. "Anyway, she's not performing an autopsy, she's doing a cursory exam. The Island doesn't have facilities for an autopsy."

"Are you heading to Rose Haven now?" Victoria struggled to her feet.

"Yes."

"Let me get my hat."

"You don't want to see this, Victoria. It won't be pleasant. I'll give you the scoop the minute I know anything that can be released to the press."

"I'll leave a note for Elizabeth, then I'll be ready."

Twenty minutes later, Howland pulled up to the rear entrance of the Rose Haven Funeral Parlor and parked in the lot next to the loading ramp. Victoria let herself out of the car.

"Victoria . . ." Howland started to say.

But she interrupted him. "I suppose we'll be using the back door."

CHAPTER 8

Toby, the undertaker, greeted Victoria and Howland at the back door of the mortuary. "Are you here for a viewing?"

"We're here for Peg Storm's autopsy," said Victoria.

"Ah!" said Toby. "Yes. Dr. McAlistair doesn't perform autopsies here on Island. This is a preliminary cause-of-death assessment. The autopsy will be performed in Boston. Dr. McAlistair and Sergeant Smalley are still at lunch."

Howland checked his watch. "It's one-thirty, for God's sake."

"We'll wait," said Victoria, and returned to Howland's car.

Smalley and Alison arrived a few minutes later. "What are you doing here, Mrs. Trumbull?" Smalley demanded.

"That's all right, John," said Alison, putting a hand on Smalley's arm. "Mrs. Trumbull is welcome to observe."

" 'John?' " said Howland.

Alison smiled.

They followed Alison up the concrete ramp and through the industrial steel doors where Toby waited. He was dressed in gray trousers, a black blazer with a red V-neck sweater showing underneath, white shirt, and black-and-white striped tie.

"Dr. McAlistair," he gushed. "A pleasure to meet you."

Alison nodded.

The room, chilly and immaculate, smelled of formalin. The cement-block walls were painted a shiny light gray, the concrete floor a dark gray. A sheet-draped form laid out on a stainless steel table occupied the center of the room.

Toby produced a clean, starched lab coat and held it for Alison, who slipped her arms into it. He turned to the others. "Stay behind that line, if you will, please." He pointed to a red stripe on the floor.

Alison donned a facemask and snapped on latex gloves. She pulled the sheet down gently, uncovering Peg's face, neck, and shoulders.

Victoria shut her eyes for a moment, then opened them again.

Alison studied Peg without touching her at first. Then she examined Peg's throat, looked into her mouth, lifted Peg's closed eyelids.

She turned to Victoria. "The fall down the steps didn't kill her."

Howland grunted.

Smalley stepped forward. "What have you found, Dr. McAlistair?"

"Strangled?" Victoria asked.

"Quite likely," said Alison. "You may cross the red line, Mrs. Trumbull. Look here." She pointed out what looked to Victoria like thumb marks on the front of Peg's neck, then turned Peg's head slightly, and Victoria saw, clearly, finger marks on the sides of her neck.

Smalley cleared his throat.

"It's not as obvious as you may think, Mrs. Trumbull," said Alison, ignoring Smalley. "Some fabric object was first pressed against her face. A pillow or towel, something like that." She moved a large magnifying lens that hung from an overhead armature to Peg's face. "You can see fibers. I'll collect and bag them, and the state police lab in Sudbury will identify them." She moved the glass so Victoria could see the marks on Peg's neck. "I don't believe she was smothered to death, though. She may or may not have lost consciousness, and was then strangled."

"Dr. McAlistair . . ." said Smalley.

Alison pulled the sheet back over Peg's face, and then removed her gloves and facemask. She tossed them into the plastic-lined trash container, then slipped off the still-immaculate lab coat. Victoria was about to protest about wasteful laundering, when Toby dropped it into a nearby hamper.

"You saw me look at her eyes?" Alison asked.

Victoria nodded.

"I found small red dots or streaks on the whites of her eyes and her eyelids. Petechial hemorrhages. Typical of asphyxiation. Caused by blood leaking from ruptured capillaries. Most assuredly, she did not die by falling down the stairs."

"You're talking to a member of the press, you know," Howland grumbled.

Smalley, who'd been pacing back and forth behind the red line, said, "This information is not to leave the room."

"We'll need to perform a complete autopsy on Ms. Storm," said Alison, nodding to both Howland and Smalley. "We'll take her to Boston for that. I'll give you what little information I can, Mrs. Trumbull."

Howland dropped Victoria at her house,

leaving with a cryptic comment about girls and sororities. Victoria didn't respond. She sat in her caned armchair at the cookroom window watching thunderclouds build up in the west and thought about Peg's death. Who would have harmed her, and why? She'd been a pleasant, friendly young woman.

And she thought about Teddy. If she were an eight-year-old boy, where would she go? The phone rang, startling her.

"Victoria? Ruth Byron here. I've been trying to reach you for the past hour. I need to talk to you." Her voice quavered with anger. "How can he consider opening the play tonight under the circumstances? Even Equity players have more sensitivity."

Victoria listened to the Island Playhouse founder until she finally wound down, then remarked, "A professional troupe, according to Dearborn, doesn't let mere death disrupt a performance."

"An actress dead and a child gone missing?"

"Tonight's performance is sold out."

"How crass," Ruth sputtered. "Any publicity is good, no matter how tasteless, according to him. I don't know what possessed my sister to marry that man in the first place. Or me to hire him," she added bitterly. "I suppose I was trying to get my sister off my back."

Victoria traced the pattern of the red-checked tablecloth with her thumbnail. "He's a good director. You recognized that. Your sister is an actress, too, isn't she?"

Ruth snorted. "So she claims. You knew Dearborn had been fired from his two previous directing jobs, didn't you?"

"No. Why?"

"Drinking. Rebecca has no talent and yet she behaves like a prima donna. No one wants to hire her. And Dearborn can't hold down a director's job because of his drinking." Ruth paused. "Nine months ago I made him an offer. I hired him on the condition that he quit drinking and join AA."

"The automobile association?"

Ruth ignored Victoria's attempt at humor. "Every time Dearborn sobers up, Rebecca finds him just too, too boring, so they separate."

"I understand that often happens when one spouse is a recovering alcoholic."

"Those two have gone through the cycle — drinking, drying out, Becca leaving, Dearborn drinking again, reconciliation — I can't tell you how many times. You'd think I'd have known better than to believe my offer would change things."

"Where's your sister now?"

"She's still in touch with Dearborn, even though they're living apart," said Ruth. "Right now they're concocting a scheme to get the theater away from me."

"Equity?"

"Convincing my backers that the theater should go Equity, yes. I didn't found the theater as a profit-making venture."

"Why is your sister doing this to you?"

"Aunt Fifi left the building to me. With the stipulation that it be used as a community theater. Rebecca has always resented that. Not real theater, says Rebecca, as if she knows what real theater is. You'll never make money, she says. Well, I don't want to make money, Victoria. Ticket sales cover the utility bills, with enough left over to keep up the building."

"Doesn't she know, a community theater is supposed to be just that? Community members having a good time putting on plays for others' enjoyment?"

"You don't need to convince me, Victoria. But those two are pushing, pushing, pushing for Equity theater, Equity actors, Equity salaries . . ."

"And Equity ticket prices. I'm sorry I agreed to write that play. I've let you down by working with Dearborn, I'm afraid."

"You wrote it at my request, Victoria. This Equity issue came up later, after we'd started rehearsals."

Victoria moved her chair so she could get a better view of the brewing storm. High up, the thunderheads were flattening into classic anvil shapes. "Howland has refused to go on stage tonight as the monster, so the understudy is taking his place."

"Roderick?" Ruth groaned. "That ham. Who's taking over Peg's role now she's dead?"

"The stage manager."

"Nora? Oh dear. And Teddy's role?"

"Dearborn had a friend's daughter in reserve." Victoria shifted the phone to her other ear. "He plans to round up actors to read the parts of Frankenstein's bride and . . ."

"Dawn Haines dropped out? That's a surprise. She's a fine actress."

"She's not fond of Dearborn."

"Who else?"

"Gerard Cohen, who plays the blind man."

"I thought Gerard was a friend of Himself?"

"Gerard was a friend of Peg's, too."

"Yes. Of course." Ruth was quiet.

"Bruce Duncan has bowed out."

"Isn't he on Dearborn's team?"

"Bruce is convinced life is following art."

"That's stretching credulity."

"Bruce is good at that," said Victoria.

"Who's taking over his role?"

"Robert Scott, who plays the Arctic explorer."

Ruth paused for a long moment. "Dearborn was asking for trouble, casting Bob in that play. In any part."

"Why?"

"I'm not sure you want to hear this, Victoria. Bob and my sister, Rebecca, had, and probably are still having, a broiling hot affair, ever since Dearborn went on his latest wagon. That's part of their cycle. When he's on the wagon, she beds down some apeman primitive. When Dearborn starts drinking again, Rebecca dumps her latest. Bob Scott thinks he's IT with Rebecca, in capital letters. He's not." Ruth changed the subject abruptly.

"You did a superb job of adapting the book to the stage, Victoria. Kept to the story while avoiding the difficult parts."

"Doesn't this kind of behavior on Rebecca's part bother Dearborn?"

"He's so involved in himself, I'm not sure he notices."

"Robert Scott seems utterly different from Dearborn, rather a natural being."

"You mean unwashed and nonintellectual," said Ruth.

"Robert Scott seems a logical substitute for Bruce Duncan," Victoria added. "He's not a bad actor, and the Arctic explorer appears only at the very beginning and end of the play. The two are never on stage at the same time."

"I can't get over how wrong Dearborn is for going ahead with opening night," said Ruth. "The entire cast should be out searching for Teddy."

"Peg was so thrilled when she got a part in the play," Victoria mused.

"Such a freak accident."

"Accident . . ." Victoria started to say more, but an image of Smalley made her stop.

"You don't think it was an accident?"

Victoria was silent.

Ruth cleared her throat. "I don't want to get into that, Victoria. Actually, I called you for another reason. My son."

"George? He's in graduate school now, isn't he?"

"Yale Drama," said Ruth. "His advisor called this morning to say George hasn't shown up for classes for a couple of days, and she's concerned."

"Do you have any idea where he might be?"

Elizabeth tiptoed into the kitchen, filled the teakettle, and plugged it in. Victoria looked up and lifted a hand.

"I'm afraid so," said Ruth. "When I told George about Uncle Dearborn and Aunt Rebecca and their latest move, he was as upset as I am, more so. He has my Irish blood. I suspect he's on his way to the Island to do battle for me."

"Good."

"No, no, Victoria. He mustn't tangle with Dearborn. He'll only make things worse. This is why I wanted to talk to you. He'll ruin his career before it starts. If you see George, please talk to him. He'll listen to you."

"I'll gladly hold his coat for him," said Victoria.

Dearborn Hill had been on the phone most of the morning trying to find actors willing to substitute for those who'd refused to go on stage tonight. Opening night. Amateurs, all of them. His hair was no longer artistically rumpled. He'd run his fingers through it so many times it was lank and disheveled. He'd had so many cups of coffee, his hands shook. He wanted a drink badly. Becca's sanctimonious sister had offered him the artistic director's job with too many strings attached, he thought with resentment. Twice he'd gotten up from his desk, ready to drive to the liquor store in Oak Bluffs. Then he realized how little time he had and went back to making his phone calls.

There'd be a sell-out crowd tonight, he told himself. Peg's death and Teddy's disappearance would guarantee ticket sales. The substitute actors would have to read their parts, but the audience would understand. Add to the enjoyment.

He'd found a new little William right away, the precocious seven-year-old daughter of a board member.

Bob Scott would play two parts, the Arctic explorer and Bruce Duncan's role as Frankenstein's boyhood friend.

Did Nature Boy think he didn't notice what was going on between him and Becca? Dearborn smiled to himself. One of these days, he'd take care of Bob Scott. No hurry.

What an ass Bruce Duncan was. Wooden when he was on stage, theatrical when he was off. Even Scott was a better actor.

He hadn't found a substitute yet for Gerard Cohen, who played the blind father. He was surprised when Cohen refused to go on tonight. Cohen was one of his supporters. He, Dearborn, could play both the blind man and Victor Frankenstein. The two were never on stage at the same time.

The bride of Frankenstein was a problem. As insufferable as she was, Dawn Haines was an excellent actress, knew her lines, didn't over-emote, knew how to cover for someone else's missed lines. Dearborn tapped his fingers on the desk and slapped his shirt pocket as though he still carried cigarettes. He'd quit smoking three years ago.

And then he had an idea. What was Victoria Trumbull's granddaughter's name? Perfect. She'd be perfect. Elizabeth Trumbull, that was it. He picked up the phone and dialed Victoria's number.

Elizabeth answered. "Absolutely not," she said, when he identified himself and told her why he was calling. "No way."

Dearborn Hill could be charming when he wanted to be. He talked about her grandmother's play. The work, the art, the soul her grandmother had put into her adaptation of the old classic. He spoke about the traditions of the theater. The show must go on. He mentioned gently and tastefully how Peg's passing would be honored. He avoided any talk of the sell-out crowd he hoped to attract. He cajoled, apologized, appealed to her loyalty to her grandmother, appealed to her sense of vanity, and, under other circumstances, might have worn Elizabeth down.

She looked up and saw her grandmother's expression.

Victoria was variously described as looking like an owl or an eagle. Now, she looked like a stone warrior. Her flushed cheeks seemed to be daubed with war paint. Her deepset hooded eyes glittered.

"Sorry, Dearborn. Find someone else," Elizabeth said, and disconnected.

On his end, before Elizabeth hung up, Dearborn heard what was unmistakably Victoria Trumbull's low, clear voice saying, "The idea! The very idea!" and he frowned as he pressed the button that cut off the connection.

"Why on earth would he call here?" Victoria sputtered. " 'The show must go on,' indeed. How unfeeling! How mercenary! My own granddaughter . . . !"

Elizabeth held up her hands to ward off her grandmother. "Hey, Gram. I told him no. Anyway, I've got to work tonight."

CHAPTER 9

Elizabeth left for the afternoon shift at the harbor, where she was assistant dockmaster, and Victoria was alone again. She tapped her fingers absently on the space bar of her typewriter until the bell dinged. Where would she hide if she were eight years old?

She went back to work on her column. Thunder grumbled in the distance. She heard a knock on the kitchen door, and she opened it to two girls wearing jeans, backpacks, and running shoes. They smiled uncomfortably.

"Mrs. Trumbull?" the shorter of the girls asked.

"Yes?"

"I'm Tracy and this is my friend Karen." Tracy was slender with short dark hair. She pointed to the taller girl. "Karen and me, we're here for the summer and need a place to stay?"

"Oh?" said Victoria.

Tracy shifted her feet uneasily. "We stopped at the police station." She glanced up at Karen. "And a woman, like, fixing their computer, told us you sometimes rent rooms?"

"Come in." Victoria opened the door wider. The clouds had begun to fill the sky to the northwest. A stiff wind tossed the tips of the cedars in the pasture and flipped the leaves on the Norway maple. "Looks as though you got here just in time."

As she spoke, lightning flashed, followed by a rumble of thunder. The girls stood uncertainly inside the door.

"Have a seat," Victoria suggested, indicating the gray-painted kitchen chairs.

They took off their backpacks and set them on the floor, then perched, as though ready to take flight.

Victoria seated herself at the kitchen table across from them. "Are you vacationing?"

"We're working at the Harborlights Motel?" said Tracy.

Karen nodded. "Waiting tables." Karen had great quantities of curly blond hair, disheveled in a way that Victoria, who was not usually critical of styles, wanted to brush into some kind of order. "We were staying in Chilmark, but . . ." Karen ran a hand through the mop of hair. She glanced

111

quickly at Tracy.

"It's kind of far to commute," said Tracy. "Your house is right on the bus route."

Victoria wondered where this was going. "Yes, it is convenient."

"We tried hitchhiking . . ." said Karen, and stopped.

"It's quite safe on the Island," said Victoria. "I often get around that way."

The girls looked at each other, then at Victoria. Tracy sighed, then blurted out. "We were hitching last night and got picked up by, like, a really weird *thing* . . ."

"I suppose it was covered with blood, with fangs and stitches and electrodes coming out of its head?"

The girls stared at Victoria.

"That's our local drug enforcement agent, Howland Atherton . . ." Victoria started to say, but Karen interrupted.

"We don't do drugs!"

Victoria held up a hand to reassure them. "The police picked up Mr. Atherton after you called nine-one-one . . ."

"That *thing* was DEA? *Undercover?*" Tracy blurted out.

Victoria got up, filled the teakettle and plugged it in. "Mr. Atherton was in costume for a play. The police have been trying to locate you."

"Us?" Karen glanced uncomfortably from Victoria to Tracy. *"Drugs?"* She ran her fingers through her hair again, and Victoria thought about offering her a comb. "My parents would kill me if they thought . . . !"

Tracy pulled a cell phone out of her jeans pocket. "Maybe the battery's low?"

The sky had darkened during the few minutes since the girls arrived. Victoria switched on the light.

"Cellular phones have poor reception on the Island. Call Sergeant Smalley at the state police right away and let him know you're safe." Victoria showed them where the phone and directory were. "After you talk to him we can see about a room."

Karen found the number and Tracy punched it in. She explained to Sergeant Smalley about Roddie, the poet at Island Java who said it was okay to hitchhike, then about the creature stopping to pick them up. She handed the phone to Victoria. "He wants to talk to you, Mrs. Trumbull."

Smalley said, "Do you know anything about this Roddie character, Mrs. Trumbull?"

"He's Dearborn Hill's nephew, Roderick Hill. He reads often at Island Java. His poetry is quite good."

"He have a job?"

"He works at Rapid Express Agency at the airport."

"How old is the guy?"

"Early twenties."

Smalley paused and Victoria could hear his swivel chair squeak. "Until I sort things out, can you put the girls up for a few days?"

"There's nothing wrong with Roderick that a few years won't cure." Victoria glanced over at the two girls and nodded. "But I'll find room for them."

Tracy and Karen looked at each other and grinned.

"Thanks, Mrs. Trumbull. We owe you. For accommodating Dr. McAlistair as well." Smalley hung up.

Lightning flashed, and an immediate clap of thunder rattled the house. Karen put her hands over her ears. The lights dimmed, then brightened again. Rain slashed against the glass.

Victoria got up again. "I'd better shut the windows before everything gets soaked."

"We'll help," said Tracy.

They went from floor to floor, closing the old sashes.

"The big attic has two more, but I'll leave those open. There's not much up there that rain can damage."

"We'll shut them, if you'd like," said Tracy.

"Thank you. That would be nice." Victoria opened the door to the steep attic stairs and the girls scampered up. They returned almost immediately.

"The one in the room with the bed was already closed, Mrs. Trumbull," said Tracy.

Victoria thought about that for a moment. "My granddaughter must have shut it for some reason. What about the other window?"

"That was open, but rain wasn't coming in."

"Does someone sleep up there?" Karen asked.

"Sometimes. Visiting great-grandchildren like to camp out in the attic."

"I didn't realize you had a dog, Mrs. Trumbull," Karen said.

"I don't have a dog," said Victoria. She studied Karen and her unruly hair. "I have a cat. No dog would dare trespass on McCavity's territory."

"Oh," said Karen, sounding puzzled.

"Let me show you your room." Victoria opened a door leading off a small hallway and the girls peered in.

"Awesome!" said Karen.

"Wow," said Tracy. "This house is huge! *Two* attics."

The small attic room over the kitchen was

bright, despite the gloom outside. Two east-facing skylights looked out on dark clouds and the tops of wind-lashed trees. A window on the south overlooked the roof of the one-story cookroom. Rain streamed down the asphalt shingles. The bare boards of the ceiling sloped steeply to low walls. A braided rug in shades of red, gray, and white covered most of the painted floor.

Lightning flashed.

Karen covered her ears.

"Did your house ever get, you know, hit by lightning, Mrs. Trumbull?" asked Tracy.

"Not that I know of."

Rain sheeted down the outside of the skylights.

"We brought sleeping bags," said Karen. "We can sleep on the floor."

"You won't need to do that." Victoria started down the enclosed staircase that led down to the kitchen, bracing her hands against the walls for support. "I have folding cots in the big attic. You can bring them down later."

"Can we move right in?" asked Karen.

"Certainly."

"We don't have a lot of money," said Tracy.

"We can work something out."

"Is someone else staying here?"

"My granddaughter, Elizabeth, lives with

me, and Dr. McAlistair will stay a few nights. She's a forensic scientist."

"Forensic, like in somebody murdered?" asked Tracy.

"Yes," said Victoria. "Just like that."

CHAPTER 10

Dearborn Hill had run out of time. He'd given up hope of getting a substitute for the role of Frankenstein's bride.

A hell of a thunderstorm was raging, clanging, dimming lights, dropping torrents of rain. An appropriate prelude to opening night of this play.

The stage manager would have to read the part of Frankenstein's bride as well as the part of Justine. He cursed Dawn Haines and her lack of professionalism. Dawn was ideal for the role, good voice, good figure, and a stage presence hard to define. Bratty, snippish, spoiled, but a fine actress.

Nora was a fine stage manager, but no actress. She had a shrill voice and no sex appeal. Resented the idea of projecting sex appeal. She'd trudge onto the stage, he knew, read the lines accurately but woodenly, and trudge offstage again.

He wanted a drink badly. To hell with AA

and the agreement with his sister-in-law. When the theater turned Equity, he'd tell the backers she had to go. Maybe then she'd understand.

A drink. Becca had always liked him best after he'd had a drink or two. Every time he'd sobered up, their marriage went on the rocks. At which thought he envisioned himself with a Jack Daniel's, rattling the ice cubes and being terribly witty.

He thought about her grubby affairs every time he went on the wagon. Bob Scott. What could she possibly see in that dirt-caked landscaper? When Scott tried out for the part of the Arctic explorer, Dearborn's first reaction had been to send him packing. His second reaction was to give the guy the role. Smother him with his lack of sophistication. He sighed. And just then, his phone rang.

"Yes?" he answered wearily.

"Dearborn, darling!"

"Becca," he said with surprise. "Where are you?"

"On Island, darling. Just got in from Boston. Getting soaking wet outside the ferry terminal. Do I hear you have a play opening tonight and no actors?"

Dearborn groaned. "A death and a kid missing."

"The play must go on."

"That's theater," said Dearborn.

"Have you talked to my holier-than-thou sister?"

"Unfortunately, yes."

"What did she say about all this?"

"What you'd expect."

"She's appalled at your insensitivity, isn't that right?"

Dearborn grunted.

"The ghoulish public will flock to the theater?"

He grunted again.

"I know my sister." Becca's voice rose. "She pulled the wool over Aunt Fifi's eyes. Actress, indeed. Ruth can't act her way out of a wet paper bag. Auntie had no right to give her that building." Dearborn could hear her tapping her fingernails on the phone. "*I'm* the actor in the family, and always have been. Ruth and her, quote, community theater. Piffle!"

" 'Piffle'?" Dearborn's spirit lifted slightly. "Do you plan to come to the opening tonight?"

"Can you guarantee that my dear sister will *not* be there?"

Dearborn thought about his wife's voice and her ability to project it. How she could move her body to denote aggression or submission or dejection or wild sexuality. He wanted her badly.

"You're not saying anything, darling," Becca purred.

"I can guarantee Ruth won't be there."

"Maybe I'll come, then," Becca murmured.

Dearborn thought for a moment, then cleared his throat. "You wouldn't consider going on stage tonight, would you?"

"Moi?" said Becca. "*Moi?* With no rehearsals? You're joking. I don't even know what the hell play you're putting on."

"Frankenstein."

Becca's laugh rose from cello through viola to violin, trembled with vibrato, tossed out a bassoon note or two, warbled into a flute aria, and ended with a tympanic rumble. "And what part am I expected to play, the bride of Frankenstein?"

"Yes," said Dearborn, astonished that she'd identified the very role he wanted her to play. "You'd be perfect."

"Darling, I'm speechless!" murmured Becca. "A bride made up of discarded human parts, partially decomposed, stitched together with wire, limbs that don't quite fit the torso?"

"No, no," said Dearborn. "That's Frankenstein's monster. He constructs the monster in his college dorm."

"Darling!" said Becca, breathlessly.

"No, no," Dearborn repeated. "Franken-stein's bride is a lovely young girl, pure, in-nocent. Fresh, untouched beauty."

"Innocent? Pure?" Laughter again. "How sweet!"

Dearborn's spirits rose further. "You can do it, Becca."

"Of course I could, darling," she said, us-ing her lower register. "But I won't."

"The audience doesn't expect you to know your lines. You can read them, and you *can*." He took a breath and heard a rumble of thunder. "The bride of Franken-stein has never been given a break before now. I can see you reading that part. The subtlety, the hidden wit, the naïve girl with a raging appetite. For unknown delights," he added.

"That's in the play?" asked Becca.

"The role is yours to do with as you wish. You'll enthrall the audience. No one has ever done this. We've been fed movie and television versions until that's all we know. This play is the real thing." He thumped his fist on the desk. "With your acting, no one will even notice the play script in your hand."

Had he hooked her yet?

"You need a drink, darling," she whispered.

"Pull this off and I'll take you to any bar on the Island."

"I suppose you'll be drinking your usual Shirley Temples?" she muttered. "I don't drink alone."

"By Godfrey, I'll join you."

"I'll think about it," murmured Becca.

"Double-time run-through in a half-hour?"

"I'll let you know."

Dearborn cleared his throat delicately. "Grand way to jerk your sister's chain."

Peal of merry laughter. "What a silver tongue you have, darling. See you in twenty minutes, then," and she hung up.

Dearborn opened his bottom desk drawer and took out the Jack Daniel's he'd bought earlier, when he'd felt his lowest. He broke the seal, twisted off the cap, poured an inch, two inches, of the tawny liquid into the bottom of the mug he'd been drinking coffee from all afternoon, and, to celebrate, downed the first drink he'd had in eight months, sixteen days, and, he looked at his watch, three hours.

Trooper Tim Eldredge reported to Sergeant Smalley at the police barracks after interviewing Jefferson Vanderhoop on his boat. He had tried, too, to track down Peg Storm's ex-husband, Leonard Vincent. Eldredge had been caught in the downpour, and was now wet, rumpled, exhausted, unshowered, and unshaven.

Smalley was still crisply pressed and smelled clean. "So the T-shirt shop doesn't know Mr. Storm?"

"Mr. Vincent, sir," said Eldredge.

"Vincent, then."

"They know who he is, but he doesn't live there."

"Or work there?"

"No, sir."

"Check with the registry. Must have a driver's license."

"No record of a license, sir."

Smalley sat at his desk. "Check the voting records, Tim."

"Yes, sir. I did. He's not registered."

"In none of the six towns?"

"No, sir."

Smalley swiveled his chair and faced the corner of the room where the flag of the Commonwealth hung limply on its staff. "A person can't hide forever on this Island."

"No, sir."

"You check at the courthouse, the address he gave in the divorce records?"

"Yes, sir. His sister's address in Jersey City."

"What did his sister have to say?"

"The address turned out to be a Chinese restaurant."

Smalley swiveled back. "Contact the Jersey City police."

"Yes, sir. No record of anyone named Vincent, man or woman. Or Storm, either."

"In the entire city?"

"Yes, sir."

Smalley ran a hand over his short hair and muttered, "Where can the guy be?"

Eldredge was about to drop into the wooden armchair in front of Smalley's desk, but propped himself up, holding its back instead. "Sir, would you mind if I went home and changed?"

Smalley stood. "Sorry, Tim. Of course." He looked at his watch. "Two hours give you enough time?"

"Yes, sir," said Eldredge, stifling a yawn.

The storm had passed and sunlight streamed through the far clouds. Victoria, wearing black rubber boots muddy almost to her ankles from the afternoon's rain, was out in the glorious afternoon, deadheading irises in the perennial border. Casey pulled up next to her in the police Bronco. The rain had left behind sweet-smelling air, puddles, and mud.

Victoria shaded her eyes with a dirt-caked hand. "Rabbits."

Casey leaned toward the window. "What about rabbits?"

"They ate every one of my tulips this spring. Just nipped off the buds, before they had a chance to bloom."

"Doesn't McCavity scare them off?"

"He watches." Victoria took a swipe at a faded iris blossom with her secateurs. "I hope you got Patrick and his friends to the beach before the storm hit."

"They had enough time for a dip."

Victoria tucked her secateurs into the pocket of her trousers. "I assume you're here on business?"

Casey nodded. "Flights from Boston to the Vineyard were canceled because of the storm, so Teddy Vanderhoop's mother took the bus to Woods Hole and caught the boat that gets in at four-thirty. I'm picking her up in Vineyard Haven."

"Why the West Tisbury police?"

"The Tisbury and state cops are working both cases — the missing boy and the death of Peg." Casey paused. "Understand you were at the funeral parlor?"

"Yes."

"Did Sergeant Smalley say anything to you, Victoria?"

"He told me, in no uncertain tones, to keep quiet."

"He told me Peg didn't die from the fall."

Victoria wiped her muddy hands on her corduroy trousers. "Give me a minute or two to wash up and change my clothes."

"Kind of wet for gardening, isn't it?"

"I've been planting some *Dodecatheon poeticum.* An Oregon friend sent me a dozen or so bulblets."

"Yeah?" said Casey. "What's the 'dodeca' part. I can guess the rest."

"Shooting star. Poet's shooting star."

"Appropriate. At least no one's tried to shoot Frankenstein yet. Maybe he'll do the shooting, since he's the star."

Victoria ignored Casey's attempt at humor. "The flowers are quite beautiful, a sort of rose-lavender. They look like miniature badminton shuttlecocks. I hope the ground isn't too wet." Victoria splashed through a small lake in the driveway and headed into the house, stomping mud off her boots on the entry mat.

Casey listened to the police radio while she waited. Communications was calling the West Tisbury police. Someone had thrown a brick through the window of the Rapid

127

Express Agency's office at the airport. Casey lifted the mike and called her sergeant, Junior Norton.

"Right, chief. On my way."

A few minutes later, Victoria appeared, clean, combed, and calling out instructions to someone behind her.

Casey opened the door. "Is your granddaughter home?"

Victoria hoisted herself into her seat. "Elizabeth's at work. But I've acquired two more guests."

Casey headed out of the driveway. "In addition to the doc?" She braked to let a dump truck go by on the Edgartown Road.

"The hitchhikers the police were looking for showed up at my house. I'm putting them up temporarily." Victoria pulled down the visor and checked her reflection in the mirror. "Will Mrs. Vanderhoop want to stay somewhere other than her own house?"

"You don't happen to have an extra room, do you, Victoria?"

"I have the downstairs bedroom. She should stay away from her own house until we find Teddy and solve Peg's murder."

"*State* police are the ones who solve murders."

The radio crackled and Junior Norton's voice came on. "Chief, you know the brick that was thrown through the Rapid Express office?"

"What about it?" asked Casey.

"A note was wrapped around the brick. On VETA letterhead."

"VETA?" asked Casey.

"Vineyarders for the Ethical Treatment of Animals. Says, 'Even cannibals don't stew innocent fish. Only REAL people do.' "

"What in hell is that supposed to mean?"

"REAL is Rapid Express Agency Limited, and fish refers to a shipment of five hundred goldfish that one of their employees left out on the tarmac in the sun over the weekend."

CHAPTER 11

The wet road steamed in the low evening sun. A passing car sprayed the windshield, and Casey switched on the wipers.

"I'm sorry about the goldfish that died," said Casey. "Seems like an awful waste. But is the brick thrower threatening revenge on Rapid Express employees because of some goldfish?"

"I shouldn't be surprised," said Victoria.

"Trouble is, I have to take this kind of stuff seriously. You never can tell with these wackos."

"What can you do?"

"I'll ask Junior to check on the Island membership of VETA and talk to whoever's in charge," said Casey.

Victoria thought for a moment. "You know Bruce Duncan, don't you?"

"Sure. He's in your play. Short, balding guy in his mid-thirties."

"He may know who was getting the shipment of goldfish. He's quite outspoken about animal rights. I suppose that includes goldfish."

"I guess."

"He works for Precious Pets, the pet store."

"Yeah?"

"Who was to receive the shipment of fish?"

"I'll ask Junior to check that out," said Casey, picking up the radio mike.

They drove down the hill where Howland had stopped for the girls the night before and continued toward the ferry dock. Vehicles were lined up in the staging area for the next boat, which was rounding the jetty.

A small intense woman with short, dark, curly hair paced back and forth outside the terminal. Victoria checked her watch. "That's Mrs. Vanderhoop. She's waited almost an hour."

"At least it's not raining," said Casey.

Teddy's mother paced to the railing that overlooked the dinghy dock, turned, and paced back toward the staging area. The arriving ferry was backing into its slip, doors open, cars ready to disembark. A steamship authority crew member, still in yellow foul-weather gear, extended an arm to stop her. She nodded, swiveled around, and paced back toward the railing.

Casey pulled into a nearby parking spot. "She's really wound up tight."

"Wouldn't you be?"

"How well do you know her, Victoria?"

"Not well. She brings Teddy to rehearsals, then watches from the back of the auditorium until he's finished. During rehearsals, he usually sits with me, then he and his mother go home together."

"A typical stage mother?"

"I suppose so," Victoria mused. "I think I might be, too, if my eight-year-old were performing in a play."

"He's not simply in a play, he's an eight-year-old who's hit the big time in television, and his whole life is about to change. I wouldn't want that for Patrick." Casey shook her head. "Not a normal life for a kid."

"He's a wonderful actor," said Victoria.

"Acting in plays at the playhouse, that's different." Casey opened the door and held it open. "I mean, that's fun, not work." She slid out and slammed the door shut. "Wait here, Victoria. I'll get her luggage."

Victoria could imagine what must be going through Mrs. Vanderhoop's mind. Casey helped retrieve her suitcases from the baggage cart, wheeled them to the Bronco, and stowed them in back. Teddy's mother climbed into the seat behind Victoria.

Victoria greeted her soberly.

Casey leaned over the seat. "Mrs. Trumbull says you can stay with her while we look for your son, Mrs. Vanderhoop."

"Thank you. I *would* feel better." She sat back, then immediately sat forward again. "Is there any word of Teddy? I've been out of touch since early this morning."

"Not yet," said Casey. "All six Island police departments and the state police are searching for him."

"Have they found any clues?"

"Tracks of bicycle tires in Ms. Storm's driveway."

"Teddy's?"

"We assume so, Mrs. Vanderhoop."

"Please, call me Amanda."

"The tracks made a sharp U-turn, and an opened-up comic book was face down on the ground as if it had fallen out of a carrier or basket," said Casey.

Amanda smiled faintly. "He must have gone home for his bike and his comic books."

"The state police think Teddy realized something was wrong in Peg's house and left in a hurry." Casey backed out of the parking spot. "Quite probably, he's hiding somewhere. Any thoughts on who he might run to?"

"None at all. Unless his father took him."

Casey said nothing.

Amanda asked, "Is anyone posted at my house? I mean, in case Teddy comes home?"

"A state trooper is stationed around the clock at Peg Storm's."

"Yes, of course." Amanda waited until Casey turned around and was headed back toward Five Corners. "Would you mind stopping at my place so I can pick up my car and a few clothes?"

"Your car," said Casey. "I'm not sure about going into your house. Straight ahead?"

"Straight, yes."

They crossed through the congested traffic of Five Corners onto Lagoon Pond Road. After they passed Maciel Marine they turned left onto the Job's Neck Road and pulled up in front of Amanda's. Next door, yellow police tape circled Peg's house.

Victoria unsnapped her seatbelt and turned again to look at Amanda, who was holding her face in her hands.

"I got to know Teddy well when we sat together at the theater, Amanda. He's a bright boy. He wouldn't allow anyone to harm him."

"His father didn't want Teddy acting

134

professionally. We argued about my son's career. When I — when Teddy, that is — got the contract, his father demanded half of everything Teddy earned. Half, of his own son's earnings."

"The state police interviewed your ex on his boat," said Casey.

"His boat. That's all he cares about. Trying to make Teddy into a fisherman like him." Amanda blotted her eyes with a wadded-up tissue.

Sergeant Smalley came down the front steps of the house next door, Peg's house, and strode over to the Bronco. He introduced himself to Amanda.

"Okay if Mrs. Vanderhoop gets her clothes?" Casey asked. "She's staying with Victoria."

"Afraid not." He turned to Amanda. "We obtained a search warrent to look through your house for traces of your son, Mrs. Vanderhoop. We need to go over it again. In the meantime, it's considered a crime scene. Sorry about that, but I'm sure you understand."

"I don't suppose the door was locked?" asked Casey.

"We left it the way it was. Back door unlocked."

"Yeah," said Casey. "Mind if we look

around?"

"Keep them on the other side of the tape."

They skirted the property, past the tall beech tree that shaded the house. At the top of the steps that lead up to the kitchen, a wooden toy box had fallen on its side, lid open, with Legos spilling out.

"I've told Teddy over and over and over to move that box before someone trips over it," Amanda scolded. "He . . ." She stopped.

"Sorry you can't go inside," said Casey.

"How long before I can get my clothes?"

"I'll check with Sergeant Smalley. Probably a day or so. After the state police finish."

Victoria moved cautiously along the edge of the crime scene tape. She stopped opposite the window and looked at the beech tree. "I loved climbing trees when I was Teddy's age. I imagine he does too?"

Amanda stared at the tree.

Victoria pointed to a broken branch. "Is that recent?"

"It wasn't broken when I left." Amanda crumpled the tissue she was holding.

"Has anyone found Teddy's bicycle?" asked Victoria.

"No, but . . ." said Casey.

Victoria continued. "If an intruder kidnapped Teddy, he probably would not have stopped to collect Teddy's bicycle."

"Victoria . . ." warned Casey

"If his bicycle is missing, Teddy must have taken it."

"I've forbidden him to ride on paved roads," said Amanda.

"Perhaps he felt this was an emergency," said Victoria, and added reassuringly, "I'm sure he's safe. And we'll find him."

Leonard Vincent had invested the money he'd gotten from his share of Peg's house in three acres of land in Chilmark and was building a four-bedroom house, a rental property that would support him for the rest of his life. In the meantime, he'd moved in with a woman friend, Penny Weiss. Penny lived in a shack, a small building Vineyarders call a camp, in the woods behind the Animal Rescue League on the outskirts of Edgartown. Her camp was about ten feet by sixteen feet, and consisted of a combination living room and kitchen, and a bedroom, which was essentially a double bed enclosed by plywood walls. A beaded curtain hid a toilet off to one side.

Leonard didn't share the double bed with Penny. He slept on the couch in the eight-by-ten-foot living room, and spent his time watching TV when he wasn't working on his house-to-be.

Penny, an artist, put up with Leonard because she liked to have a man around the house to open jars and scare off intruders, and because he was nice looking and could be a lot of fun. She painted watercolors of fishing boats and seagulls, which she sold at the Chilmark flea market. She supported herself, though, by cleaning houses.

She'd waited at a client's house until the storm was over before returning to her camp.

Leonard, dressed in his usual baggy, black long-sleeved shirt and black jeans, was watching a soap opera.

"Lennie, honey, I've got some bad news for you."

"Yeah?" Leonard moved his head because she was blocking his view of the program.

"I heard it on Island Radio in the car. Your ex was found dead last night."

"Yeah?" He glanced up at her.

"She fell down the cellar stairs." Penny set the grocery bags on the floor. "The police are looking for you. They want to question you."

"Tough. I got nothing to do with her."

"I guess they question everybody in a case like that."

"If she fell down the stairs and killed

herself, what do they think I can tell them?" Leonard said. "I'm not hiding."

"Want me to drive you to the police station?"

"Hell, no." Leonard stretched out his arms, displaying fine pectoral muscles. "They want me, they can find me."

CHAPTER 12

Ruth Byron's son, George, had come over on the four-thirty boat, the same one Teddy's mother was on. Both sat in the ferry lunchroom, Amanda in one of the booths, George on a fixed stool at the windows that faced forward. They didn't know each other, so when the boat docked in Vineyard Haven, George hitchhiked to his mother's in West Tisbury, while Teddy's mother made her phone call to Casey to pick her up at the ferry terminal.

George, a lusty young man in his early twenties, burst in through the back door of his mother's small cottage, found her washing dishes at the sink, snatched her off her feet and up into his arms, and kissed her soundly on both cheeks.

"Well!" said Ruth, once he set her down. "It's good to see you, too." She picked up the dish towel she'd dropped and wiped her wet hands on it. "George, dear, why aren't you in class?"

"I've come to rescue you from Uncle Dearborn."

"What makes you think I need rescuing?"

"You called."

Ruth grimaced. "That was just to be motherly. And to tell you about Victoria Trumbull's play."

"After your call, Cousin Roderick phoned. Upset because Howland Atherton got the part of the monster. All Roderick got was the understudy role."

"Ah. Roderick."

George was a giant male version of his mother. A wide mouth that turned up in a perpetual grin. Deep creases where his mother had dimples. A turned-up nose flanked by wide-spaced hazel eyes and an overall merry expression. Clearly, they were mother and son. George perched on a barstool he'd pulled out from under the counter.

"How long do you plan on staying, George?"

"Until I straighten out Uncle Dearborn."

Ruth gave him a wry look. "That might take a while."

"You need my support against that pompous ass and your green-eyed sister."

Ruth tossed the towel onto the counter.

"Dear George, love, I don't want you involved."

"I already am." He got up from his seat, snatched up the dish towel, and began to wipe a plate.

"You'll have to sleep on the couch. I'm having your room papered."

"I'll only be there at night."

"I had all your bedroom furniture moved to the barn."

"I'll sleep in the barn, then. Is that all right?" George finished wiping the plate and put it away.

"The costume barn is awfully dusty."

"I don't mind. We kids used to jump up and down on the prop furniture to see the dust rise."

Ruth smiled. "No wonder the cast griped about the springs."

"And we used to try on the costumes — sequined gowns, moth-eaten white flannel trousers, armor, flapper hats . . ."

"Cloches," Ruth mused. "From a Noel Coward production."

"We'd stage wars with the weapons — daggers and swords, guns and cudgels. It's a wonder we didn't kill each other."

"I'll get you clean sheets and a fresh pillow."

"I know where they are."

"You heard what happened yesterday, didn't you, George?"

"Not really. I've been on the road for two days."

"Two days? From New Haven? Surely you didn't walk?"

George grinned and snapped the dish towel playfully at his mother. "You were about to tell me something."

"Peg Storm is dead . . ."

George set down the half-dried knives and forks. "No!"

"Teddy has vanished and tonight is opening night."

"What happened?"

"The police found her at the foot of her cellar stairs."

"Why the police . . . ?"

"Teddy's mother called the police when there was no answer at Peg's house." Ruth emptied the dishpan into the sink.

George watched the soapy water spiral down the drain. "So he's had to cancel opening night. Serves him right."

"But he hasn't canceled, George." Ruth glanced at her son.

George sat again. "You're kidding!"

" 'The show must go on.' "

"And the actors?" He thrust his hands into his pockets.

143

"About half of them refused to go on stage tonight."

"What about the other half, Mom? Surely . . ."

"They agree with Dearborn — 'the show must go on.' " Ruth opened the cupboard under the sink and stowed the dishpan.

"With a dead actor and a missing kid?"

"Box office," said Ruth. "Equity points."

"No one will show up. That's totally off the wall."

Ruth shrugged. "This is summer. Off Islanders probably haven't heard about the death yet. Or if they have heard, they'll want to attend all the more. One thing I can assure you, George, dear, theater audiences are unpredictable."

"But who'll play the missing actors?"

"Various people. They'll have to read from the play script. I imagine your Uncle Dearborn has been on the phone most of the day. He tried to enlist Victoria's granddaughter, Elizabeth."

"For what?"

"The bride of Frankenstein."

George burst out laughing. "Nuts and bolts?" He bent over hooting with laughter. "Spare parts?" he sputtered. "Screws?"

"Stop it, George. This adaptation of the book is not like the movies and television."

George wiped his eyes on the back of his hand. "Is Uncle Dearborn going to read the part of the bride of Frankenstein, then?" He laughed some more. "In drag?"

"I have no idea who'll read. They're doubling up on parts. Bob Scott, who's playing the explorer, will probably read the part of Frankenstein's friend who tries to prevent him from creating the monster."

George laughed louder. "Bob Scott — the one who's having it off with Aunt Becca?"

"Don't be crude, George." Ruth frowned. "It's a serious play. Mary Shelley's book is full of symbolism and social meaning, and Victoria Trumbull's adaptation has captured that."

George stifled his mirth. "Sorry, Mumsy. This play is going to lay one large egg tonight. Just what we need to expose Uncle Asshole Dearborn."

Ruth shook her head. "George, dear, I don't think you understand how serious the problem is. Uncle Dearborn is a manipulator, and angels love to be manipulated. If he can convince them to back an Equity theater over my objections, that will be the end of the community theater I founded."

George held out his arms to his mother and embraced her. "You happen to have a comp ticket I can use tonight?"

"Surely, you're not thinking of going to the opening?"

"I might."

"But your Uncle Dearborn . . ."

"I can handle Uncle Dearborn."

"You think so? Aunt Rebecca as well?" Ruth pried herself out of her son's arms and fished through her purse. "Here's the ticket, George dear. I hope you know what you're doing."

"Trust me," said George, slipping the ticket into his shirt pocket and grinning. "I believe I *will* enjoy myself."

The costume barn was at the far end of Ruth's property, hidden by cedar and locust trees, high-bush blueberry, and wild grapevines that had overgrown the meadow. Carrying the clean bed linens, George loped down the dirt road that led to the barn, shoved the wide barn door to one side, and stopped in surprise.

His bed was off to one side, where the movers had probably left it, but it was roughly made up with sheets and a pillow. A lamp had been placed on a box next to the bed, where the movers would have no reason to set it, and a half-dozen new comic books were stacked next to the lamp. His bedroom bookcase had been shoved to one side of the bed, and its shelves were stocked with cans of baked beans, Vienna sausage, bags of chips, cookies, candy bars, a box of crackers, and bottles of soda.

The racks of costumes and stage furniture had been pushed to the back of the barn to make space for the impromptu bedroom.

Was someone staying here? The bed didn't look as though it had been slept in. His mother had said nothing about another visitor. George dropped the clean linens and his backpack on the bed and hurried back to the house in time to see the taillights of his mother's car disappear around a bend in the road.

Sergeant John Smalley, with Alison by his side, followed Casey into Victoria's drive.

"We just saw you at Peg's house, Sergeant," Victoria said.

"John picked me up in Vineyard Haven," said Alison. "I was shopping."

Teddy's mother had driven her own car from her house, and parked next to the police Bronco. Smalley carried her suitcases from the Bronco into the house, while Amanda waited uncertainly.

"Let me show you around," Victoria told her. "I won't take you up to the attic. The stairs are steep and I wouldn't want you to fall."

"Thank you, Mrs. Trumbull. I didn't look forward to being alone in my own house. And with Peg gone . . ."

When they returned to the kitchen, Smalley, Alison, and Casey were still talking cop talk.

"Have you had your supper yet, Sergeant?" asked Victoria.

"I'll pick up something on my way home, Mrs. Trumbull."

"There's enough soup for all of us."

"You sure? I don't want to . . ."

Victoria lifted the lid of the large, steaming soup kettle.

Smalley looked in and breathed deeply. "Lentils. I accept."

"My granddaughter made the soup. I usually add frankfurters just before serving." She looked in the small freezer above the refrigerator and shuffled things around. "I thought I had an opened package, but I seem to be mistaken." She found a new one, and Smalley opened the tough plastic with his pocketknife.

"Thanks for putting up the girls and Dr. McAlistair," he said. "Mrs. Vanderhoop, too. Looks like we've set you up in the hotel business."

"I can use the extra money," said Victoria.

Amanda got up quickly from the kitchen table. "Let me pay you now, Mrs. Trumbull, before I forget."

"A check is fine. Or cash." Victoria quoted a rate that seemed unreasonably high to her.

"Are you sure?" Amanda asked. "That seems awfully low."

Casey looked at her watch. "I've got to get home to Patrick, Victoria. See you all tomorrow?"

"Take care, chief." Smalley folded his knife and put it back in his pocket. "I was telling the chief I'm not comfortable with Roddie, the man who picked up the girls at the coffeehouse, Mrs. Trumbull."

"He's really only a boy. He is a bit different, but then he's a poet."

"I want to keep an eye on the girls until I know what he's up to."

"He's Dearborn Hill's nephew, his brother's son, and as I told you, he works for the Express office at the airport."

"He spends a lot of time at Island Java."

Victoria dropped the last slices of hot dog into the soup and set the lid back on the kettle. "I often read *my* poetry there. Poetry finally is regaining popularity after years of self-indulgent navel gazing." She took a breath. "It's about time people recognize how powerful poetry . . .”

Smalley quickly cut in. “This is different.”

“Poets should be among the highest paid . . .” she searched for the right word, and Smalley interrupted again.

“He attaches himself to girls sitting together, talks about his art and himself, and lets them pick up the tab.”

“He wouldn’t be the first impoverished artist. Did the girls complain?”

“No.” Smalley shook his head. “Where are they now?”

“They’ve been fixing up their room most of the afternoon.”

On cue, the girls came down the back stairs into the kitchen.

“We heard voices,” said Tracy. “Okay if we come down?”

“Of course,” said Victoria. “This is Sergeant Smalley. You spoke to him earlier today on the phone.”

“Hear you had quite a fright last night,” he said.

“Yes, sir,” said Tracy.

Amanda returned with her rent money and gave it to Victoria, who put the bills in her pocket, then introduced her to the girls. “Mrs. Vanderhoop will be staying with us for a day or so until we find her son.”

"Ma'am." Karen stood uncertainly by the stairs.

"Mrs. Trumbull will find your son," Tracy reassured her.

Amanda smiled faintly.

"Would you girls like to have supper with us?"

"Thanks, Mrs. Trumbull. But, like, we don't want to . . ."

Victoria waved the weak protest aside. "Set the table for seven. The dishes are in there." She pointed to the cupboard.

"Seven?" said Amanda.

"You, Sergeant Smalley, Tracy and Karen, and me. Alison, the forensic scientist, is staying with us, and you know Howland Atherton from the play, of course. Frankenstein's monster?"

Tracy stopped gathering utensils. "Mr. Atherton? The monster? The DEA agent? He's coming?"

"You'll get to see what he really looks like," said Victoria.

Karen glanced around. "Is he here now?"

"He'll be back shortly. He went home to feed his dogs."

The evening was cool and the aroma of the hearty soup, cooked all afternoon, filled the house.

By the time Howland showed up, Smalley

was ladling soup into bowls as Alison set them on the table. Howland looked quizzically from one to the other. "Had you two met each other before today?"

"I knew Alison by reputation." Smalley passed her another filled soup bowl.

Alison smiled.

"Meet your hitchhikers, Howland." Victoria introduced the girls, then ushered everyone into the dining room and seated herself at the head of the table.

The girls looked at each other nervously.

Howland turned his attention to them. "I wasn't thinking when I pulled over for you two. Sorry about that."

"Please everyone sit," said Victoria.

There was a general shuffling.

Alison said to Amanda, who was sitting next to her, "I'm so sorry you're going through this. I know what you're feeling."

Amanda looked down at her untouched soup and nodded.

CHAPTER 13

During supper, Amanda picked up her spoon, stirred her soup listlessly, and set the spoon back on her plate.

Victoria turned to Smalley, who was on her right. "Howland tells me you're a *Frankenstein* scholar."

"I wrote my senior thesis on *Frankenstein*," he said. "I understand your play follows Mary Shelley's book closely."

"Her book has been terribly misinterpreted." Victoria's eyes were bright. "I hope my adaptation will help people understand that *Frankenstein* is about social issues of the time, not the horrific aspects of the monster."

Tracy and Karen looked at each other and giggled.

"You see?" said Howland, reaching for the bread. "The monster has far more allure than man playing God."

"Same issues as today," said Smalley.

"Mary Shelley was concerned about technology. Today, we replace knees and hips with hi-tech materials, transplant kidneys, and pluck living hearts out of dead people. We keep the dead alive with technology."

"Brain transplants, next," said Alison. "Pass the bread."

"You're not implying technology is evil, are you, Smalley?" Howland handed the breadbasket to Alison. "Frankenstein's problem was that he was underfunded and unsupervised. For a first-year college student, a teenager working on his own, he did pretty well, scrounging body parts from cemeteries and morgues and stitching them together secretly by candlelight."

"Imagine the poor ventilation," said Alison. "He had to work in a hurry, once he acquired a corpse."

"Yuck!" said Karen.

"The monster had to be huge, so Frankenstein could work on the fine stitching," said Howland.

Victoria coughed politely.

Howland continued, "At least Frankenstein didn't have to worry about malpractice suits."

Alison broke off a corner of her bread. "The cost of malpractice insurance is why I'm in forensic medicine."

"The malpractice lawyers would have had a field day," said Howland. "The poor monster wasn't to blame. He was an innocent."

Amanda had been stirring her soup without eating. She spoke up for the first time. "The monster may have been innocent to begin with." She set her spoon on the side of her plate. "But three or four murders is hardly the work of an innocent."

"The second murder," said Victoria, "was the work of a flawed justice system. The monster killed little William, Justine didn't. She was innocent, yet she was convicted and hanged. Murdered by the so-called justice system."

"You see?" said Smalley. "Nothing's changed."

"May I have the butter?" Karen asked in a small voice.

"Bread, too?" asked Howland.

"Yes, please. Thanks."

Smalley folded his napkin and set it next to his empty soup bowl. "Two hundred years ago Mary Shelley saw technology as a threat to personal freedom. Nothing's changed there, either," he said. "Will we implant chips in people so medical records can be accessed, personal freedom be damned?" He turned to Victoria. "I want very much to see your play, Mrs. Trumbull. It's time to clear away the sensationalism that's overlain the book."

"Bravo!" Howland applauded. "Do any of you intend to go to opening night?" There were emphatic denials around the table. "What about you two?"

"We don't have tickets." Karen shook her head and her hair swirled about her face.

"Do you want to go? I have comp tickets I won't use."

"Really?" said Tracy.

Howland reached into his shirt pocket and handed two tickets to Tracy.

"Thanks, Mr. Atherton!" said Tracy. "Do we have time to get to the theater?"

Victoria checked her watch. "The bus goes past the house in a little over ten minutes. That will get you there in time."

After the girls left, the remaining diners sat around the table for a long time, finishing their coffee and conversing.

At eight, Victoria looked at her watch. "Curtain time."

"It must be difficult to be the playwright and miss opening night of your play," said Alison.

"Under the circumstances . . ." Victoria stopped in midsentence. "I have trouble understanding such insensitivity."

Howland laughed. "Dearborn? *Insensitive?*"

Tracy and Karen arrived at the playhouse in plenty of time and stood in a rapidly growing line.

"It's almost like a Broadway opening," said Tracy. "Look at the crowd."

Karen stood on tiptoe. "The line goes all the way down to Main Street."

"We're lucky to have tickets."

The doors opened, and the line slowly moved into the theater, which had been a barn when Ruth Byron's Aunt Fifi willed it to her. An usher took their tickets, and they moved up the steep steps with the crowd into what had been the hayloft.

Tracy and Karen found seats next to a cute guy who was sitting alone, about a third of the way up the tier of seats.

"Hi," said Tracy. "Are these seats taken?"

The guy smiled. "They are now."

Once Tracy and Karen had settled themselves, Tracy turned to him. "Do you live on the Island?"

"My mother does. I'm visiting her. How about you two?"

"We're working for the summer. The Harborlights Motel?"

"Nice place. Right on the harbor. Where

157

are you staying?"

"West Tisbury?"

He grinned. "That's where my mother lives. How did you get here to the theater?"

"By bus. And you?"

"Hitchhiked." He held out a hand to Tracy, then Karen. "I'm George Byron, by the way."

The girls introduced themselves. "We tried, like, hitchhiking last night," said Karen with a giggle. "You'll never guess what happened." She and Tracy told him about Frankenstein's monster picking them up, and how the monster was really a DEA agent, and they just had supper with him, and how they're living with the playwright.

"Victoria Trumbull is the playwright," said George. "She and my mother are good friends. My mother, Ruth Byron, owns the theater."

"Wow!" said Tracy and Karen together.

"This conversation is typical Island," said George. "Everyone's connected."

The lights dimmed and Dearborn Hill stepped onto the stage.

"That's my uncle," whispered George.

"Wow!" said Tracy and Karen together, again.

The audience fell silent.

Dearborn held his hands in a sort of

benediction and looked up to some unseen divine being. "Tonight's performance," he said in mellow tones, "is dedicated to Peg Storm, who died last night."

A gentle murmur from the audience.

"Peg was new to the stage. But Peg was a professional in every sense of the word. She would have wished the play to go on. We honor her wish with tonight's performance. *Frankenstein Unbound.* First, a moment of silence." He bowed his head.

Somewhere in town, a clock tolled eight.

Dearborn lowered his hands and looked over the audience. "Peg's part, Justine Moritz, will be read tonight by Nora Epstein, our stage manager. The monster will be played by Roderick Hill . . ."

"My cousin," George whispered.

Dearborn continued, ". . . Robert Scott, who plays the Arctic explorer, in addition will read the part of Frankenstein's friend Henry Clerval. And the bride of Frankenstein will be read by Rebecca Hill."

"My aunt," whispered George.

Dearborn started the applause, and the audience joined in. "Ladies and gentlemen, let the play begin!"

Scene One was set in the cabin of a ship held fast in the ice while on a voyage to discover the fabled Northwest Passage. The crew had rescued Victor Frankenstein from a cake of ice that he'd been rowing, desperately in pursuit of a gigantic figure the crew had seen racing across the ice with a dog sled. The explorer, delighted with his new friend, listened to Frankenstein's strange story.

Toward the end of the first scene, someone in the back of the auditorium snickered.

Before the second scene of Act One had played for more than a few minutes, someone else in the audience guffawed, and then laughter broke loose and rippled through the auditorium.

The setting was Frankenstein's college dorm room, where he was stitching together miscellaneous body parts, accompanied by stage thunder and lightning. Dearborn, as Frankenstein, had donned a black wig to make himself look eighteen. The wig perched on his white hair like a crow nesting in cotton wool.

After the second scene, the actors could do no wrong. The audience laughed, howled, stamped their feet, applauded, whistled, booed. There were shouts of "Bravo!"

Early in the second act, the monster begged Frankenstein to create a mate for him. Weak from laughter, the audience could only groan with pleasure.

"I am thy creature!" cried Roderick, the monster. "I ought to be thy Adam . . ."

Tracy turned to George and whispered, "Who did you say the monster is?"

"My cousin Roderick," whispered George in reply.

The man in front of them turned and shushed them.

When, in the third act, Frankenstein tore to pieces the Eve he was creating for his Adam, and tried to dispose of the leftover body parts, the audience went berserk.

The actors picked up the energy from the audience, and audience and actors rose to higher and higher pitches, each feeding off the other.

Frustrated at the destruction of his mate-to-be, the monster hunted down Frankenstein's friend, Henry Clerval, and strangled him. Roderick, as the monster, was so caught up in the enthusiasm, he was perhaps a bit too realistic. Robert Scott, who played Clerval, collapsed, as he was supposed to, and was carried off stage, as the script called for, and the audience forgot him as the play moved on to further delights — Frankenstein's honeymoon with his bride of not quite one day.

Becca was at her emoting best in the

honeymoon hotel. Stage thunder and lightning presaged the coming of the monster. The bridegroom heard her scream, dashed into the honeymoon suite, saw his bride lying limp on the bed and the monster scrambling out of the window.

"Bravo! Bravo!" Whistles. Rhythmic and prolonged applause.

In the wings, Dearborn, sweating profusely under his black wig, directed the substitute players to their places.

"Explorer! Where's the explorer?" Dearborn called out, and when no one responded, he shouted again: "Nora! Act Three, Scene Five. Read Scott's part at my deathbed. On stage, everyone! Quickly, quickly!"

"Frankenstein! Explorer! Monster! Places!" Nora called out. She picked up a copy of the script and took her own place at Dearborn's side, where he had flung himself onto his bed.

Although the stage was fairly dark for the scene change, the audience could still see enough to feel a part of the show, and called out instructions to the stagehands and actors.

Dearborn, as Frankenstein, gasped his last. Nora, as the Arctic explorer, promised woodenly to carry out Frankenstein's deathbed wish to kill the monster. Roderick, in trying to climb through the porthole, tore it out of its plywood setting and ended up with it around his neck like a horse collar.

"Shit!" shouted Roderick.

Dearborn sat up.

Nora pulled the constricting porthole off Roderick's neck.

Dearborn lay down again. The monster raged. Nora thumbed through the script, seized the pistol that lay beside the bed, and aimed it at Dearborn.

"Not Frankenstein!" shouted the corpse. "The monster!"

"Bravo!" shouted the audience.

Nora lifted the pistol and aimed it at the monster. The audience hushed as the monster waited for Nora to pull the trigger, and when the shot finally came, ending the play in a glorious explosion, a brilliant burst of flame, a cloud of smoke, and the smell of gunpowder, the audience rose as one in a standing ovation that went on and on and on and on . . .

Curtain call. A second. A third. After the fourth curtain call, the monster tugged off his bathing cap wig and pulled off the makeup that had taken him an hour to apply.

Karen and Tracy together shrieked,

"Roddie!"

"I'm heading for Island Java," said George, as they stood up and waited for their turn to leave the auditorium. "Care to join me?"

Karen and Tracy looked uncertainly at each other. "The last bus is at midnight."

George grinned. "We can always hitch-hike."

"Why not?" said Tracy, and the three, holding hands in the flush of excitement over the play, ran down Church Street to Main Street, and from there to the coffeehouse, giggling.

CHAPTER 14

The cast repaired to the Sand Bar in Oak Bluffs. The Sand Bar waiters had pushed tables together for the cast party and decorated them with skeletons and bats left over from Halloween, a theme the management felt was appropriate to the play.

Dearborn and Becca sat at the head of the table.

"A Jack Daniel's for mine host, garçon!" Becca called out to a passing good-looking primitive.

"Fuck off," he said.

"He's not the waiter," said Dearborn.

Becca shrugged.

A plastic tumbler of Jack Daniel's was placed in front of Dearborn. A plastic tumbler of scotch was placed in front of Becca. Pitchers foaming over with beer arrived. Pretzels and popcorn and hilarity abounded.

Dearborn stood and held up his portion

of Jack Daniel's. "To a successful run!"

"Hooray!" cried the cast, holding up cups of beer.

"Who in hell do they think they are?" the man Becca had hailed as a primitive said to the man he'd been obliged to sit next to at a small table. The place was packed.

"Act-ors," said the lean, slightly oily-looking man he'd joined. "Frankenstein."

"They went ahead with the play?" the first man said, raising his shaggy eyebrows. "Tonight?"

"Why not?" said the second. "Opening night."

"Peg Storm, that actress died yesterday, and . . ."

"My ex," said the second, and held out a hand. "Aren't you Vanderhoop? We were next-door neighbors for a few months. Lennie Vincent. How're you doing?"

"Me? It's my boy who's missing. Teddy."

Lennie waved the hand he was still holding out. "Put 'er there, Jeff."

"They call me Jefferson," said Vanderhoop, ignoring Lennie's hand.

"Have it your way, *Jefferson.* Buy you a beer?"

"I buy my own," growled Vanderhoop.

"Sheesh!" said Lennie.

"Look, asshole, my kid's missing, and I don't like your attitude."

"That right?" said Lennie, looking interested. "My ex is dead, and I'm celebrating."

Vanderhoop reached over and grabbed the front of Lennie's black T-shirt, and yanked him to his feet. "Yeah? Never did like you much."

"Hey! Take it easy, will you?" Lennie smoothed his hair. "Sorry about your kid."

Vanderhoop let go of the T-shirt and sat down again. "Sorry about the wife."

"Ex. Don't be. Change your mind about the beer?"

A loud cheer rose from the Frankenstein table, and Dearborn stood. He held up his hands. "People . . . !" he started.

"There's your problem, right there," said Lennie.

"Thinks my kid should be an actor." Vanderhoop jerked his thumb at Dearborn. "Like him."

"Who's the old lady with him?"

Vanderhoop squinted. "Don't know. Never seen her."

". . . to the bride of Frankenstein!" Dearborn announced, holding up his Jack Daniel's to Becca.

"Hooray!" shouted the cast at the table.

"There's your answer," said Vanderhoop.

"My kid would be going fishing with me tomorrow, if it wasn't for that asshole."

"Took my ex out to dinner couple of times," said Lennie. "Suppose he was screwing her?"

Vanderhoop looked Dearborn up and down. "Him? Doubt it."

A waitress plopped a beer pitcher on their table. Lennie poured and handed a cup to Vanderhoop. "Here's to good times!"

Vanderhoop held up his beer, but didn't drink.

Lennie took a swig and wiped his mouth with the back of his hand. "Think your old lady ran off with your kid?"

"Goddamned bitch," said Vanderhoop.

"Where's Bob Scott?" someone at the Frankenstein table called out.

"Where's the monster?" someone else yelled. "Roderick! Where's Roderick?"

Victoria was puttering around in the kitchen when Elizabeth arrived home after midnight. She greeted her grandmother. "Are you waiting up to read the reviews in the early editions, like they do in New York?"

"The *Enquirer* comes out next Friday, a week from now," Victoria said, ladling out a bowl of soup for Elizabeth. "The usual Island grapevine will have the reviews long before then." She handed the bowl to Elizabeth. "I expect the girls to come home any minute. I'll be interested in their reaction."

"Girls? What girls?"

"Karen and Tracy, the hitchhikers Howland stopped for."

Elizabeth laughed. "Don't tell me the girls are staying here, too? In addition to Alison?"

"Yes. Tracy and Karen. Howland gave the girls his tickets. They should be home by now."

"Since this is opening night, they may have been invited to the cast party."

"Perhaps," said Victoria. "But the bus stops running at midnight, and it's after that now."

"Someone will give them a ride home. The monster again?"

Victoria smiled. "Roderick Hill is playing the monster tonight. He's the understudy."

"Maybe one of the off-Island dailies will review the play," said Elizabeth, once they'd settled in the cookroom. "It's certainly newsworthy. I'll pick up copies at Alley's tomorrow morning." She glanced at her watch. "This morning."

Victoria nodded.

"You know, Gram, Dearborn Hill staging the play tonight under the circumstances. That's likely to make major headlines . . ."

Victoria tapped her fingers on the table and changed the subject. "I was glad you made such a large pot of soup. We had quite a crowd."

"Really? Who was here?"

"Karen and Tracy, the two girls. And Sergeant Smalley . . ."

Elizabeth frowned. "What was he doing here?"

"Alison had to examine Peg's body at Rose Haven. Sergeant Smalley picked her up here, then brought her home. He wanted to make sure Amanda was settled in."

Elizabeth set her spoon down. "Who on earth is Amanda?"

"Teddy's mother. She'll be staying with us temporarily."

"Wait," said Elizabeth shaking her head. "Didn't Howland and Alison go to the beach together?"

"Sergeant Smalley came by before Howland arrived." Victoria said. "Your soup is getting cold."

"She and Howland seemed to be hitting it off."

"Howland thought so, too," said Victoria. "But she's calling Sergeant Smalley 'John' I noticed. Howland stayed for supper and was quite entertaining."

"Seven is a lot for dinner." Elizabeth

started to eat again. "So how many people are staying here in the house?"

"Only four. Alison, Teddy's mother, and the two girls. I'm curious to know how opening night went. I was hoping someone would call." She stood up. "Your soup was delicious. Everyone complimented you on it."

"Your recipe, Gram. Lentils, leftover carrots, celery tops, spaghetti sauce, and lots of garlic to pull it all together. And, of course, sliced hot dogs last minute. Thanks for taking care of that."

"I had to open a new package. I thought we had half of one in the freezer."

"We did," said Elizabeth.

"I didn't see it."

"Maybe the old one slipped behind the ice cream?"

"I looked," said Victoria.

Elizabeth shrugged. "We've got four guests in the house, now. Maybe one of them raided the fridge."

"It's not important," said Victoria, thinking about a missing boy and a missing dog.

Roderick had put his bathing cap wig back on and had applied enough of his makeup to look convincing. The day before, he had bruised his shin and it was still sore. He limped to the coffeehouse from the theater.

"Roddie's here!" screamed Karen from the table where she and Tracy and George were seated. "Come sit with us!"

George stood up and held out his hand. "Cousin Roderick, I presume? I almost didn't recognize you."

"How exciting! A real actor!" said Tracy. "We thought you were just a poet."

"You're totally famous," said Karen.

George grunted. "Are you performing here as well?"

"Good publicity for the play," said Roderick, fingering his fangs, which were wrapped in a damp paper towel in his pocket.

"Wow!" said Karen.

"And you're at our table!" said Tracy.

"What'll you have?" George asked the girls.

"Apple juice," said Tracy.

"In a coffeehouse?" asked Roderick.

"Well, latte?" said Tracy.

"Me, too," said Karen.

"Espresso for me," said Roderick.

While George was getting the coffee, a spot lit up the stage, someone did a drumroll on a tabletop, and the emcee adjusted the mike. "Tonight, we have our own, our inimitable — da, da, da — Roddie the Body as Frankenstein's monster! Give him a big hand, folks."

Roderick slipped his fangs into his mouth, straightened the stitches on the side of his skull, tugged down his black sweatshirt, and lumbered onto the stage, furry, clawed hands almost dragging on the ground.

It was well after midnight when George, Tracy, and Karen left the coffeehouse, and went up the hill leading out of town.

George stuck out his thumb.

"I wouldn't mind if the monster picks us up tonight," said Tracy, grinning happily.

But a red Volvo station wagon driven by an elderly woman pulled unsteadily over to the side. George, Tracy, and Karen got in, and the driver, who knew Victoria Trumbull well, and George's mother slightly, dropped George off at his mother's, then turned the car around and drove the girls slowly to Victoria's. All the lights were off in Victoria's house, and the girls, who were relieved to be home safely, slipped upstairs quietly to their nicely fixed-up room.

Roderick limped to his car, which he'd left near the theater, and drove back to the room he shared with Uncle Dearborn. The door to the cellar room was locked, and George looked for the key in its usual spot under the brick. Not there. He pounded on the door. No answer. He pounded again and yelled, "Hey, Uncle Dearborn! It's me!"

A window in the house next door was flung open. A man poked his head out and shouted, "Some people are trying to sleep!" and slammed the window down again.

Roderick waited around for a while. He saw Uncle Dearborn's car parked in front of their cellar room. And then it came to him — Aunt Becca was in town. He could feel his temper rising. Aunt Becca. The self-centered broad. After his triumph at the theater, the second triumph at Island Java . . .

What an injustice. His own uncle and god-damned aunt-in-law locking him out. Where did they expect him to sleep tonight?

He thought about that. Where could he sleep? He wasn't about to sleep in his car, parked in front of the house where Aunt Becca would see him. He was still in costume, and the makeup was beginning to itch. He couldn't get the stuff off without cold cream, and that was in the bathroom cabinet in his and Uncle Dearborn's apartment. Damn Aunt Becca. He got back in his car and drove slowly through the darkened town of Vineyard Haven to the just-as-dark town of Oak Bluffs. He came to the wide sweep of State Beach, and there he stopped.

He might as well pull over to the side of the road and sleep in his car, he thought. Not a bad place. Quiet, with the beach and Nantucket Sound to his left, the soft murmur of water lapping on the gravelly strand, the pleasant iodine smell of beached seaweed. He'd been high on adrenaline during the performance, high again at the coffeehouse, he felt exhausted, drained, let down.

Goddamned Aunt Becca!

He pulled an old blanket out of the back of his car and made a pillow of it, leaned his monstrous head on the blanket pillow, which he propped against the window, and slept.

He had no idea how long he'd been sleeping. He was awakened by a bright light shining through the windshield, and he sat up, wondering where he was and what was going on.

"Sir?" said a voice behind a flashlight beam. "Oh shit, not again!"

Roderick shook his head to clear it.

"Not Mr. Atherton?"

"What?" said Roderick.

"You have some identification, sir? A license or something?"

Roderick looked around and saw a police car stopped in front of him, its blue lights flashing. He fished in the glove compartment and handed his license to the state trooper. Then he recognized the trooper.

"Tim! It's me. Roderick. Roderick Hill."

"Yeah?" said Eldredge. "You'll have to come with me."

"What's up, Tim?"

"Step out of the car."

"Where are you taking me?"

"To the jail," said Eldredge, sighing. "Déjà vu all over again."

CHAPTER 15

Victoria awoke before dawn, dressed quickly, and slipped out of her room, shutting the door softly behind her. She crossed the study, avoiding the floorboards that creaked, and tiptoed to the door of the attic. Elizabeth's room was nearby, and she could hear her granddaughter snoring lightly.

She held her hand against the door to keep the old hinges from squealing and gently tugged the knob. She went up the steep stairs slowly, one step at a time.

She was halfway up when she heard a low moan. She smiled. Last spring during play readings, she had shown the house, including the attic, to the players. Ghosts, indeed, she thought. When she reached the top, she stepped carefully onto the wide floorboards.

A wooden wall with an open doorway divided the attic into two large rooms. Victoria rapped on the side of the opening.

"Teddy?" she whispered.

She heard the moan again.

"Teddy?" She turned on the light, and saw a small, filthy dog curled up on one of her old quilts.

A small figure with tousled red hair, dressed in jeans and T-shirt, sat up in the bed, blinking. He tossed back the covers, slid off the high bed, and landed on the floor facing her.

Victoria went toward him. Teddy backed against the wall, eyes wide.

"It's all right, Teddy," Victoria whispered. "No one else knows you're here."

"What are you going to do?"

"May I sit down?"

Teddy moved the chair that had been under the window, brushed off the seat, and held it for Victoria. She sat.

"Sandy . . . ?" said Teddy.

"Peg's dog?" Victoria nodded to the dog on her quilt.

"The bad guy hurt him, and I found him in the woods. We have to get him to a doctor. Peg doesn't know where Sandy is, and she'll be worried."

Victoria folded her earth-stained hands in her lap, examined them minutely, and decided to wait before telling him Peg was dead. "I suppose you don't want anyone to know where you are?"

"The bad guy was after me."

"Could you tell who he was?"

Teddy shook his head. "I couldn't see all of him. Everything he had on was black and floppy. He talked in a funny high voice like a girl."

Sandy lifted his head, and dropped it down again.

Victoria looked over at the shivering mutt. "We need to talk. First, I'll see that Sandy gets to the doctor, and soon."

Teddy knelt by Sandy. The dog was panting. Teddy moved the water bowl closer. The dog opened his eyes and shut them again.

"I'm scared, Mrs. Trumbull. Suppose Sandy dies?"

"We'll make sure he doesn't." Victoria twisted her thin wedding band on her finger. It would never slide off over her swollen joint. "Your mother's here, Teddy," she said.

"Here? In this house? She came back from California?" He stopped. "Why? Does she know I'm here?"

"Not yet."

"Please, Mrs. Trumbull. Please don't let her know I'm here."

"Why, Teddy? She's your mother. She needs to know you're safe."

Teddy lifted his shoulders. "She's got this

creepy boyfriend."

"He won't hurt you, Teddy."

"He wants the money. He'll make me go to California."

Victoria stopped twisting her ring. "Don't you want to go?"

"No." Teddy shook his head vigorously.

"You're a wonderful actor."

"I don't want to be an actor. I want to be a fisherman."

"Well," said Victoria, "You did the right thing to come here. When your mother couldn't reach you last night, she flew back from Los Angeles. She has to be told you're safe. All the police forces on the Island are looking for you. They need to be told, too."

"I could write a note saying 'Don't worry. I got away from the burglar.'"

"That would be a good idea," said Victoria. "But your mother and the police need more than just a note saying you're safe. You could add that you're staying with a friend and that you'll call your mother. Today is Saturday. Tell her you'll call on Monday. That should give us enough time."

Teddy squirmed.

"You mustn't allow your mother to worry . . ."

"She's only worried about the TV show and the money and her boyfriend."

Victoria shook her head. "No, Teddy. She needs to know you're all right. The police do, too. It's not right to let them think you've been kidnapped. Or worse."

"I'll write the note," said Teddy, looking down at the dog.

"I'll make sure your mother gets it." Victoria rose to her feet and looked out of the window. "First, we'll take care of Sandy, but we have to wait until everyone leaves. Your mother is going to your house this morning to help the police."

"The police!" Teddy scrambled to his feet. "Because of me?"

Victoria said nothing.

"Is Peg all right? Did the burglar hurt her?"

"I'm afraid so."

"She screamed for me to run, and I ran."

"She wanted you to run," said Victoria.

"How bad did he hurt her?"

"She's dead, Teddy."

Teddy closed his eyes. "Poor Sandy."

Victoria gave him a few moments of silence before she said, "After everyone leaves, carry Sandy downstairs."

Teddy nodded. "What will Sandy do without Peg?"

"We'll think of something. I'll call Joanie, the animal control officer, and tell her I found a sick dog . . ."

"That's true, isn't it?"

"Yes. I'll ask her to take Sandy and me to the doctor. You'll find notepaper and envelopes in that desk." Victoria pointed to the rickety old desk under the eaves.

Teddy wrote the note and Victoria read it. "Good. Address the envelope to your mother, and I'll leave it on the kitchen table where she'll see it."

Teddy sighed. "I'm not really scared of my mother."

"Of course not."

"You won't give me away, will you?"

"Not until we talk."

"I'm not scared of my mother," he said again. "But I don't want her to tell him where I am."

"Him?" said Victoria. "The boyfriend?"

Teddy nodded.

"Why don't you like him?"

"He makes me eat awful stuff."

"What kind of awful stuff?" Victoria asked, concerned.

"Snails and octopus." Teddy shuddered. "Slimy black stuff. He pretends to be so lovey-dovey to my mother, but he's only after her money. He says she's going to be rich because of my television show."

"What's his name?"

"She calls him 'honey' or 'darling' mostly."
Teddy put his hands to his throat and stuck
his tongue out. "Yuck!"

"Don't you know his real name?"

"I think it's Reilly."

Victoria got up slowly. "I have to go now.
When everyone leaves, carry Sandy downstairs to the kitchen."

"The cat doesn't like Sandy."

"I'll take care of McCavity," said Victoria.

Victoria was still talking with Teddy in the
attic when Elizabeth came downstairs to
make breakfast. Alison and Amanda joined
her, and they talked together quietly so they
wouldn't awaken Victoria. Alison measured
coffee grounds and water into the coffee-
maker and turned it on.

"What do you like for breakfast,
Amanda?" Elizabeth asked.

"Just coffee, thanks," said Amanda. "I'm
going to my house, see if I can help the
police."

The last drip of coffee sputtered into the
glass pot, and Alison poured some into a
mug. "Pretty hot. Why don't you take this
with you."

"Thanks. I'll bring the mug back."

After Amanda had gone, Elizabeth said,
"She doesn't seem as broken up about her

son as you'd expect."

"She may be in shock," said Alison. "Or denial. People handle awful situations differently."

"It's as if she's only pretending she's worried sick."

"She doesn't want to admit to herself that something might have happened . . ." Alison turned away and didn't finish her sentence.

"My grandmother's sleeping awfully late," Elizabeth said. "She must have been exhausted. She didn't get to bed until well after midnight. How about you, did you sleep okay?"

"Eventually." Alison wrapped her hands around her coffee mug. "Before Victoria comes down, let me ask you something."

"Sure."

"Howland was teasing her about ghosts. I know she doesn't believe in them. But I heard some strange noises last night."

"Where were the noises coming from?"

"The attic."

"You're not the only one to hear ghosts up there. But the explanation is simple." Elizabeth poured bacon fat from the pan into a can marked "Grease for Kyle."

"Who's Kyle?" said Alison.

"A green friend of Victoria's. An environmental type who runs his car on grease. Ask Victoria about him." She put a lid on the can and stowed it in the freezer. "About noises in the attic, there are generations of mice up there who have eluded McCavity. Occasionally a squirrel gets in. We had a raccoon in the chimney last year."

"It sounded a bit like scratching, but it also sounded like something moaning."

Elizabeth glanced at Alison. "Do *you* believe in ghosts?"

Alison set her coffee down. "I'm a scientist. People have been seeing, hearing, and feeling spirits for centuries. I'm not about to disregard all those sightings. What about you?"

Elizabeth shrugged. "My grandmother has programmed me into being sensible, which means, according to her, there's no such thing as a haunted house. Everything has a logical explanation. Want to go up to the attic and look around?"

"Not now." Alison checked her watch. "Sergeant Smalley is picking me up any minute. By the way, thanks for lending me your jeans. They fit perfectly."

"You're welcome to borrow whatever you need."

"I hope we find Amanda's boy soon." Alison paused and looked at the distant spire

185

of the church. "Do you know Teddy?"

"Not well. He seems like a bright kid. My grandmother and he became close pals during rehearsals. The oldest and the youngest players. She's terribly fond of him. And worried."

"We all are." Alison turned away. "In a past life, I had a son. He was Teddy's age . . ." she stopped.

Smalley drove up at that point, and Alison hurried out of the door before Elizabeth had time to react.

Elizabeth tried to absorb Alison's remark about a son. She had assumed the forensic scientist was divorced, but hadn't thought beyond that. What had happened to her son?

She looked at her watch. Time enough to drive to Alley's and pick up the off-Island dailies.

When she returned with the newspapers, ten minutes later, Victoria was in the kitchen, pouring herself a mug of coffee.

"Morning, Gram."

Victoria turned guiltily.

Elizabeth studied her. "Are you okay?"

"Of course. Why do you ask?"

"You seem sort of flushed."

"A sign of good health."

Elizabeth looked at her grandmother again

and shrugged. "I bought the newspapers. Let's see what they say about your play."

Victoria carried her coffee into the cook-room, and they both sat. Elizabeth laid the papers on the table in front of her grand-mother. "After the way Dearborn has tried to undermine Ruth . . ." She corrected herself. "The way he and Ruth's own *sister* have worked against her, I wouldn't blame you for hoping everything will go wrong with the play." Elizabeth looked around. "I haven't met the two hitchhikers yet. They must be asleep still."

"They left early." Victoria had seen them from the attic window, standing at the end of the drive, waiting for the bus.

Elizabeth noted the flush return to her grandmother's cheeks. "What time did you get up?"

"I've been awake for a while." Victoria turned her attention to her cereal.

Elizabeth smiled. "Alison heard noises in the attic. I'm afraid we may have mice again."

"Why, did she hear them scrabbling around?"

"She asked me if we had a ghost . . ."

"Oh for heaven's sake," said Victoria. "Howland thinks it's so comical to go on and on about ghosts in our house, and now everyone who stays here thinks the house is haunted." She shoved her cereal bowl away from her.

"We should probably set mouse traps up there." Elizabeth grinned. She, too, thought about the missing boy. Now there were noises in the attic and her grandmother was being secretive. "I'll set some mouse traps in the attic right after breakfast."

"Don't bother," said Victoria, quickly. "Let me see what the newspapers have to say." She opened up the Cape Cod paper and stared at the front page.

"What is it?" Elizabeth pushed her chair back.

Victoria handed her the paper.

"Ohmygod!" cried Elizabeth.

Chapter 16

The headline read, "Comedy Ends in Tragedy."

"Comedy!" exclaimed Victoria.

"Tragedy?" Elizabeth leaned over her shoulder. "Want me to read it?"

"I wish you would."

Elizabeth sat down and spread out the paper. "The subhead says, 'Actor dies of apparent heart attack.'"

"Good heavens!"

" 'During the opening performance last night of *Frankenstein Unbound* at the Island Players, Robert F. Scott, 48, who was performing two roles . . .'"

"Robert Scott!" exclaimed Victoria. "He was reading Bruce Duncan's part as Frankenstein's friend."

Elizabeth looked over the top of the paper. "Yeah?"

"Bruce had been cast in the part of Henry Clerval."

"Oh?" said Elizabeth, lowering the paper.

"Henry Clerval is murdered by Frankenstein's monster."

"Bruce Duncan is the guy who . . . ?"

"Yes," said Victoria. "Bruce was almost hysterical when he learned about Peg's death. He was convinced he was next."

"In order of appearance?" said Elizabeth.

"Go on reading," said Victoria. "Heart attack?"

" '. . . performing two roles, collapsed after reading the part of Frankenstein's friend, Henry Clerval. Mr. Scott was found backstage by the cleaning woman, Maria Gallante, and was taken to the Martha's Vineyard Hospital, where he was pronounced dead on arrival of an apparent heart attack.' " Elizabeth glanced up. "The article goes on from there. Do you want to hear it?"

"The headline said comedy?"

"Let me find that part." Elizabeth ran her finger down the page. "Here we go. 'The play, adapted by the poet Victoria Trumbull from Mary Shelley's book *Frankenstein* and directed by Dearborn Hill, was produced despite objections from some of the cast. Peg Storm, who played the part of the Frankensteins' housekeeper, had been found dead the night before, and Teddy

Vanderhoop, eight, who played the part of the five-year-old William Frankenstein, was still missing as of press time.' "

"Comedy?" said Victoria.

"I'm coming to it. 'Last night's production of the play, which deals with weighty social issues, was staged as a farce, much to the delight of the standing-room-only crowd.' "

"Standing room only? Farce? The idea," said Victoria. "The very idea!"

"Want to hear more?"

"I don't think so," said Victoria, picking up the phone.

George Byron was reading the same article to his mother at their breakfast table when the phone rang.

"I was about to call you, Victoria," Ruth said. "Have you read past the farce bit?"

"That's when I decided to call."

"You'll never guess who acted Frankenstein's bride, the part the paper refers to," said Ruth.

"Dearborn?"

"Guess again."

"His nephew?"

"Rebecca," Ruth cried. "My beloved sister!"

"Rebecca?" Victoria repeated.

"My sister played the part of Elizabeth Lavenza, the bride of Frankenstein!"

"There's nothing farcical about the bride's role."

"Rebecca adores acting. She loves to emote. Did you read the passage in the paper about 'high camp'?"

"I don't think I want to," said Victoria. "The first I knew about Robert Scott's death was when we read about it in the paper just now. Forty-eight is young to have a heart attack."

"George went to the performance last night, Victoria."

"Did George tell you what scene Robert was playing when he collapsed?"

"The monster had strangled him."

"The monster, as played by Roderick?" Victoria asked.

"Yes."

"Was Roderick too enthusiastic in his acting?"

"Hard to know, Victoria. Bob was alive when the stage crew dragged him off. So much was going on, no one paid much attention to him." Ruth paused. "He apparently lay down on the sofa backstage, which is where the cleaning woman found him."

"No one missed him in Act Three?"

"Dearborn was drunk. The play was not

going as expected. The audience was having a ball. The cast went along with the audience and treated the play as a farce. When Bob didn't appear on cue, Dearborn substituted Nora, who read the part, woodenly, of course. The audience loved it."

"Now that the play has been reviewed as a farce, I suppose we must continue to treat it as such?"

"We have no choice, Victoria. At the end of the run I'll fire Dearborn, of course."

"You may have some dissent from your backers, if you fire him after a commercial success." Victoria paused again. "This is exactly what I was hoping to avoid. Mary Shelley wrote a serious book. Despite all the best intentions of the past two centuries, the public is not interested in the message. They crave sensationalism and grotesquerie. And now we have two deaths associated with the play."

"The two faces of Janus," said Ruth. "The Roman god of beginnings and endings."

"Front page," said Dearborn to Becca, laying out the Cape Cod, New Bedford, and Falmouth papers. "Even *The Globe* has a front page item. Look here." He pointed.

"Ummm." Becca nuzzled his neck, then picked up *The Globe* and studied the four-inch item below the fold. "Guess that will show dear, sweet sister Ruth. Sell-out crowd, the rafters fairly pealed with laughter. We held them in our hands." She tossed down the paper and strode across the room. "How dare she dictate behavior to you." She tapped her chest with her fingers. "To me. How insulting, when you produce an audience pleaser the way you did last night." She turned. "The way you always do, darling."

Dearborn cleared his throat. "Helped to have Bob Scott die after he was strangled. Not sure we can duplicate that."

"I didn't mean to sound insensitive, darling. Forgive me!" She went back to Dearborn and threw her arms around his neck. "Of course, that was sad. Tragic. As you know." She cast a lingering look at her husband. "Bob meant a great deal to me at one time." She took long, sweeping steps across the room, hands clasped under her chin.

"Sometimes I wonder about your taste," Dearborn muttered.

"But what a noble way to go," said Becca. "Not exactly on stage, but performing to a full house." She repeated the two words. "Full house, darling. *Full house*."

"He didn't die on stage."

"You know what I mean."

"I'm sure he felt no pain," said Dearborn.

"Did you like the way I handled my role? Sweet, innocent bride, hmmm?" Becca asked.

"The audience loved you," Dearborn said.

"Do you really think so?"

"You heard the laughter."

"At all the right places."

"All the right places," Dearborn repeated.

"I'm glad he didn't die until after my death scene," said Becca. "I'd have resented him, really, for upstaging me." She went back to her pacing. "The idea of my sister implying that you can't hold your liquor. Of course you can. You've never in your life *had* to take a drink."

"Just three drinks all evening," said Dearborn, looking pleased. "Plus one or two before the performance, of course. Fortification for opening night."

"How humiliating to make you go to public meetings and confess something that's not really a problem." She picked up the New Bedford paper. "My sister has always known how to make a person grovel."

"She meant well, I suppose," said Dearborn, sounding unconvinced.

"Darling, it's sweet to be back together. We'll show that bitch, won't we?"

Dearborn slapped the back of his hand on the Cape Cod paper. "We couldn't have gotten better press than that."

Joanie Adams, the animal control officer, showed up ten minutes after Victoria called. She parked her truck in the driveway and slipped into Victoria's kitchen. Sandy lay where Teddy had left him, huddled and shivering, in a cardboard box lined with an old quilt.

Joanie examined the small, scruffy, filthy dog.

"Peg Storm's mutt, Sandy. How'd he get here?"

"You heard that Peg died?"

"No! What happened?"

"She was found at the foot of her cellar stairs," said Victoria, careful not to mention marks of fingers around Peg's throat.

"How awful! She was much too young."

"We all are," said Victoria.

"Did she trip or something?"

"No one's said."

"Well, Sandy needs to get to the vet, that's for sure, and soon. Sandy first. We can talk about Peg later."

"May I come along?"

"Glad to have the company, Mrs. Trumbull."

The vet, Doc Atkins, a young man in his mid-fifties with a bushy, black mustache and a thatch of black hair, met them at the door of the clinic and carried Sandy to an examining table.

"What's Sandy doing with you, Mrs. Trumbull?"

"It's a long story," said Victoria.

Doc Atkins moved his hands gently over the dog's body and legs. "Couple of bad bruises. Must hurt you, pup." Sandy lifted his head. "Back leg dislocated. How'd you do that, boy?" Sandy laid his head on his paws. "I'll fix that right now. Put it back in place without anesthesia, less traumatic. Come hold him, Joanie."

Sandy yelped when Doc Atkins tugged his leg into place, then lay his head down and panted.

"Good boy." Doc Atkins patted the dog's head. "That's all there is to it, Sandy, old pal." He took Sandy's temperature and felt around the swollen areas. "No apparent internal damage. No fever. Tell Peg I'm putting Sandy on antibiotics and painkillers. Keep him quiet for a day or two. Let him determine himself how much he can do."

Victoria twisted her ring. "Peg's dead."

He swiveled around. "No!"

She told him about the police finding Peg at the foot of the cellar stairs.

He shook his head. "I can't believe it. Freakish thing to happen. Don't worry about Sandy. I'll keep him overnight, give you a call tomorrow."

"Thank you," said Victoria, and she and Joanie drove back to Victoria's big old house.

Tim Eldredge reported to Sergeant Smalley and saluted smartly. "I've located Lennie Vincent."

Smalley looked up from the papers on his desk and sighed. "Eldredge, relax, will you?"

Tim Eldredge set his feet apart and put his hands behind his back.

"Vincent?" asked Smalley.

"Peg Storm's ex."

"Of course." Smalley tugged off his reading glasses. "Where is he?"

"Building a house in Chilmark."

"By himself?"

"Pretty much, sir. He's handy."

"How'd you track him down?" Smalley waved his glasses at the visitor's chair. "Have a seat, Tim."

"I asked the register of deeds, sir, to see if

a Leonard Vincent bought property recently."

"Good thinking."

"Thank you, sir. He got a fair amount of money in the divorce settlement."

Smalley nodded. "Is he living at the new house site?"

"No, sir. I followed him when he quit for the day. He's staying in a camp behind the Animal Rescue League. Belongs to an artist."

"Good man," said Smalley.

"Want me to bring him in, sir?"

Smalley swung his glasses by the earpiece and considered. "He's not likely to go anywhere. We can wait."

"Yes, sir." Eldredge stood, saluted, and left, shutting the door behind him.

"You don't need to salute!" shouted Smalley to the closed door and muttered to himself, "Hot shot."

After the animal control officer dropped her off at home, Victoria opened the door at the foot of the attic stairs and called up. "Teddy?"

"Ma'am?"

"Everyone's gone. Sandy's at the doctor's and he'll be fine. Elizabeth made a great quantity of breakfast, and we need to talk.

Come downstairs."

Teddy appeared at the foot of the stairs, disheveled and dirty.

"Bath, first," said Victoria. "In the bureau near your bed are clean clothes someone left last summer. You can wear them while I put yours in the washing machine."

Teddy turned slowly and started up the stairs.

"Don't linger," said Victoria. "I'll be in the cookroom."

Ten minutes later, Teddy, clean and combed and wearing jeans and a T-shirt, both several sizes too large, sat in front of a large plate of bacon and eggs, and toyed with his food.

"Aren't you hungry?" Victoria's recollection of small boys was of their large appetites.

"I guess." Teddy took a dutiful bite of eggs and chewed and chewed.

"Don't you feel well, Teddy? It's no wonder, after all you've been through."

"I'm okay," said Teddy, resting his head on his hand.

"I was at the theater when you and Peg left. What happened?" She passed him the basket of toast.

"Peg let me off at my house to get my bike."

Victoria nodded.

"I picked up my comic books, too."

"Yes."

"I rode into her driveway and she screamed, 'Run, Teddy, run!' I never heard anybody scream like that. And I ran."

"That was the right thing to do," said Victoria.

"Maybe I could have saved her."

"No. She wanted you to run, she told you to run, and you did what she asked. Go on," said Victoria. "What happened next?"

When he'd heard Peg cry out, Teddy told Victoria, he had wheeled his bicycle around. One of his comic books slipped off the top of the pile in his basket and hit the ground with a splat. He pedaled as hard as he could down the road off the point. Where three roads forked off, he paused, out of breath, heart pounding. He set one foot on the ground and looked over his shoulder. Car headlights jounced down the road behind him. Quickly he turned left onto the shell-fish hatchery road, which dead-ended at Lagoon Pond. The road was only about a quarter-mile long, but he hid in the dense shrubbery to the side.

He saw a light-colored car turn off Job's Neck Road and head toward town. The

Lears' car, he thought at first, then realized it was not the Lears after all. He didn't recognize the car.

Teddy set his uneaten toast next to his plate.
  "What happened then?" Victoria asked softly.

CHAPTER 17

"Go on, Teddy," said Victoria.

"My teacher told us to call nine-one-one whenever you're scared like that," Teddy said.

"But you couldn't, could you? You'd have to find a telephone. What about your neighbors?"

"They weren't there. They're mostly August people and their houses are still closed up. I thought about going to the Cohens' house, but Mrs. Cohen died last year."

"And Mr. Cohen is in the play and was still at rehearsal."

Teddy told Victoria he had decided to go back to his own house and call Peg from there. Suppose Peg had screamed because someone was coming after *him?* He'd thought about the car leaving the point. Maybe someone had kidnapped her.

Maybe he shouldn't go back to his house

after all.

Yes, he'd decided. He'd sneak up like a Ranger. His dad had been a Ranger. He'd pretend someone was out there trying to murder Peg, and he, Teddy, would arrive in time to capture the bad guy. He'd tie him up and call the police and while they were on the way, he'd rescue Peg, who would be gagged and tied up, sitting on a kitchen chair with her hands behind her back. He'd take out his pocketknife and cut the ropes, and she'd be grateful and tell his mother, who would tell his dad. The police would be amazed that he, Teddy Vanderhoop, eight years old, was so brave. And his parents would be so proud of him. His mother would forget about her boyfriend, and his mother and dad would get together again and he wouldn't have to move to California and be an actor.

Teddy paused and Victoria said, "You *are* brave, Teddy. Your parents and the police will think so, too." She poured orange juice and moved the glass toward Teddy. "Go on," said Victoria.

He had pretended this was only a game, he told Victoria. He reached the rail fence that marked his property. The lights were off at

Peg's. But lights were on in his house. He didn't remember turning them on. Maybe Peg had escaped to his place and was looking for him. Maybe the bad guy had left Peg tied up and was stealing the TV from his house. A burglar, maybe.

The game had moved in a direction Teddy didn't much like. He'd leaned his bike against the fence and, crouching beneath overhanging tree branches, he crept toward his house. This was like the time he and Joey snuck up on Joey's sister's slumber party, hoping to hear the girls scream. Exciting, but scary, because Joey's father might catch them.

Who might catch him this time?

He had lowered himself to his stomach, and, slithering through the shrubbery, reached the big beech tree next to his house. He kept the tree trunk between him and the lighted windows.

Teddy paused again, lifted the glass of orange juice and set it down without drinking any.

"I remembered then I *did* turn the lights on, Mrs. Trumbull. To get my comic books. My mother always tells me to turn off the lights, but I must have forgot."

"Go on," said Victoria.

■ ■ ■ ■

From where he'd stood, he explained to Victoria, the windows were too high for him to see in. The light from the windows shone on the tree. He jumped up and caught a low branch in his hands, swung his legs up, and hoisted himself onto it. Now he could see into the dining room. If he moved forward on the branch, he would be able to look through the archway into the living room and kitchen.

Teddy stopped talking.

"What did you see?" Victoria felt as though she was prying into Teddy's private life. But this was police business and she was trying to help him. She hoped she was using proper interrogation techniques.

"Someone opening drawers in my mother's desk."

"Could you tell who it was?"

"I guess it was a man, but it could have been a girl. He was all in black. I could only see his lower half."

"Then what happened?"

"My foot hit a big dead branch."

Victoria recalled the fresh scar on the beech tree next to Teddy's house. "And the branch broke." She leaned forward.

"It made the loudest snap I ever heard in my life."

"And the intruder heard the sound?"

"He came to the window and looked out." Teddy shivered.

Victoria got up and put a sweater around his shoulders.

"I'm not cold, Mrs. Trumbull."

"I know you're not."

"The burglar wore something over his face, a black hat pulled down."

"Like a ski mask?" asked Victoria.

"I guess. He called out in a weird voice, like a girl's, 'Is that you, Teddy?' " Teddy closed his eyes. "He said, 'I've got something for you, Teddy, a video game. Come on in, and I'll show you!' " Teddy pulled the sweater around his shoulders.

"And then what?"

"He said, 'You're playing a game, aren't you? I'll come out and we can both play.' Then he went toward the back door."

Teddy's thoughts had spun around, he told Victoria. Maybe the burglar had a gun and would shoot him. Or capture him. What had happened to Peg? He had to get out of the tree. Bullets would reach higher than he could climb. Should he go to Peg's and rescue her? No, he had to find a telephone and dial nine-one-one. He had to get to his bike, and quick. He dropped off the tree limb and landed on his knees and hands. He crouched and darted under the overhanging branches, plunged through the underbrush, and, just as he heard the back door slam, he saw the glint of starlight on the metal handlebars of his bike.

"You could hear the back door shut?"

Teddy nodded. "I heard a thump and something fell." He looked up. "It sounded like the big box where I keep my Legos. My mother is always telling me someone is going to trip over the box and hurt themselves, and I guess he did."

Victoria laughed. "That was one time it's lucky you didn't obey your mother. What happened next?"

"The bad guy hollered . . ." Teddy didn't finish the sentence.

"Something rude?"

"Yes. I figured maybe he'd broken a leg and that would keep him from running." Teddy closed his eyes.

The split-rail fence had shown up as a lighter shadow in the night, Teddy said. Now he could see his bike clearly. He scrambled over the top of the fence, and when he reached the bike, turned it around and ran until it was going fast. He hopped on and forced his feet to turn the pedals faster and faster. Then he raced down the road that led off the point.

He gazed at Victoria with tired eyes. "I didn't know where to go," he said. "I thought maybe I could borrow a dinghy and row out to my father's boat."

"That would be a long way to row."

"I was scared that the burglar might have a gun, and he would see me in the dinghy and shoot me."

Victoria nodded.

"I was scared to go to my dad, anyway."

"Scared?"

"It's my fault they're getting a divorce."

Victoria shook her head. "Grown-ups have problems, and the problems have nothing to do with their children. It's not your fault. So what made you decide to come to me?"

He looked up at her again, his eyes meeting her deep-set, ones. "You're my friend."

"I am," said Victoria, and smiled.

"Do you want to hear how I found Sandy, Mrs. Trumbull?"

"Yes, I do."

"I decided to take the lane that ends at

209

the Vineyard Haven-Edgartown Road, then the bike path to your house. Well, when I got to the turnoff to the lane I heard this moan."

"That must have been frightening."

"I was really scared. I didn't know what it was."

"And it turned out to be Sandy."

Teddy nodded. "I could tell he was hurting, Mrs. Trumbull."

"So you rode to my house with Sandy in your arms?"

"I put him in the bike basket on top of my comic books. I knew we could hide in your attic, Mrs. Trumbull. I thought it would be okay to sneak a little bit of food."

"Under the circumstances, yes."

"I knew Sandy would have to go to the bathroom. Me, too." Teddy blushed. "Sandy could use old newspapers and I could wait until no one was home." He looked at Victoria, still blushing.

"Go on," she said.

"Then, after I picked up Sandy, I heard another car coming off the Job's Neck Road."

"Did you know whose it was?"

"Not real well. I thought maybe the first car was the bad guy's helper, and the second car was the bad guy."

"That was a long bike ride to my house in the dark."

"I had to wait, because I saw a police car in your driveway. When the lights went out and the police car went away, I sneaked into your house with Sandy. I was almost at the stairs when something hissed. I thought a ghost was after me. But it was only your cat."

"You needn't worry. There are *no* ghosts in this house."

"He made cat-fight noises. I was afraid he'd wake up Elizabeth."

"McCavity is a good guard cat," said Victoria. "Once you made a bed for Sandy and got him settled, you came downstairs and found the hot dogs?"

"I hope that wasn't stealing?"

Victoria smiled. "Where were you when the girls came upstairs? They saw Sandy's bed."

"I built a cave under the big bed."

"It's very high, isn't it?"

"It was starting to thunder, and I'm scared of lightning."

"And that's where you were hiding when they came up to shut the windows."

CHAPTER 18

While Victoria listened to Teddy, and while Teddy picked at his food, Dearborn was still at the theater, on the telephone again, hair askew, a newly opened bottle of Jack Daniel's on the desk beside him, his coffee cup in one hand.

Becca paced back and forth, reading her lines for the bride of Frankenstein aloud from the play script. She stopped when she reached Dearborn's desk. He had just set the phone down. "The matinee is sold out, Becca. Standing room only, and most of that's sold out, too."

"Marvelous, *mon cher!*" She lifted her script and resumed her pacing. " 'Something whispers to me!' I'll try that again. 'Something *whispers* to me . . .' la, la, la, 'but I *will* not *listen* to such a *sinister* voice.' "

Dearborn ran his fingers through his hair. "Who am I going to get to play the two parts — Clerval and the Arctic explorer —

on such short notice. Scott picked a hell of a time to die."

Becca lowered her script. "What about our nephew?"

"He's got his hands full with the monster part. His makeup alone takes almost an hour to put on. I thought you couldn't stand him?"

"Not *Roderick,* darling. *George.* He's perfect. Yale Drama School. He was at the opening last night."

"He'll never agree. He and his mother . . ."

"Pooh, darling. George is a professional. He won't let a little thing like a family squabble keep him from the stage." Becca set down her play script, clasped her hands under her chin, and began pacing again. "And such an opportunity. *Two* roles he can add to his credits. He won't even have to learn his lines." She stopped in front of Dearborn's desk again, and tapped her lacquered nail on his blotter. "Call him. This minute."

George hung up the phone with a broad smile.

Ruth came into the study, where her son was sitting in her armchair. "Who was that, George? You seem pleased."

"I am pleased." George bounced to his

feet. "Uncle Dearborn has asked me to take over Bob Scott's roles — two roles — for the matinee this afternoon."

Ruth took a deep breath, and let it out. "Absolutely not." Her face turned bright pink. "Don't you dare accept." Her expression was stormy. "That . . . that . . . that *filth!*"

"Don't you see, Mom, this puts us in a great position."

"What I see, George, is Uncle Dearborn and Aunt Rebecca manipulating you and making a fool of me. And sabotaging a serious play."

"It's too late for sabotage. Uncle Dearborn has already turned the play into a farce."

Ruth's face got pinker still. "Victoria Trumbull put an incredible amount of thought into editing out the sentimentality and the sensationalism of the book and focusing on Mary Shelley's all-too-modern message."

George shook his head. "Too late, Mom. The play's sold out. After all that buildup, the audience won't stand for 'serious message.' " He made quote marks in the air with his fingers.

Ruth set her hands on her hips. "He was drunk . . . drunk!"

"Fire him when the run is over." George put his arm around her shoulder. "You can't fight it. Look at the reviews." He flipped through the newspapers and pointed. " 'High camp!' 'Summer farce!' 'Franken-stein run sold out!' 'Engaging comedy!' " He flipped the newspapers back onto the study table. "Trust me. I'll get even with those two yet."

Ruth wrapped her arms around herself as if she were cold.

"Besides, if I've got a part in a play — two parts in a play," George grinned, "my advisor won't hassle me when I return late to school. By the way, I meant to tell you about the costume barn."

But Ruth had turned her back on her son and left the room.

Victoria gave Teddy a new toothbrush, and he scrubbed his teeth while she folded his clean clothes.

"I've got to tell some of your story to the police, Teddy," said Victoria. "You may be the only eyewitness to the killer."

Teddy made a gurgling sound.

"You're very brave. Much braver than I would have been."

"Really?"

"No question about it. I promised you I'd

keep your secret and make sure you're safe, and I will. But I've got to talk to the police about what you saw. Will you trust me?"

"Can I still stay here?"

"For a while, at least."

"People!" Dearborn clapped his hands. "People! Your attention. There's work to be done, and we have only four hours before curtain."

Becca looked up from her script and slipped off her reading glasses, "We have a sold-out house, cast. For a matinee!"

"Double-time," said Dearborn, "let's get with it. I'll skip over my part as Frankenstein." He waved his script at the players. "Now, George, for your benefit, the play starts, like Shelley's book, after Frankenstein has been picked off an ice floe in the Arctic Ocean."

George wet his thumb and turned pages of his script.

"Frankenstein is suffering from hypothermia. You put him to bed and summon a crew member to bring him hot gruel. You sit by his bedside — that's about all you need to do — and listen sympathetically while he tells you his story."

"Got it," said George.

"You have adequate time to change from

your captain's uniform."

"I thought I was the explorer?" said George.

"In Mrs. Trumbull's adaptation, the explorer *is* the captain. You'll have plenty of time to change into the Henry Clerval costume. Clerval doesn't appear until almost the end of Act Two, after the monster begs me to create a mate for him."

"Righto," said George.

"At that point, you see, I'm in a quandary. Shall I create a mate? Release into the world another monster like the first? Will the couple have children? What will the children be like? You can see why the play is an audience pleaser."

"End of Act Two?" asked George.

"I, Frankenstein, have almost completed the female monster when I have second thoughts and tear her to pieces. The monster goes berserk and, to get even with me, strangles you, my only remaining friend."

"Do I know about the mate in the making?" asked George.

Dearborn shook his head. "You know only that your friend Victor is suffering."

"Clerval is not to be played as a comic, then?"

"No, no, no. You play both parts straight, as Mrs. Trumbull intended, the explorer and

Henry Clerval. Her adaptation is entirely serious. She points up the pathos of the unfortunate monster, his innocence, the injustices heaped on him." Dearborn looked up and smiled. "But last night's audience read into the entirely serious lines of some actors a certain dark humor. And as actors, we must give the audience what it wants, correct?"

"Yes, Uncle Dearborn," said George, turning pages.

"After the monster strangles you, you'll be dragged off stage by stagehands in the blackout, and then you'll have time to change back into the uniform the explorer wears."

George thumbed more pages. "Near the end of Act Three."

"Actually, the very end. In the book, as you know, Frankenstein was rowing a cake of ice across the Arctic Ocean in pursuit of the monster when he was picked up by the Arctic explorer's ship. In the end, of course, he dies from the effects of exposure."

George said, "Of course."

Dearborn smiled. "You see, not only difficult to stage, but there's a certain unintended humor in the scene." He cleared his throat. "On my — Frankenstein's — deathbed, I exact a promise from you, the ex-

218

plorer — that you will *kill* the monster."

George looked up innocently from the script. "So then I get to shoot Cousin Roderick?"

Dearborn cleared his throat again. "In the book, the monster capers across the ice pack, howling in frustration and rage because his creator has thwarted him by dying. But in Mrs. Trumbull's adaptation, you will take the gun Frankenstein left beside his bed, the gun with which he intended to kill the monster, and yes, you will shoot Roderick. The monster." Dearborn looked around at the small cast gathered around him. "Any questions, people? Any comments for George, here?"

"Did somebody fix the porthole, Uncle Dearborn?" asked Roderick.

Dearborn looked at his other nephew over the top of his glasses. "It was enlarged to accommodate you."

"That was a wonderful scene. We should keep it," said Becca, slapping her hand on her copy of the script.

"I could have been hurt," said Roderick.

"I noticed you were limping," said Becca. "Did you stumble into something on stage?"

"No." Roderick turned away. "I tripped on a rock."

George raised a hand. "Is the gun loaded

with blanks?"

"Naturally," Dearborn said. "Our stage manager, Nora Epstein, has seen to that. Other questions? Fine." He clapped his hands. "Quickly, quickly." He looked at his watch. "Take it from Act One, Scene One. We open with you, George, by my bedside."

"Splendid, splendid," said Dearborn, getting up from his — Frankenstein's — deathbed at the end of the run-through. He looked at his watch again. "You have three-quarters of an hour, people, before you need to get back to the theater. Don't wander too far away."

George went backstage to the prop table, where he examined the gun he would be using to kill Roderick. The gun looked both real and lethal, and when he picked it up, it was heavy.

He checked his own watch. Enough time to get to Shirley's Hardware and back before getting in costume for the matinee.

The morning was bright. The previous day's thunderstorm had cleared the air. Victoria walked the quarter-mile to the West Tisbury police station, and when she got there, Casey was at her computer. She looked up.

"Hey, Victoria. Nice day."

"Would you mind taking me to the state police barracks?"

Casey swiveled around. "Now what?"

"I have to talk to Sergeant Smalley."

"Yeah?"

"It's the state police who are investigating the murder, isn't it?"

"What's up, Victoria?"

Victoria sat down in her usual chair. "Since the state police are in charge, I'm trying to go through proper channels. If you won't take me . . ."

"I suppose you'll hitchhike." Casey got up with a sigh. "I'll drive you. I wasn't getting anywhere with this awful Island-wide computer network, anyway. Do you intend to tell me what this is all about?"

"I can't," said Victoria. "I've given someone my word."

Casey looked up at the ceiling and sighed.

Trooper Tim Eldredge was at the desk when Victoria and Casey walked in. He looked tired and his uniform was wrinkled. "Morning, Mrs. Trumbull, Chief O'Neill."

Casey nodded and stepped aside.

Victoria said, "You look as though you've had another busy night, Tim."

"Yes, ma'am, Mrs. Trumbull. Bob Scott's death, you know."

221

"I read about it in the off-Island papers early this morning. It seems very strange."

"Yes, ma'am. I guess you and the chief want to see Sergeant Smalley?"

"Victoria wants to see him, not me," said Casey.

"I'll buzz his office. The forensic scientist, Dr. McAlistair, is with him now."

"Thank you," said Victoria.

"Go right on up, Mrs. Trumbull. He'll meet you at the head of the stairs."

Casey studied the posters and notices on the station house wall. "I'll wait, Victoria. I've got paperwork I have to fill out."

Victoria held the banister tightly as she went up the stairs. Smalley greeted her, ushered her into his second-floor office, and held a visitor's chair for her.

"Hello, again, Mrs. Trumbull." Alison turned to Smalley. "Thanks for letting me take the state police vehicle. I'll be at the funeral home if anyone needs me."

After Alison left, Smalley took his seat behind the desk. "What can I do for you, Mrs. Trumbull?"

"I'm on a sensitive errand, and I'd like to tell you about it indirectly, if you don't mind."

"Concerning what, Mrs. Trumbull?"

"Suppose a child witnesses what might

have been a killer rifling through a desk, and that child manages to get away and hide someplace safe."

Smalley leaned forward. "The boy? Teddy Vanderhoop?"

"I can't identify anyone because I've given my word."

Smalley leaned back again. "If I understand you, Teddy is safe and you know where he is?"

"Possibly." Victoria nodded.

"Thank God." Smalley breathed out. "Continue your story."

"The hypothetical child's mother is involved with a man who frightens the child. The child doesn't want his mother to know where he is because he's afraid the man will come after him."

"We've got to let his mother know he's okay. Otherwise she'll go nuts."

Victoria nodded. "This is still hypothetical."

"Yes," said Smalley. "Strictly hypothetical."

"Let's say the child has written a note for his mother saying he's safe, that he got away from the burglar, and he'll get in touch with her on Monday."

Smalley looked at his watch. "This is Saturday." He looked up at Victoria. "Would it be advisable for me to call off the all-Island search for Teddy?"

"If I were you, yes. I would call off the search."

"And if you were me, would you notify the Island police departments that the boy is safe and is in hiding?"

"If I were you, yes." Victoria sat forward in her own chair. "How much may I tell you before the law gets involved and you must act on what I have to say?"

"If I were you," said Smalley, smiling, "I would continue to talk theoretically. But in detail, please."

Victoria told him how Teddy had heard Peg scream for him to run, how he had seen an unfamiliar light-colored car turn off the Job's Neck Road and head toward town, how he'd gone back to his house and climbed the beech tree.

"That explains the broken branch," said Smalley.

She told him how Teddy had found Peg's dog, Sandy, hurt, and had decided to ride his bike to her house and hide in her big attic. She repeated what Teddy had said about a second car that had turned off the Job's Neck Road, also heading toward town.

"Theoretically, could the boy identify either of the cars?" Smalley asked.

"He might."

Smalley made some notes. "I need to question the boy, Mrs. Trumbull."

"I gave him my word that I'll keep his secret until Monday."

Smalley shook his head. "Terribly irregular, Mrs. Trumbull. You can work unofficially, whereas I am legally obligated to inform the parents, regardless of my personal feelings."

"Do you want me to question him about the cars and the intruder?"

Smalley leaned back in his chair and swiveled it toward the flag in the corner. "Since you're asking me hypothetical questions about a hypothetical child, let me give you a list of questions that would aid the police, should this turn into a real situation. I need his answers as soon as possible." He swiveled back to his computer, tapped away at the keyboard, and printed out a list of questions.

Victoria examined the list. "Thank you."

"You realize, of course, Mrs. Trumbull, just how irregular all this is?"

Victoria nodded.

"You realize, too, what a chance I'm taking by going along with your idea of a hypothetical child?"

"It's not much of a chance," said Victoria.

"Monday, then, you'll notify us?"

"I've promised I'd keep his secret until Monday."

"Can you tell me if the boy is in any danger at present?"

"No," said Victoria firmly. "At least, I don't think so."

"On your say-so, I'm calling off the search. However, I'm stationing Trooper Eldredge near your house, just in case."

Victoria got up from her chair. "Tim is welcome to stay with me. I have an extra bedroom. He won't have to sit in his car."

CHAPTER 19

While Casey waited for Victoria in the reception area of the state police barracks, she studied a report she'd brought with her. She looked up and closed the folder when she heard her deputy coming down the stairs.

As Victoria reached the last step, the buzzer on the desk sounded, and Trooper Tim Eldredge picked up the phone. "Eldredge, here." Pause. "Yes, sir. She's still here." Pause. "Right." He stood. "Chief O'Neill, the sergeant wants you."

"Now?"

"Yes, ma'am."

"Did he say why?"

"No, ma'am. You can go right on up. He'll meet you at the head of the stairs."

Victoria smiled and seated herself on the bench. "I'll wait. I've got a poem I'm working on. A triolet."

"A *what?*"

"Triolet. The first line is repeated as the fourth and seventh lines, and the second line is repeated as the eighth, and last, line — the rhyme scheme is A B a A a b A B."

"Say what?"

"That's the rhyme scheme for a triolet, A B . . ."

"Okay, Victoria." Casey shook her head and trudged up the stairs. She followed Smalley into his office and sat in the chair Victoria had vacated.

"Victoria was giving me a poetry lecture. You want to see me about something she said?"

Smalley grinned. "I'm not at liberty to divulge Mrs. Trumbull's confidences. However, in my opinion, we can call off the search for the boy. You might want to notify your people."

"Yeah? So Victoria's found him and is hiding him?"

"Can't say." Smalley's grin grew wider. "That was one reason I wanted to see you. The other reason has to do with Bob Scott." Smalley's grin faded. "The actor who died last night."

Casey sat forward. "Something fishy about his death?"

"Decidedly fishy. Since Dr. McAlistair is still on Island, Toby the undertaker took

228

Scott's body to Rose Haven Funeral Parlor, and the doc will do a preliminary cause of death exam there."

"He didn't die naturally of a heart attack, then? Did Frankenstein's monster strangle him too realistically in the play?"

"We don't think so. Maria Gallante, the cleaning woman, found a plastic cup next to the sofa where Scott was lying. She was smart enough to pick up the cup with a tissue, put it in a paper bag, and give it to the ambulance crew when they arrived."

"One benefit of watching TV," said Casey. "Poisoned?"

"Could be."

"With what?"

"The lab in Sudbury is testing the residue in the cup as we speak." Smalley shrugged. "We won't know until the tests are in. Won't know for sure that he *was* poisoned."

"Mind if I share this with Victoria?"

"She's your deputy. I'd say she's pretty good at keeping confidences." Smalley grinned again. "Tell her the information is to go no further."

"When will we get back the tests?"

Smalley looked at his watch. "They're doing a rush job. But that won't be tomorrow."

"Can we assume Teddy's safe?" asked Casey.

"Theoretically and hypothetically, yes."

"We still have two suspicious deaths."

Smalley nodded. "The boy may have been — in fact, still may be — an intended victim. I'll ask Trooper Eldredge to keep an eye on Mrs. Trumbull's house for the next few days."

"So that's where he is. That figures," said Casey. "What about the boy's mother?"

"Mrs. Trumbull is handling that."

"Lord!" said Casey. "I should ask the selectmen to send her to the police academy for some basic training."

"She doesn't need further training," said Smalley. "In fact, we could learn a thing or two from her."

"The stakeout of Victoria's is unofficial?"

"You could say that."

Casey took a deep breath. "I'll talk to my sergeant, Junior Norton. Ask him if he would mind very much, if it's not too inconvenient, sitting in on an all-night poker game with his buddy Tim Eldredge at Mrs. Trumbull's."

"Nicely put," said Smalley.

"Would you mind stopping at the pet store?" Victoria asked Casey, as they headed back

230

to West Tisbury from the state police barracks. "I need to buy cat food."

"Sure, Victoria. But I thought McCavity
only ate food from those fancy little cans
you get at Cronig's." Casey eyed her deputy,
who stared straight ahead. "Ah," she said.
"You want to talk to the guy who works
there. Bruce Duncan. About the goldfish,
right?"

Victoria nodded. "That, too."

Precious Pets was down a slight hill,
behind and below Radio Shack in what
amounted to the ground-level basement of
the shops above. Casey pulled up in front of
the store. A sleepy Black Lab, who'd been
dozing in the shade of an overgrown lilac
bush, got to her feet, shook herself, and
stood expectantly, tongue out, tail wagging.
Victoria held out her hand, and the dog
sniffed.

"She must smell McCavity," said Casey,
holding the door.

Victoria went in first. She breathed in the
odors of puppies and kittens and hamsters
and fresh cedar shavings. Casey followed
her past an open pen of snuggled-together
black puppies, past shelves piled with col-
lars and pillows, rawhide bones and catnip
mice, bags of cat chow, dog chow, litter,
cedar shavings, and birdseed. At the end of

the aisle were a half-dozen fish tanks.

Bruce Duncan stood on a step stool, siphoning sludge from the gravel at the bottom of one of the tanks. He wore his usual black T-shirt with VETA in large green letters on the front and Vineyarders for the Ethical Treatment of Animals on the back. "Can I help you?" he said before he turned and recognized Victoria. "Mrs. Trumbull. What can I do for you?"

"I wanted to buy a few goldfish for my pond," Victoria said, examining the tanks.

Bruce lifted the siphon, and the stream of muddy water in the plastic hose gurgled back into the tank. He stepped off the stool and winced as he put his weight on his right foot.

"Are you all right?" Victoria asked, concerned.

"Barked my shin couple days ago." Once he was off the stool, Bruce was almost a head shorter than Victoria. "You want goldfish?" He pointed to one of the empty tanks, and his face darkened. "That idiot, excuse my French, Mrs. Trumbull, that idiot at the express office *killed* them."

"Oh?" said Victoria.

"At the airport." Bruce dropped the siphon into a bucket partially filled with sludge.

"I don't understand."

Bruce smoothed down the thin strand of hair he'd combed over the top of his head. "You know Roderick Hill?"

"Yes. From the play. The stand-in for the monster."

"That's the one. The monster. The store got an air shipment of five hundred goldfish this weekend, and he killed them."

"I still don't understand," said Victoria.

"You know he works at the express agency at the airport, don't you? Rapid Express." Bruce's face became even pinker. "He left the container of goldfish out on the tarmac over the weekend. They stewed to death in the hot sun."

Casey had been standing next to Victoria. She coughed politely. "I'm going to look at the Black Lab pups, Victoria," and she strolled toward the puppy pen.

"Surely, he didn't do it on purpose. Wasn't there a sign on the carton? 'Live Fish' or something like that?"

"He didn't even look. Didn't notice the four-inch-high fluorescent red letters saying 'Live Fish'. Wrapped up in his own sweet self. Can you imagine what it must have been like for those fish in the hot sun?"

"No, I can't imagine," said Victoria, sympathetically. "I don't even want to think about it. Will you be getting a new ship-ment?"

"Not if he's still employed by those Rapid Express people, we won't." Bruce picked up a plastic lid from the floor and uncovered the bucket. "I don't think he'll be with them much longer. Not if I have anything to say about it."

"That certainly was irresponsible." Victoria leaned on her lilac-wood stick. She'd been standing a long time.

"Irresponsible! He takes after his uncle. Self-centered, vain, thoughtless, stupid . . ."

"I don't believe he's stupid," said Victoria.

"Well, he obviously can't read. I'll fix him one day."

"Don't do anything rash," advised Victoria.

Bruce went on as if he hadn't heard. "Does he have more rights than any one of those goldfish? They were simply trying to live their own lives." He smacked a fist into his palm. "I'd like him to know what it's like to be boiled alive."

"That sounds a bit extreme," said Victoria.

"To think that he and his uncle went ahead with the play even after . . ." He paused. "Even after . . ."

"You were right to refuse to go on stage last night. It was crass and insensitive for

Dearborn to continue with opening night. Box office, he said." Victoria looked around for a place to sit and ended up leaning against the table.

Bruce lifted the bucket and set it on the table. The sludge smelled strongly of ammonia. "I was the next victim, Mrs. Trumbull. You know that, don't you?"

"I think you're being overly . . ." Victoria didn't finish. The man who'd taken over Bruce Duncan's role was dead, and she didn't know if Bruce had heard yet.

"I'm not being overly anything. Two deaths in order of appearance, little William and the housekeeper Justine. The third victim, Frankenstein's friend Henry Clerval, is me!" He pounded his chest.

"Have you seen any of this morning's off-Island newspapers?" Victoria raised her eyebrows.

"I haven't had time," Bruce said.

"The papers report that Robert Scott died of an apparent heart attack."

"No!"

Victoria waited.

"You see? That death was intended for me."

"The papers claimed he died of heart failure."

"That's what death is. Heart failure. Now

it's three people. If I'd gone on stage last night . . ." He didn't complete the thought.

"Teddy isn't dead."

"He was the first one killed by the monster."

"Peg's death was attributed to an unfortunate accident. Robert's to a heart attack."

"Coincidental? Two deaths, maybe three?" Bruce lifted the siphon out of the bucket and shook a few drops of water from it. "You think I'm crazy, don't you?"

"Not crazy," said Victoria. "Sensitive, perhaps. Or, like many actors, superstitious. It's a coincidence that two members of the cast have died. But Teddy is alive," she repeated.

Casey returned from the Lab puppies. "Did you need cat food, Victoria?"

"No," said Victoria, turning back to Bruce. "Who do you think killed them?"

"I'm not saying, Mrs. Trumbull. But I think you can guess."

Victoria shifted her weight to a more comfortable position. "You were disturbed by something else in the play, Bruce. Would you mind telling me what?"

Bruce laid the siphon on a tray in front of the empty goldfish tank. "The costumes."

"Oh?" asked Victoria, puzzled.

"The explorer's parka, the monster's

hands and feet, the housekeeper's coat collar, the bride's wrap."

"What about them?"

"Fur," Bruce said. "Fur! Animals killed to amuse some uncaring audience. Wolf ruff. Dog hair. Mink collar. Beaver coat."

"I believe it's rabbit, not beaver," said Victoria.

"You think rabbits are inferior to beaver?"

"Rabbits ate my tulips this spring. All of them."

"They've got to eat, too."

"They simply nipped off the buds. Wasted the rest of the plant. Tulips have as much soul as rabbits," said Victoria, shifting away from the ammonia smell. "At any rate, all of the costumes came from items found at the West Tisbury dump."

"It's still fur," repeated Bruce. "Animals killed for their fur."

"Talk to Dearborn about the costumes."

"Lot of good he is, Mrs. Trumbull. He was drunk as a skunk last night."

"Was he?"

"At least, that's what I heard."

"You intend to continue acting in the play, don't you, Bruce? Now that we've paid tribute to Peg by not performing in opening night. If you're concerned about Henry Clerval's death, I don't suppose he's likely to die a second time."

Bruce thought for a moment. "I wouldn't be too sure."

"You cared a great deal for Peg, didn't you? She was a lovely person. I know she cared about you, too."

He turned, and Victoria saw that he was angry, not sorrowful. "Cared about me?"

"Certainly. She thought highly of you."

"She didn't care about me, Mrs. Trumbull." He picked up the slop bucket. "She despised me."

CHAPTER 20

Casey dropped off Victoria at her house, and Victoria, after checking to make sure no one else was home, went upstairs and knocked on the attic door. She heard sneakers on the steps and Teddy opened the door. He was pale.

"Are you feeling all right?" she asked.

He rubbed his eyes. "I fell asleep. How's Sandy?"

"I haven't talked to Dr. Atkins since this morning, but he seemed to think Sandy would be fine. But I did talk to Sergeant Smalley at the state police barracks."

"No!" wailed Teddy.

"It's all right, Teddy. He's promised to keep your secret, at least until Monday. All of the Island police were searching for you. He needed to let them know you're safe. He's also given me a list of questions to ask you. Would you like to come downstairs, for a change? You must be tired of the attic."

"It's okay. I like it up here. What did my mother say about the note?"

"The note is still on the table. She must not have seen it yet. Come along."

Teddy followed her to the kitchen, where she made a peanut-butter sandwich for him, and they moved into the cookroom. She rummaged in her cloth bag until she found the list of questions Smalley had given her.

"The police need to know everything you can possibly remember about what you saw and heard the night before last. That was Thursday."

"Dress rehearsal," Teddy said, nibbling at his sandwich.

"Did you hear anything at the theater that was unusual? I was there with you, of course. But you're supposed to say what you heard."

"Only that after everyone left, someone in back of us made a noise Mr. Hill didn't like."

"That's right. I remember that, too." Victoria jotted down a note in the space Smalley had left after the question. "Mr. Hill looked up and asked who was there, and no one answered." She referred to the list. "He wants to know if, on your way home, you noticed anything different?"

"We stopped at Louis's and picked up the

pizza, and then Peg drove home along Lagoon Pond Road. Someone was in a dinghy going behind the point."

"Motorboat?" asked Victoria, writing.

Teddy nodded.

"A man or a woman?"

"I couldn't tell. I think it was a man."

"Was he on the same side of the point as you?"

"Yup." Teddy thought a moment. "No, he wasn't. He went around behind the point."

"Could you tell anything about the person or the boat?"

"Lots of people on Lagoon Pond have dinghies with outboard motors," he said. "I didn't notice anything special about it."

"No telling what might be useful to the police," said Victoria. "Did you see any strange vehicles when you drove onto Job's Neck?" she asked after he'd settled back in his seat.

He shook his head. "Peg let me off in front of my house and drove on to her house next door. I can't think of anything I haven't told you. I got my bicycle from the shed and then I went into my house."

"Was the door locked?"

"Just the front door. Not the back. We never lock the back door."

"Go on. You were saying you went in . . ."

241

"I went in and turned on the lights so I could find my comic books, because it was beginning to get dark. I'm pretty sure I turned the lights out when I left, Mrs. Trumbull. My mother makes a big deal about not wasting electricity."

"She's quite right. Go on."

"I turned out the lights and put my comic books in the basket on the front of my bike."

"Did you have many comic books?"

Teddy nodded. "A big pile. One fell out. I didn't ride my bike over to Peg's, I wheeled it, because she's right next door."

"I see."

"I was going to leave my bike in her shed. Then, like I told you, I heard Peg scream, 'Run, Teddy, run!' just like that." He'd imitated the scream in an eerie way. Victoria shivered.

"So you ran."

"I shouldn't have. My dad wouldn't of."

"Teddy, you did exactly the right thing. Your dad was trained to be a Ranger. You haven't been, not yet."

Teddy picked up his partly nibbled sandwich and put it down again.

"Aren't you hungry?" Victoria asked.

He shook his head.

"What happened next?"

"Pretty soon I saw this light-colored car

242

go by. I thought at first it was Lears' car, but it wasn't."

"Can you tell me anything at all about the car? Was it big, like an SUV, or small, like a sports car?"

Teddy thought. "It was kind of medium. I couldn't really tell the color. Maybe light tan or gray or blue." He shrugged. "Not white. Sort of an old lady's car. Four doors and kind of a dopey shape, you know?"

Victoria sighed, and thought of the green Citation she no longer was permitted to drive. All because of backing into the Meals on Wheels van. Her Citation had not been an old lady's car. "Could you tell how many people were inside?"

"Just one. A man, I think. I couldn't really see him, but the top of his head was taller than the top of the headrest."

Victoria noted this. "Was it possible that the man driving the light-colored car was a neighbor? Someone you knew?"

Teddy pushed his sandwich away from him. "I know most all the cars on the point. Could've been a summer renter or a visitor."

"But you don't think you knew him?"

Teddy shrugged again. "I didn't get a good look at him."

Victoria turned the page of her list of

questions. "Then you went back to your house. Why did you do that?"

Teddy shrugged. "I was scared to go back to Peg's, because of the scream, you know?"

Victoria nodded.

"I figured I could call her from my house, and if she didn't answer, I could call nine-one-one. That's what they tell us to do at school." He looked up. "And the lights were on downstairs. I know I didn't leave them on."

"I'm sure you didn't. Tell me, again, everything you saw. The person rifling through your mother's desk. Can you possibly recall whether it was a man or a woman?"

Teddy wiped his mouth with the back of his hand. "The person was kind of a blob. All dressed in black."

Victoria noted that. "Could you tell how tall the person was? When you were in the tree, where was his head with respect to pictures on the wall?"

Teddy thought for a long time. "He was bent over the desk, so I couldn't tell."

"Did he ever stand up straight?"

"When I broke the branch, yeah. But I was so scared, I didn't really look at him."

"Try to remember. Did he come to the window before you climbed out of the tree?"

"Yeah. He came over and opened the window and put his hands on the windowsill, and that's when I saw this ski mask, and he looked up and he was looking right at me. I could see his eyes."

"Were his eyes a dark color or a light color?"

Teddy shook his head.

"But he seemed to be taller than your mother. Was he as tall as your father?"

"He didn't seem real tall. Medium, I guess."

"As tall as I am?"

"Shorter than you, Mrs. Trumbull. You're pretty tall."

Victoria smiled and turned to another page. "When you climbed out of the tree, you heard him go out the back door."

"He tripped over my Lego box and must have hurt himself, because he swore something awful. My mother told me that was going to happen. Someday, somebody's going to get hurt, she's always saying."

"Well, this time she'll be glad you didn't listen to her."

"I always *listen* to her." Teddy grinned. "But I don't always do what she says. Her creepy boyfriend stays with us sometimes. When I don't do what my mother wants." Teddy sighed. "She likes him better than she likes me."

"I doubt that," said Victoria. "She likes him in a different way. She'll never stop liking you best of all."

Teddy settled back in his chair.

"When he banged into the Lego box and swore, did it sound like a man or a woman?"

Teddy sat up straight. "A man. Definitely a man."

"Then you dropped out of the tree, managed to reach your bicycle, and turned onto the lane that led to the main road. That's when you found Sandy. And I know from what you told me earlier, you saw two cars turn off the Job's Neck Road. Which car did you see while you were rescuing Sandy?"

"The second. It was light colored, too, but it was more like an old VW bus. Sort of boxy, but not real big."

"The license plate. Could you tell anything about it?"

"It was too dark out. . . . I just remembered something, Mrs. Trumbull. The first car, I could see the license plate, but I couldn't read the numbers. But it had all numbers. The second car, the license plate was all letters."

"That's helpful," said Victoria. "Could you tell anything about the driver?"

"Nope."

At that point, a police vehicle pulled into Victoria's driveway.

"Quick, Teddy. Upstairs. Take an apple from the bowl for dessert."

And Teddy scurried away.

She checked for crumbs and evidence of a small boy eating an early lunch, and then she looked out the cookroom window. The vehicle had parked under the Norway maple, and Alison stepped out. Victoria had forgotten that Sergeant Smalley had loaned her a state police car.

Alison brought a faint smell of formalin with her into the kitchen.

Victoria was innocently wiping the kitchen counter and looked up. "Did you learn anything from Robert Scott's body?"

"You don't want to talk to me until I have a shower, Mrs. Trumbull. I won't be long."

Less than fifteen minutes later, she emerged, in bare feet and wearing a pair of Elizabeth's jeans and a T-shirt. She was combing her newly washed hair.

"Have you had lunch?" Victoria asked.

"John's taking me out to lunch, thanks."

"John?"

Alison smiled. "Sergeant Smalley."

"Yes, of course," said Victoria. "Have a cup of tea, then, and tell me what you can before he gets here."

"Not much to tell. Robert Scott didn't die from strangulation, although he had some serious bruises around his neck. And I found no evidence of heart anomalies."

"In other words, not a heart attack?"

"Not a heart attack caused by a pre-existing condition."

"Was he poisoned, then? The cup that the cleaning woman found . . ."

"It looks that way," said Alison. "If it was poison, I'll be interested in learning what the killer used. Quick acting and fairly humane, I would guess. Bob Scott didn't suffer."

CHAPTER 21

Dawn Haines, free of her role as the bride of Frankenstein, stood in the pet food aisle at Cronig's Market trying to decide which delicacy her cat, Perky, would deign to eat. Just this morning, Perky had delivered a headless mouse to her doorstep, his contribution to the dinner table. But Perky, himself, must be offered salmon treat. Or was it chicken livers this week?

She was poring over the small cans of gourmet cat food when a voice behind her said, "They're impossible, aren't they?"

Dawn turned, and there was Trooper Tim Eldredge, still looking rumpled, wheeling a grocery cart half-full of sensible items like potatoes, onions, and oatmeal. He reached for a large can of generic cat food.

She brightened. "Hi, Tim. You have a cat?"

"Three."

"My condolences. You're not still on duty,

are you?" She indicated his disheveled uniform.

"Sergeant Smalley gave me a couple of hours off. To get cleaned up."

From head to foot, he was a picture of exhaustion, needing a shower, a shave, clean clothes, and a good night's sleep.

He asked, "You're not going on stage for the matinee?"

Dawn chortled. "I think I'll defer to the new bride of Frankenstein. Becca Hill and her idiot husband, Dearborn, can have the play, as far as I'm concerned."

"I hear it's a howling success."

"What they've done to it stinks," said Dawn.

A woman behind Tim said, "Excuse me."

"Sorry," said Tim, and he pushed his cart to one side to let her pass.

"A bunch of us didn't act on opening night out of respect for Peg Storm. Now Bob Scott's dead, and it's like Mr. Hill can only think about the box office and more, more, more receipts." She beckoned with her free hand in a come-to-me gesture.

"Makes you wonder who's next."

"Mr. Hill's an A-number-one hypocrite," she said. "Like he's always ranting and raving about professionalism, yet look what he's done to Mrs. Trumbull's play. No one will ever again be able to produce it the way she meant it to be."

"Who's the next one killed in the play?" Tim asked again.

"The bride of Frankenstein."

"You?"

"Not any more, it isn't." She flicked her long braid over her shoulder with one hand. "Dearborn the drunk and Becca the super ham are producing the play this afternoon, no matter that Peg and Bob are dead. 'Box office, box office, box office.' And Teddy's still missing."

"Sergeant Smalley called off the search for him."

"No!" Dawn cried. "They haven't given up . . . ?"

"I don't know what it means. The sergeant wants me on duty at Mrs. Trumbull's tonight." He covered his mouth and yawned. "Informally, you know. I'm supposed to be playing an all-night poker game with Junior Norton, the West Tisbury cop."

"Two of you? Mrs. Trumbull's not in danger, is she?"

Tim looked around before he answered. "I have a feeling Teddy may be at Mrs. Trumbull's."

"But that's where his mom is staying. The forensic scientist, too."

"Mrs. T's got a pretty big house."

Dawn set her basket on the floor. "They don't really think Peg's and Bob's deaths are accidents, do they? I mean, it's too weird."

Tim shrugged. "Cops don't like coincidences, even though we see them all the time."

"It's almost like Bruce Duncan is right about the actors getting killed in order of their appearance."

Tim shrugged again.

"So if Teddy is alive somewhere, you must be scared that some killer is out there, trying to find him?"

"Teddy plays the first victim of the monster, right?"

Dawn nodded. "Victor Frankenstein's little brother, William."

"And Teddy went missing. Then the next one killed in the play is the housekeeper, the part Peg Storm played."

"Justine. She's hanged."

"And now Peg is dead," said Tim. "Then who gets killed in the play?"

"Henry Clerval, the part Bob Scott played."

"And Bob Scott is dead."

"It wasn't even Bob Scott's part. He was substituting for Bruce Duncan, who didn't go on stage out of respect for Peg, like a lot of us. Bruce had a thing for her."

"Heavy stuff." Tim checked his watch. "I gotta get these groceries to my grandmother before I clean up and get over to Mrs. Trumbull's. You want to join us in the poker game?"

"Maybe."

"I'll pick you up in an hour."

"You know where I live?"

Tim grinned. "Sure do." He piled a half-dozen cans of cat food and a twenty-five-pound sack of cat chow into his cart. "Which way are you going?"

"Next aisle. Cereals and juice." Dawn picked up her basket and dropped four small cans of gourmet cat food into it.

They left the pet food aisle, walking slowly and talking. "You really think Teddy is at Mrs. Trumbull's?"

"You better not talk so loud. I don't think anyone's supposed to know," said Tim. "Was she Bruce Duncan's girlfriend?"

"You mean Peg? No way. She tried to discourage him politely, but he just didn't get it. Finally, she was almost rude, at least for her. Now he's going crazy about her death."

"Probably feels guilty."

She shrugged. "I doubt it. Not Bruce."

"Then the bride of Frankenstein?"

"Not me. Dearborn's wife, Becca, was so awful, the audience loved her. Dearborn was drunk, and they loved that. Roderick was clumsy, and Nora, the stage manager, read her lines in a monotone. The audience loved everything." She glanced at Tim, who stifled another yawn. "You need to get some sleep."

"I wish."

"I don't think they meant to turn the play into a farce. It just happened." Dawn turned the corner past the sushi, and Tim followed with his cart. "Poor Mrs. Trumbull. After all the work she did on that play."

Tim yawned again and checked his watch. "Carrots. My grandmother needs carrots. See you later." He wheeled his cart toward the checkout, and Dawn continued to the dairy aisle. She was looking for a half-carton of eggs when she saw Bruce Duncan's reflection in the glass of the refrigerators.

"What d'ya say, Dawn. Fancy meeting you here." He, too, carried a basket, his with crackers and cheese in it. "Mrs. Trumbull's granddaughter is over in pickles and olives, and Gerard Cohen is in frozen foods."

"He's not acting in the matinee either?"

"Doesn't look that way. I suppose you could call us cast-out outcasts."

"Unh," said Dawn.

"Well," Bruce went on, "Dearborn's wife is the next victim. You should be glad you're not on stage for this performance."

Dawn nodded. "Mr. Hill seems to have everything under control."

"Except the murders," Bruce Duncan said.

Gerard Cohen wheeled his cart to a stop behind them. "What murders?"

At Shirley's Hardware, George wrote out a check for his purchase. "Wasn't sure you had this in stock." He held up what looked like a large pistol and a box printed with flags.

"If you don't see what you want, ask. We'll special order it for you," said Mary, writing George's phone number on his check. "That's our motto." She handed him the receipt.

Jessie, the owner, stopped at the counter. "Going hunting?" he said, and laughed. George was tall, but Jessie towered over him and outweighed him by a good fifty pounds.

"Someone showed me," said George.

"While you're at it," Mary said, "do you suppose you could come over to my place and shoot at a few deer? They've eaten everything in my garden." This week, her hair was a bright metallic green.

"Frighten 'em to death, most likely," said Jessie.

Mary slammed the cash register drawer shut. "Want a bag?"

"Yes," said George. "I'd rather not be seen carrying."

"Don't blame you." Jessie laughed again. "How's school?"

"Not bad," said George.

"Haven't seen your mother around lately."

George glanced at his watch. "She's busy. I've got to get back to the theater. Matinee this afternoon, and I have to change into my costume."

"Hear the play's a big hit," said Jessie.

"Guess so," George replied. "See you."

"Break a leg," said Mary, returning her pen to her hairdo.

George looked again at his watch and hustled out of the door, got into the car he'd borrowed from his mother and drove back to the playhouse. He parked on Franklin Street, as close as he could to the theater so he wouldn't have far to walk, and strode down the hill and through the wide front door. People were already lining up, an hour and a half early.

The line trailed down two blocks to Main Street. Scalpers were out, hawking tickets at Broadway-plus prices.

George hurried. He and the dying Frankenstein were the first on in Act One, and he
had to change into his explorer's costume.
After he'd done his listening-to-
Frankenstein bit, he'd have plenty of time.
He laughed when he imagined the audience
reaction to what he was about to do.

He supposed Dearborn must be wondering where he was. Unless Uncle Dearborn
had already drunk enough to anesthetize
himself.

CHAPTER 22

The play, if possible, was a bigger hit than on opening night. The audience expected high camp and got it. The first scene was on the ship where George, as the Arctic explorer, had picked up Frankenstein from his ice floe. He had listened sympathetically to Frankenstein's fantastic story, as told by Dearborn. As George had suspected, his uncle had fortified himself before going on stage. With every astonishingly well-articulated word, he puffed out fumes of semi-metabolized whiskey. George held his nose and instinctively backed away from the deathbed. The audience cheered, shrieked, whistled, clapped, and shouted out suggestions. Dearborn added a few extemporaneous lines, to which George replied with his own.

At the end of Act One, Scene One, George hustled backstage to the dressing room, dumped out his purchase from Shirley's

Hardware, opened the box with the realistic-looking pistol he'd bought and loaded it the way Jessie and Mary at the hardware store had shown him. Then he made his way to the prop table.

Nora Epstein, the stage manager, was still in the women's dressing room, practicing her part as Justine, so the prop table was unguarded, as it had been for two nights.

George knew nothing about guns. He substituted his newly purchased gun for the stage gun, dropped the stage gun into a cardboard box that was under the table, and covered it with a moth-eaten woolen scarf.

He thought briefly about fingerprints, but since he had no gloves or even a handkerchief with him, he decided the hell with fingerprints. No one had seen him, he was quite sure.

He went back to the men's dressing room and changed into his Henry Clerval costume. It occurred to him that Roderick, as the monster, would be strangling Henry Clerval. Him. So, George fished around in the costume box until he found a metal collar that must have been part of the Tin Man's costume from some long ago production of *The Wizard of Oz* and wrapped it around his neck — just in case. He practiced his lines, stretching up his chin to minimize the odd metallic rattle from the tight collar and figured no one would notice.

The strangling scene went well. So well, that when the monster grabbed him around the throat, it was the monster who shrieked in pain, hopped on one foot holding both hands down at knee level and started after Henry Clerval for real, with a drawn-out growl. The stage darkened and the stage-hands dragged off Clerval's limp body with its dented tin collar. The body's face had a broad smile.

The audience took up the cry of "Encore! Encore!" and stamped its collective feet until the floorboards shook.

George had a bit of trouble removing the dented collar, but at last he was freed of it. He could hardly wait until the final scene, when he, the explorer, would carry out the dying wish of Frankenstein, and shoot Roderick. Wouldn't matter that his fingerprints were all over the weapon, he thought. They were supposed to be.

He watched from the wings as Act Two wound down. This was the act where the monster would strangle Becca, lying in her nuptial bed as the bride of Frankenstein. Would Roderick forget his strength? Would he be so angry with Aunt Becca that he would deliberately go too far? Would his hands be sore from strangling the tin collar of Henry Clerval? George watched with interest.

Roderick, as the monster, climbed through the hotel window into the bridal suite, and this time the entire window frame detached itself from the plywood wall, dropped onto the stage, and entangled itself around his feet. He stumbled and fell. Picked himself up, picked up the pieces of the frame, apparently got splinters in his hands in the process, and, howling, flung the pieces into the audience, to the delight of all.

Becca, the bride, screamed, as she was supposed to, and Roderick growled his lines about the wedding night, reached into his coat pocket, plucked out the gun, and waved it around.

"No, no, you fool!" Becca screamed. "You're not supposed to shoot me, you're supposed to strangle me!"

Damn, said George to himself. *I'm* the one who's supposed to shoot *Roderick.* Roderick's not supposed to shoot Aunt Becca!

He nearly darted onto the scene, but the noise from the audience was deafening.

"You stupid oaf," shrieked Becca. "Failure! Actor? Hah!"

Roderick shouted above the din, "This is all your fault, Aunt Becca! You'll be sorry!"

He bent his knees, held the gun the way he'd seen it done on television . . .

Cheers, whistles, catcalls!

. . . and aimed the gun at his own temple.

What on earth is he doing? George held his hands over his eyes and missed the action.

"Stop!" shrieked a voice from the wings.

Roderick turned his head toward the voice just as he pulled the trigger. There was a puff of smoke, a brilliant scarlet flash popped out of the gun, unwound itself into a six-by-nine-inch flag that said, in dense black letters, "BANG!!!!!!"

With that, the monster fled from the stage, leaving the bride un-strangled.

Becca sat up in the nuptial bed and cried out after him, "Can't you do anything right?" Then, apparently recalling where she was, she peered out at the audience through myopic eyes and addressed the blur of faces in a high, wavery voice. "I've been strangled!" She placed her hands around her neck. "My throat! My poor throat!" She gasped, stuck out her pink tongue and crossed her eyes. "He's killed me! I'm dead," and she slumped back on the bed.

It was impossible to top the murder of Frankenstein's bride, but the audience didn't care. They were weak from laughter and hoarse from shouting, their hands smarted from applauding, their feet stung from stamping.

In the last act, when George, as the Arctic explorer, produced the gun, the same gun, the gun with which he was to shoot Roderick the monster, the audience shouted warnings to the monster. George tugged the limp flag out of the muzzle, held the gun in both hands, pointed it at Roderick, crouched in a coplike manner, pulled the trigger, and shouted at the top of his lungs, "KA-POW!"

The audience roared.

The play ended. There were three curtain calls, and the audience demanded a fourth. After the fifth curtain call, George, from the wings, started the cry of "Author! Author!" and every voice in the audience joined in. "Author! Author!"

Backstage, Dearborn slumped over the prop table, asleep with a half-finished plastic cup of Jack Daniel's in front of him. The room trembled with the cries of "Author! Author!"

Becca rushed into the room. "Darling, wake up!"

"Umpf," said Dearborn.

"Author! Author!"

Becca shook him. "You have to go on

stage and say something."

"Nothin' to say," said Dearborn.

"They'll tear the place down."

"So what," said Dearborn.

"Author! Author!" The howl from the audience was even more insistent.

Becca shook him again, and tried to pry him out of his chair. "They're turning mean." She looked around frantically. "Roderick! George! Do something!"

"Go find good ol' Vicky," mumbled Dearborn.

"We already tried," screamed Becca. "No one answers the phone at her house." She turned to George. "Where is she?"

George, whose grin showed a set of fine teeth, shrugged.

"Roderick, *darling*," she snarled.

"Don't 'darling' me, you, you . . . phony!" Roderick shouted above the roar. "She's reading her poetry at Island Java."

"Get her!" screamed Becca. "Now! Hurry!"

Dearborn, eyes closed, snorted.

Becca grasped him by his hair and pulled him to a sitting position. "Get up, get up!" she hissed.

George had moved to one side, where he stood with arms folded, still grinning.

Becca turned on him. "Help me get him

to his feet, George. He's got to go on stage."

"He won't make it," said George.

"He has to. He will." Becca tugged on Dearborn's — actually Frankenstein's — coat collar.

"Author! Author!" came the rhythmic howl from the audience.

"Roderick!" screamed Becca. "Go! Get Mrs. Trumbull!"

Roderick, still in monster makeup, turned a leering, bloody face to her, thrust a finger in the air, and lurched off.

George stepped away from the wall he'd been leaning against. The wall trembled with the roar of the crowd. He stood behind Dearborn and, together with Becca, lifted him to his feet, turned him around, marched him toward the stage, and gave him a grand shove.

Miraculously, Dearborn straightened up, smoothed his mussed hair, and strode onto the stage, both hands high in the air. The stamping, clapping, and whistling stopped abruptly.

"Friends!" said Dearborn, in what sounded like a sober voice. "We have located the author."

"Hooray!" someone shouted, and others took up the cry. "Hooray! Hooray!"

Dearborn continued to hold up his hands

and waited a dramatic moment. "Our author, Victoria Trumbull, is on her way to the theater as we speak."

Backstage, Becca frowned. George laughed out loud.

Victoria, sitting in an armchair on the platform that served as a stage at Island Java, roughly two blocks from the theater, had opened her latest chapbook to a sestina entitled "Minerva's Bird" that she was about to read. Coffeehouse patrons leaned forward at the crowded café tables to hear every word.

"A sestina has six six-line stanzas and a tercet," Victoria explained.

Her enthralled audience nodded.

"The end words of the first stanzas . . ." Victoria never finished. She'd heard a stirring among the café tables and looked up to see Frankenstein's monster shambling toward her, knocking tables over in his blind haste.

Victoria stood, and her book dropped onto the stage, followed by her lilac-wood walking stick. "Roderick! What's the trouble now?"

"Author," Roderick huffed, out of breath. "They demand author . . . they're rioting . . . tearing apart the theater . . ."

The coffeehouse was silent.

Victoria bent down, holding an arm of her chair, and picked up her dropped book and her stick.

"Please, Mrs. Trumbull . . . they want the author . . . please come with me."

Victoria looked around at the quiet, sober faces around her and back at the monster in front of her with his fangs, stitches, electrodes, and blood.

"Hurry, Mrs. Trumbull . . . my car . . ." Roderick gasped.

Victoria made a quick decision. "I'm taking a short break," she told her audience. "I believe Jefferson Vanderhoop is here tonight?"

The coffeehouse faces looked around, and Jefferson Vanderhoop, standing by the coffee urn, raised his hand.

"Do you have some of your fishing poems with you?" Victoria called out.

"Yes, ma'am."

"While I'm gone, I'd like you to read them. I hope the rest of you will welcome a new poet to our gathering." Victoria started the applause, and the gathering politely joined in.

Roderick held out his arm. Victoria took it and stepped down from the platform. She marched between the tables, nodding first to one side, then the other, as her listeners stood respectfully. Roderick trailed behind her, limping and shuffling as rapidly as he could.

As Roderick closed the door of the coffeehouse, Victoria could hear a second round of polite applause for Jefferson Vanderhoop who was taking his place on the platform.

"Teddy's father?" Roderick said.

"Yes."

"Didn't know he wrote poetry."

"It's quite good," said Victoria. "Rough-hewn, but powerful. Not quite as polished as yours, of course."

Roderick had driven the two blocks to the coffeehouse and parked his car in front of Island Java, engine still running. He helped Victoria into the passenger seat and handed her the lilac-wood stick.

"Thank you."

Roderick plopped into the driver's seat, and Victoria turned to him.

"What's this all about, Roderick?"

He explained about the sold out theater, the scalpers, the gun that went "BANG!!!!!!" He described the five curtain calls and the cries of "Author! Author!"

"I refuse to acknowledge that I've had any part of the play as it's being performed," said Victoria, the wrinkles around her mouth forming straight horizontal and vertical lines.

Roderick told her the cheers and whistles were beginning to turn mean when he left to get her.

"I'm not surprised," said Victoria.

"They'll destroy Aunt Ruth's theater."

Victoria sighed and stared straight ahead. Roderick made a U-turn at the Black Dog Tavern and waited at Five Corners for a break in traffic.

While they waited, he pounded the steering wheel. "It's all my fault, Mrs. Trumbull."

Victoria turned and stared at him.

"It is. I'm a failure. A total failure. I didn't mean to strangle Bob Scott, but I did. I killed him. I didn't mean to smother Peg Storm, but I did. I killed her, too." He touched his forehead to the wheel. "I killed her!"

Victoria turned again and looked out at the traffic. "You can go now, Roderick. The Hummer is flashing its lights to let you through." She lowered her window and waved thanks. The driver, waiting patiently for Roderick to go ahead, did a sort of double take as Roderick, his antennae quivering, drove into the intersection and turned to go up the hill. Victoria looked into the side rearview mirror and saw that the driver was out of his vehicle, standing in the middle of Five Corners. Traffic had backed up as far as she could see in all five directions. The Hummer driver was pointing at the monster and his white-haired passenger and shouting into a doll-sized cellular phone pressed to his ear.

Chapter 23

"Everything I do," said Roderick, pounding the steering wheel, apparently unaware of the pedestrians turning to stare at him. "Everything I do, I fuck up."

Victoria looked straight ahead. "After I've pacified the audience at the theater, I want you to drive both of us to the state police barracks so you can explain to Sergeant Smalley what you've just told me."

"That's only part of the problem," Roderick said, glancing at her.

Victoria waited.

"This afternoon, I tried to kill myself. And failed."

"On stage? You attempted suicide? How?"

"I tried to shoot myself."

"With the stage gun? Why, for heaven's sake?"

He closed his eyes.

"Watch it!" Victoria braced a hand on the door frame as the car swerved. For a moment, she thought Roderick was about to succeed in his attempt and take her with him.

Roderick opened his eyes again and blinked, then turned right onto Main Street. "The world would be better off without me, Mrs. Trumbull." He sighed. "No one cares." Victoria saw a tear glistening at the corner of his eye. "By doing away with myself, I could get even with Aunt Becca."

"That's hardly getting even with anyone, Roderick. Suicide is the most selfish act anyone can perform. You'd be safely out of whatever mess you've made, leaving others to clean up after you. Jobs you've left undone, financial problems, unanswered questions, sloppy relationships . . ."

Roderick glanced at her with astonishment.

"Let alone the nuisance of disposing of your body and cleaning up *that* mess."

"I . . . I . . . I . . ." said Roderick.

"I'm not one bit sympathetic," she continued. "If you think you killed Peg Storm and Bob Scott, stand up on your hind legs and take your medicine."

Roderick hunched his monstrous shoulders and stared straight ahead, both hands high on the steering wheel. He passed the Bunch of Grapes Bookstore where Ann Bassett, the events coordinator, was putting flyers for coming book signings in the rack out front.

Ann turned, caught a glimpse of the nightmarish apparition driving a worried-looking Victoria Trumbull, and hustled back into the store. At the front desk, she called nine-one-one and explained, in a voice that was calmer than she felt, what she'd just witnessed. Tim Eldredge happened to be monitoring nine-one-one calls at the state police barracks while the usual operator was on coffee break. He gave a long, drawn-out sigh. "Yes, ma'am. We're aware of the situation. Mrs. Trumbull actually has everything under control. Thank you for calling, Ms. Bassett."

In Roderick's car, Victoria, exasperated by his talk of suicide, had not noticed the drama involving Ann Bassett and continued to berate him. "Fortunately, that was another failure. How were you intending to kill yourself?"

"I took the blanks out of the stage gun and loaded it with real bullets."

"And instead of killing yourself when you squeezed the trigger, a red flag shot out. Someone switched guns, apparently. The flagstaff, itself, could have done serious damage if you'd had the gun pressed to

273

your head."

"Somebody shouted from the wings and startled me."

He turned left onto Center Street and drove slowly up the hill toward the theater.

"What did you do with the blanks that were in the gun?"

"I have them right here." He leaned forward and reached one hand into his pocket. Victoria took the three bulletlike things from him and stared at them. "Roderick," she said with a touch of awe. "These are not stage blanks. They're real bullets."

"Say what?" said Roderick.

But they had arrived at the theater, and Victoria had no time to discuss what type of bullets had been in the stage gun. "Let me out, and you go and park. Don't forget, we're going to the police station afterward." Victoria wrapped the bullets in a paper napkin from her pocket and tucked them into her cloth bag. "I'll keep these and show them to the police. I'll meet you at the theater in about fifteen minutes. Don't do anything foolish in the meantime."

She eased herself out of the car and went toward the theater. Bruce Duncan opened the door.

"Bruce, what on earth are you doing here?"

He escorted her past the ticket booth before he spoke. "Lucky you got here, Mrs. Trumbull," he said, without answering her question. "The audience was going crazy."

"I thought you were boycotting the theater out of respect for Peg. What *are* you doing here?" Victoria repeated.

"Can't stay away." He shrugged. "I'll follow you up the stairs."

Victoria started the long climb up the steep stairway, one hand on the railing, the other holding her stick. Partway up, she stopped to rest. Her sore toe had begun to throb despite the hole her granddaughter had cut in her shoe.

"I've been rushing so, I'm a bit out of breath," she explained to Duncan, who waited on the step below her. She listened for the crowd noise she expected, but heard only one voice, one person talking, apparently on stage. Otherwise, the theater was quiet. "From what Roderick told me, I expected pandemonium."

"It *was* a near riot, Mrs. Trumbull," Bruce said. "They kept shouting 'Author!' The whole place was shaking. That's Dearborn on stage now. He told them you're on the way and he's taking questions until you arrive."

"Roderick picked me up at the coffee-house."

"Where's Roderick now?"

"Parking." Victoria resumed her climb and said over her shoulder, "The play as it's being acted is hardly the play I wrote." As she got closer to the top, she could hear Dearborn, who sounded quite sober. Not what she had expected.

"Yes," she heard him call out. "The lady in the pink blouse, fifth row."

Victoria couldn't hear the question, but she heard Dearborn's response. "Mrs. Trumbull's adaptation follows the original very closely. She uses Mary Shelley's exact wording where possible. Yes? You in the third row."

Victoria reached the top of the stairs. Duncan escorted her backstage, down a few steps into the dressing room and up more steps into the wings.

"Good luck, Mrs. Trumbull. I'd tell you the audience is a bunch of animals, only that would insult animals," and Duncan turned and left.

Dearborn glanced over at Victoria, and then called out to the audience, "You wanted the author? Well, here she is, ladies and gentlemen. Give her a hand! Our one and only inimitable, indomitable, invincible

Victoria Trumbull!"

The applause, as Victoria stepped onto the stage, swelled to a resounding accolade. She'd been so consumed by Roderick's strange confession, she hadn't thought about this moment. What could she possibly say? She wanted nothing to do with the farce her play had turned into. How could she disassociate herself from it, let the audience understand how Dearborn Hill had transmogrified a serious adaptation of a serious book, let them understand how he was destroying the theater with his talk of Equity and professionalism.

She couldn't.

She looked out over the packed auditorium below her and felt the energy and enthusiasm and sheer joy rising up from it. The audience stilled, waiting for her to speak.

Victoria leaned on her stick. "Thank you," she said in her deep, firm voice. "A play is what the director makes of it. All of the credit for this production must go to our director, Dearborn Hill." She gestured at Dearborn, who stepped forward. A haze of whiskey fumes preceded him, and Victoria held her breath. But he was steady on his feet as he advanced toward her, arms out to her. Victoria turned her head and took a quick gulp of fresh air. She shuddered as he enfolded her, and the audience rose to its feet in a standing ovation.

Backstage, when the audience had finished cheering and left the theater with the sounds of a satisfied mob, Dearborn collapsed into his chair, and was soon snoring, his feet stretched out in front of him, his arms folded across his stomach, his head lolling on his chest. A thin, silvery stream of drool trickled out of his mouth and onto his Frankenstein jacket.

Victoria seated herself on the couch where just last night, Bob Scott had breathed his last. She was searching through her cloth bag for a pen and paper when Becca pranced up to her. "We just *love* your play, Mrs. Trumbull. It's so much *fun!* Thank you, darling, for what you said about Dearborn, recognizing what a genius he is. You're such a dear, sweet lady."

Victoria scowled. Dear, sweet biddy, she thought. Cast members swirled around her, flinging off costumes, laughing, high on their successful performance. She felt as though she were sitting in the dead, unmoving center of the Oak Bluffs carousel with horses flying around her. Becca had been the only cast member to notice her presence.

She looked at her watch. More than fifteen minutes had passed.

"Has anyone seen Roderick?" Victoria asked as actors bustled past.

No one had.

Gradually, the backstage area emptied. Becca urged Dearborn to his feet, and he stumbled down the steep stairs. Shouts and laughter died away.

At first, Victoria was annoyed that Roderick was late. Then angry. Then worried. Finally, very worried. She made her way carefully down the stairs to the ticket office and the room where theatergoers could buy lemonade and gingersnaps during intermission. She stood outside in the afternoon sun, surprised that it was still daylight. After a few minutes, she returned to the ticket office. Nora Epstein was behind the cage, counting receipts.

"Hello? Oh, Mrs. Trumbull. I didn't realize you were still here."

"I'm looking for Roderick Hill," Victoria said to the stage manager. "Have you seen him?"

"Not since he dropped you off about three-quarters of an hour ago."

"Is Bruce Duncan still around?"

Nora sniffed. "Bruce Duncan hasn't

shown up since dress rehearsal two nights ago. Excuse me. I've got to count this."

Victoria walked around the small cafélike area. Chairs and small tables were set up with candles in bottles. The walls served as a sort of art gallery, with a dozen indifferent watercolors of Island scenes and several excellent oils of male torsos shown from the waist down, which she studied. She returned to the ticket booth. Nora had finished counting and was putting money into green, zippered bank bags.

"As stage manager, you're in charge of props, aren't you, Nora?" Victoria asked.

Nora flushed. "I didn't put that gag gun on the prop table, Mrs. Trumbull. I don't know who did. Dearborn has me playing so many parts, there's no way I can watch over the props."

"I understand," said Victoria. "You *did* load the gun with blanks, didn't you?"

"The *stage* gun. Of course I did. Someone substituted that gag gun. Certainly you're not implying, Mrs. Trumbull, that I don't recognize a toy gun when I see it?"

"Not at all," said Victoria. "But before someone switched the guns, he took these out of the stage gun." She opened the napkin and held it out with the three real bullets.

Nora paled. "Real bullets!" She clasped her hands on either side of her face. "I didn't load the prop gun with those, Mrs. Trumbull. I certainly did not. Never." She stopped. "The prop gun wouldn't accept real bullets, anyway."

"Do you have any idea who could have done this?" asked Victoria.

"Those *are* real bullets, aren't they," Nora said again.

"Yes," said Victoria.

"Someone might have been killed."

"Yes."

"I told Dearborn," and Nora emphasized each word, "someone has to watch the prop table." She brushed her hair out of her eyes. "He won't listen. Actors can miss their cues if the props aren't where they're supposed to be."

"Indeed."

"And, as I said, someone could have been killed."

"Yes."

"He's got me playing three parts. Three. First Justine, then when she's hanged, I've got to read the part of Monsieur De Lacey's daughter as well as the part of Monsieur De Lacey's adopted daughter. Until George Byron agreed to be in the play, Dearborn even had me reading the part for the Arctic explorer. Sheesh! At least he doesn't expect me to memorize my lines."

"The prop table . . ."

"You're asking who could possibly have substituted the guns? Anyone, as I told you. I keep telling Dearborn, over and over, no one should be allowed to go near that prop table."

Victoria half-closed her eyes and leaned on her stick. Nora had loaded the stage gun with blanks, according to her. Some unknown person had substituted a real gun loaded with real bullets for the stage gun. Roderick, apparently thinking the gun was loaded with blanks, had taken out the real bullets and loaded the gun with a second set of real bullets. At some point, another person had substituted the gag gun loaded with the gag flag for the real gun. One of the guns was missing. Which one?

When the matinee was over, George Byron hitchhiked to his mother's house in West Tisbury and burst in through her kitchen door.

"Hey, Mom!" he shouted, when he didn't see her. "Mother?"

Ruth appeared at the door of her study, scowling. "Well? How did the matinee go?"

"You're not still angry, are you?"

282

"I must say, George, I'm not thrilled with you. Aren't you supposed to be at the theater?"

"I've got about three hours. I come in peace." He held out his arms.

Ruth folded hers. "I can't stay angry with you, George dear. But I am disappointed. What possessed you to side with that . . . that . . ."

"I'm not siding with them, Mom. I know what I'm doing."

Ruth turned away from her son. "How's the barn working out?"

"I meant to tell you about that, Mom. Did you know that someone . . ."

At that moment, the phone rang. Ruth went into the study to answer.

When she returned, she said, "George, dear, I've got to pick up some copy at Tisbury Printer before they close. Don't forget what you were about to say. Ta, ta!"

"I was about to tell you someone had set up a hideaway in the barn," George said to his mother's back, but she was already in the car with the windows shut.

CHAPTER 24

While Victoria was on stage graciously crediting Dearborn Hill for his production of *Frankenstein Unbound,* Roderick was backing his car into a parking place he'd found in the shade of a maple tree on Franklin Street. He left the keys on the floor, made sure the window was open, shut the door, and started to walk back to the theater. The evening production wouldn't begin for another four hours. He thought about leaving his makeup on until then, since applying it took such a long time, but the afternoon was warm, his face itched, and he was fed up with the reactions of people on the street.

"Roderick," someone said, behind him.

He groaned, expecting another wisecrack about how great he was looking, then recognized Bruce Duncan, wearing his usual black T-shirt with the fluorescent green letters, VETA.

"What d'ya say, Bruce." He pointed at the shirt. "Don't you ever change clothes?"

Bruce looked at his shirt. "I've got four of these."

"Someone should start a VETP," said Roderick, with a smirk.

"P?"

"Plants. Vineyarders for the Ethical Treatment of Plants."

"Very funny. You heading back to the theater?"

Roderick nodded, and the electrodes on the sides of his head bobbed. He pointed to his stitched-up face. "Stuff is driving me crazy. Gotta get it off."

"I was talking to Mrs. Trumbull before she went on stage," said Duncan, looking up to Roderick who was much taller, even not wearing his costume boots.

"I'm picking her up in another ten minutes or so," said Roderick. "She wants me to take her to the police station."

Duncan ran his hands over his T-shirt. "Police station?"

Roderick heaved a great sigh. "Yeah."

"Police station," Duncan murmured almost to himself. Then to Roderick, "That must have been what Mrs. Trumbull wanted."

"What do you mean?" asked Roderick,

lumbering off in the direction of the theater.

"Hold on," said Duncan. "She wants to talk to Nora."

Roderick stopped and looked over his shoulder. "Nora? The stage manager? Why Nora?"

Duncan nodded. "I'm sure that's what she meant. She said she'd be a while. Come on." He turned back to Roderick's car. "Might as well go in your car. You drive."

Roderick stood where he was. "I want to get this stuff off my face before I do anything else."

"They've got heavy-duty cleaner in the police station, for sure," said Duncan. "Let's go."

"Mrs. Trumbull asked me . . ."

"I told you, Mrs. T. is going to be tied up."

"But . . ."

Duncan took Roderick's arm and steered him toward his car. "We can call her from the police station. Save her the trouble. Give her a chance to talk with Nora."

Back at Roderick's car, Duncan opened the unlocked passenger side door and got in.

Roderick stood by the driver's side. "As stage manager, it's Nora who's supposed to put blanks in the stage gun."

"She's supposed to guard the props, yes,"

said Duncan. "Make sure nobody messes with anything. Somebody obviously did, loading a joke gun with that flag. Come on, get in."

"Unless Nora did it to be funny."

"Nora? She doesn't know how to be funny," said Duncan. "Zero sense of humor."

Roderick paused. "I really ought to go back and make sure Mrs. Trumbull . . ."

"Hurry up. You've got a performance tonight, don't you?"

"I guess." Roderick opened his door, reached for his keys, and slid onto his seat. "Nora put real bullets in the gun."

"What?"

Roderick realized he'd said too much.

"You said she loaded it with real bullets? No way."

"I misspoke." Roderick turned the key in the ignition.

"State police barracks," said Duncan. "Near the hospital."

"I know where it is." Roderick checked the rearview mirror and pulled out of the parking space. "I still think Mrs. Trumbull should know . . ."

"Hurry up," said Duncan.

Tim Eldredge got up from his seat behind

the front desk as Bruce Duncan and Roderick, with flakes of makeup sloughing off onto the clean linoleum floor, walked in. "I don't believe it," he said. "Goddamned nightmare."

"This man has a confession to make," said Duncan, taking the lead. "You want to tell the trooper here about the murders?"

"Murders!" said Eldredge. *"Plural?"*

"Right," said Duncan. "Murders."

"More than one murder?"

"Five hundred," said Duncan.

"What did you say?"

"Not that many," said Roderick, hanging his head.

"Five hundred," Duncan repeated.

"I gotta get this makeup off," said Roderick. "It's driving me crazy."

"Right," said Eldredge. "Men's room is this way. Plenty of paper towels. Good soap. Biodegradable. Follow me."

Roderick shambled after the trooper. "I didn't kill five hundred people. He's crazy."

"Right-o. While you're cleaning up, I'll see if Sergeant Smalley is free to talk to you."

"Thanks," said Roderick. "I can't tell you what a relief this is."

"I bet," said Eldredge, closing the men's room door behind him. He returned to the reception area, where Duncan was examining the Wanted posters. "Sir, about this five hundred alleged deaths . . . ?"

"Five hundred," said Duncan, smoothing the front of his T-shirt. "Probably a few more. Confirmed, not alleged."

"Can you give me any details, sir?"

"They arrived on the Island by plane . . ."

"They? All five hundred?"

"Let me finish. They arrived on the Island by plane, and he," Duncan pointed in the direction of the men's room, "left them out on the tarmac over the weekend."

"What . . . ?"

". . . on the tarmac. In the hot sun over the weekend. Do you understand? All of them died."

"Unh," said Eldredge. "You better talk to the sergeant."

"Fine." Duncan returned to the Wanted posters while Eldredge called upstairs to Sergeant Smalley.

He cupped his hand over the mouthpiece and mumbled into the phone, "Couple of loonies to see you, sir."

Alison McAlistair had finished the preliminary examination of Peg Storm's and Bob Scott's bodies, all she was able to do, given the Island's limited facilities.

Both deaths were suspicious, no question

289

about it. She'd shown Mrs. Trumbull the finger marks on Peg Storm's dead throat, and the Boston lab was testing the residue in the plastic cup the cleaning woman had found next to Bob Scott's body.

When Alison got back to her own lab, she would do the full autopsies. By then, the toxicology results should be in, and she'd know whether Scott had been poisoned or not, and possibly, who killed him, if he had been poisoned.

She drove the borrowed police car back to Victoria's. The first thing she saw when she entered the kitchen was an envelope addressed to Mrs. Amanda Vanderhoop in childish printing, and her heart raced. A note from Teddy? She picked it up. The envelope was sealed, and Alison was too firmly entrenched in her respect for privacy to open it.

Teddy's mother probably was still at her house, going through papers that might give some clue as to where Teddy could be. She looked up the number and dialed. No one answered, and no answering machine picked up. She tried the cell phone number that Victoria had noted on a Post-It and got the message that the phone was out of service.

Alison thought about her own lost son, Douglas. The ache never eased. Douglas, too, had disappeared, vanished on his way home from school. Now, fourteen years later, she still had dreams about him, hoped he was alive somewhere. What would he be doing now? She often played that game. What would he look like? He'd be twenty-two now.

She knew, though, the chances of his being alive were nonexistent. She had been involved in too many cases of missing children she would later find dead.

She changed back into the clothes she'd worn to the Island the morning after dress rehearsal. Had it been only two days? She'd arrived early Friday morning and now it was Saturday afternoon. A lot had happened in that short time.

She dropped her borrowed clothes into the washer, added soap, and started the machine. The Saturday matinee of Victoria's play must be over by now. She looked at her watch. Almost five o'clock. She wondered how the play had gone. Ironic that it had become a hugely successful farce, despite all Victoria's efforts at serious drama.

John Smalley had asked her out to dinner this evening, her last night. After dinner, she'd catch the late ferry and be home before midnight. She and John had worked so closely during the time she'd been on the Island, she'd had no chance to get to know Howland Atherton, the drug agent and the original monster in Victoria's play. She might come over to the Vineyard some weekend to accept his rain check for a swim at his beach.

While Elizabeth's jeans and shirts were thrashing around in the washer, Alison thought about Victoria, bravely reading her poetry at Island Java, ignoring the debacle her play had become. When Alison returned, perhaps Victoria would let her stay with her again.

She laughed out loud when she remembered how all three men, Toby the undertaker, John Smalley the police sergeant, and Howland Atherton the DEA agent, had tried to protect Victoria from the unpleasantness of Peg Storm's death. Victoria had marched right into the funeral parlor over their protests and had studied with interest the marks on Peg's throat that Alison had shown her. Bravo, Mrs. Trumbull!

When the washer finally shuddered to a stop, Alison switched the laundry into the dryer and pushed in the dial. As the ancient machine started up, she heard a squeal, almost like a child's cry. Thinking the squeal came from the dryer, she opened the door, but the sound continued. She looked around for McCavity. He was asleep in a patch of sunlight on the cookroom floor.

The squeal turned into a cry that came from the foot of the front stairs. "Mrs. Trumbull?"

Alison swiveled around. "Teddy?"

A small, redheaded, barefoot boy stumbled into the kitchen. He was hugging a fuzzy blanket. "Where's Mrs. Trumbull? I want my dad."

"Teddy?"

"I don't feel so good."

"Teddy!" She threw her arms around the boy, the size and shape of her lost Douglas.

"My head hurts." He snuggled against her. "I want my dad." He was fiercely hot. She held him away from her and looked him over. His face and arms were covered with spots.

Chicken pox.

CHAPTER 25

Chef Callaghan had demonstrated to the authorities that he was conscientious, reliable, responsible, punctilious, and clearly remorseful. He was a model prisoner, hardworking and quiet. He tended the garden behind the jail, and from the fresh vegetables he'd grown in the two months he'd been incarcerated, he prepared delectable and healthful dishes for the other inmates and the county officers, who'd taken to dropping by the jail at mealtimes. He was a fine role model for the other seven prisoners, who were young enough to be his sons — and daughter (who had a cellblock to herself). He still had sixteen months of his drug sentence to serve.

On Howland Atherton's recommendation, since it was Howland who had apprehended Chef Callaghan, the chef was given the cushy job, along with two other trusted inmates, of picking up trash along State

Road. The three would walk on either side of the road followed by a county vehicle with rotating orange lights that warned approaching or passing vehicles of men — or women — at work.

Driving the county van at two miles an hour behind the jailbirds was an achingly, awesomely boring assignment.

Early that morning, Chef Callaghan had baked bread, cookies, and brownies before he prepared breakfast for his patrons. At seven-thirty, the sheriff came into the dining room. He inhaled the aroma of newly baked bread and the sweet scent of chocolate.

"I'll be sorry when your time's up, Chef," he said.

Chef Callaghan grunted. "Not me."

"Approval came through for roadside cleanup duty this afternoon."

"I heard."

The sheriff shook his head. "The grapevine. You guys hear stuff before we do."

"Figures," said the chef.

Alison held Teddy tightly against her. His body was hot. "Where are you sleeping, Teddy?"

"The attic."

"I'm making up a bed for you on the

library sofa. Sit here while I do that." She gently maneuvered him into Victoria's caned armchair, found a blanket in the linen closet, and draped it over his shoulders. She soaked a face cloth with witch hazel from Victoria's medicine cabinet and handed it to him.

"Hold this against your forehead, Teddy. Do you itch?"

He shook his head.

"You will. Witch hazel helps. Where's your dad?"

"On his boat."

"Does he have a cell phone?"

"Yes."

"You don't know the number, do you?"

Teddy nodded and gave it to her.

"I'll make up your bed, then I'll try to reach your dad. I called your mother at your house, but there was no answer."

"She's got a boyfriend." Teddy turned away. "She's probably with him." He looked up at her, his eyes red and swollen. "I don't like him."

"Well." Alison decided not to comment. She gathered up bed linens, made up the sofa in the library, settled Teddy with a glass of orange juice mixed with sugar water. Then she called the state police barracks.

"Teddy's safe, John. He's been here at Victoria's."

"What I suspected. Good. See you around seven?"

"Lovely."

Then she dialed Teddy's father. A robotic voice came on and she left a message for him to call her right away.

Five minutes later, the phone rang.

"This is Jefferson Vanderhoop. You called?" He spoke above the sound of guitar music and laughter.

"Dr. Alison McAlistair here, and I've found Teddy."

"What did you say?"

"I've found Teddy."

"Wait a second while I step outside where I can hear."

Alison heard a door open and shut, and then only the sound of a seagull crying and water lapping. "We've found Teddy."

"Where is he?"

"Safe. At Mrs. Trumbull's."

"Thank God! Who are you?"

"A forensic scientist called in to help locate Teddy. I've been working with the authorities on another matter."

"Have you contacted his mother?"

"I haven't been able to reach her."

"Not surprised. I'm at Island Java right

now," he paused. "Reading poetry. It'll take me fifteen minutes to get there. Is he okay?"

"Not feeling great at the moment. He's come down with chicken pox, and he's calling for you."

"Tell him I'm on the way." The connection cut off.

After lunch, Red Callaghan filled a thermos with coffee and another thermos with lemonade for Mr. Ferreira, this week's driver of the county vehicle, and wrapped a half-dozen brownies in aluminum foil. One entire pan full. He set the thermoses and the paper bag of foil-wrapped brownies on the kitchen pass-through.

Gus Ferreira, a portly man in his early sixties who'd taken a job with the county after he'd retired from an off-Island career, had lost the coin flip this week. Actually, Gus was one of the few county employees who didn't mind the slow pace of roadside cleanup duty.

He nodded to the thermoses and paper bag. "What've you got for me today?"

"Brownies, lemonade."

"Cream in the coffee?"

"Double cream, double sugar."

"Good man. Hear you're one of the roadside crew this afternoon."

"You heard right."

"Nice duty. Get you out of doors."

"Something different," said the cook.

At the state police barracks, Sergeant Smalley shuffled papers in a businesslike manner, deliberately paying no attention to the two loonies Trooper Eldredge had sent to him, when one of them coughed and he decided it was time to look up.

"Can I help you?" he asked.

The shorter of the two men standing in front of his desk smoothed a long strand of hair over his scalp and said, indicating the tall, younger man, "He's got a confession to make."

The younger man nodded and smiled. His black shirt and trousers seemed to be soaked with blood.

"Your name, sir?" Smalley asked the shorter man, while he studied the gore on the black garments of the taller.

"Bruce Duncan. Five hundred. Dead. Every one of them. Boiled to death."

"No, no," said the taller man. "No, he's wrong."

"Five hundred," repeated Bruce Duncan, jabbing a finger at his companion, while still staring at Smalley.

"Just a moment." Smalley leaned back in

his chair so he could look up at the taller man. "Your name, sir?"

"Roderick Hill." Roderick clasped his hands behind his back and shifted from one foot to the other. "He's mistaken. I came here because I wanted to tell you . . ."

Duncan glared up at his companion before he spoke to Smalley again. "Not mistaken, officer."

Smalley couldn't take his eyes off of Roderick's costume. "Would you mind explaining that, Mr. Hill?" He gestured at the gore.

"This?" said Roderick looking down at his gut. "I've been shot. I'm in the play at the playhouse and it's blood. But what I wanted to tell you . . ."

"Stage blood?"

Bruce Duncan interrupted. "He left them out on the tarmac in the sun over the weekend, and they boiled to death."

"What?" said Smalley.

"Goldfish."

"Fish?" said Smalley.

"No, no," Roderick insisted. "That's not what I wanted to tell you. I came here because . . ."

At which point the phone rang. "Excuse me," said Smalley and picked up the phone. "Smalley here." After listening for a moment, he put his hand over the mouthpiece.

"I've got to take this call. Leave your names and phone numbers with Trooper Eldredge downstairs. Let him know where we can get in touch with you if we need to."

"But . . ." said Roderick.

After giving Jefferson Vanderhoop directions to Victoria's house, Alison headed for the library to tell Teddy that his father was on the way, when the phone rang.

"Alison? It's Victoria. Can you give me a ride? I'm at the playhouse and I seem to have been stood up."

"Teddy's out of hiding, Victoria."

There was a long silence at the other end.

"Victoria? Mrs. Trumbull? Are you still there?"

"I'm thinking," said Victoria.

"He's come down with chicken pox. I made up a bed for him in the library."

"I thought he seemed awfully quiet. You'd better stay with him, then. I'll ask Howland for a ride. Have you called Teddy's mother?"

"No answer at her house. Do you have any idea where she might be?"

"None whatsoever. His father is at Island Java reading his poetry. You can probably reach him there."

"I already did."

"Cellular phone. Of course."

"He'll be here in about fifteen minutes."

"Have you told Sergeant Smalley the situation, that Teddy is no longer hiding and is at my house?"

"It's the first thing I did," Alison responded.

"I'll call Casey while I'm waiting for Howland," said Victoria and she hung up.

CHAPTER 26

Howland was walking his dogs on the beach below his house when Victoria reached him on the phone.

"There's something to be said for cellular phones, I suppose," Victoria said, when he told her where he was.

"What's going on, Victoria?"

"I'll explain when I see you."

"It'll take me about twenty minutes to get to the theater. See you then."

Victoria thanked Nora for the use of the playhouse phone, went outside, and sat on the low stone wall to wait.

Where could Roderick be? What had he been thinking when he'd told her he had killed both Peg and Bob Scott? He'd seemed relieved that she'd insisted he go with her to the police. She simply could not believe that he had killed anyone, despite his confession.

Yet, obviously something was bothering him.

She shifted on the uncomfortable stone wall and thought some more. Perhaps Sandy could help. Dogs were intelligent. Look at the K-9 service dogs, the drug-sniffing dogs, the guide dogs. Someone had hurt Sandy, and that person was quite possibly the killer. Sandy might be able to identify him.

She took out a scrap of paper and a pen and made a note to retrieve Sandy from Doc Atkins's. Where would be the best place for Sandy to examine the suspects? At the police station? At the theater? At her house?

Actually, what suspects were there? According to Sergeant Smalley, it was too early in the investigation to point to anyone.

She shifted position once more, then stood and laid her baseball hat on the stones as a cushion, and sat again.

Was it even remotely possible that Roderick was the killer? She had to consider that he might be. He was a bit of a bungler, that was true. Might he somehow have killed Peg accidentally? And thought he'd strangled Bob Scott during the play? She was one of the select few who believed Bob Scott had been poisoned by some as yet unidentified substance. She shook her head and shifted on her not-that-well-padded seat.

Killers had to have motive and means, of course, but opportunity was crucial. Who among the theater people and Peg's friends and relatives had opportunity?

Sergeant Smalley said Peg had been killed between the time she'd left the theater at eight and midnight, when Teddy's mother called the police. Actually, Victoria realized, Peg was probably killed close to eight-thirty, because Teddy's mother had started to call her house around then and had gotten no answer. And that was when Teddy had heard her cry out for him to run.

Victoria stood up, shook out her hat and placed it back on the stone wall, looked at her watch, and sat down again. Howland should be here shortly.

She noted on her paper to check where Peg's ex-husband, Leonard Vincent, had been two nights ago, and where Teddy's father had been. And who was Teddy's mother's mysterious boyfriend? She added Ruth Byron and her son, George, to her list, reluctantly. Ruth was certainly angry enough at Dearborn and Becca to sabotage the play, but that seemed far-fetched.

Aside from those five, the most likely suspects would have to be among cast members. Everyone who'd been at rehearsal during the second and third acts could be eliminated as Peg's killer. Or could they? Peg's home was less than ten minutes from the theater. Five minutes, if there'd been no traffic. Had anyone been missing for a half-hour or so. Even fifteen minutes, but that would be cutting things close.

Dearborn. She wouldn't mind pinning the murders on him. Had he been at the play-house the entire time? She recalled his strid-ing back and forth in front of her, calling out directions and nattering on about how a professional cast would run through dress rehearsal without a break, unlike this ama-teur lot.

Victoria jabbed her lilac-wood stick into the soft dirt next to the stone wall. Much as she would like to cast Dearborn as the killer, she couldn't imagine how he could have found the time. Was it possible that Peg had been killed later than the police estimate? She didn't think so. The murder was prob-ably somewhere between eight-thirty and nine o'clock.

Victoria went through the cast in order of appearance. Bob Scott. Had he killed Peg, then taken his own life in remorse? The poison apparently acted painlessly. Not a bad way to commit suicide. She wrote "Robt. Scott" on her paper with two ques-tion marks next to the name.

Howland? No, not Howland. Why, though? Because he was her friend and a law enforcement agent? No, Howland had been sitting in the second row, just ahead of her when he wasn't on stage. In fact, when he'd realized the antennae on his monstrous head were blocking her view, he'd apologized and moved over two seats. Later, after the rehearsal, when he was driving home and the police picked him up, Peg must already have been dead.

What about Bruce Duncan? She couldn't recall whether she'd seen him in the theater when he wasn't actually on stage. His role was an important one, trying to reason with his friend, Victor. Bruce had been terribly upset when he'd learned of Peg's death. But at the pet store, Bruce had said something that revealed how hurt he'd been by her rejection. He was a sensitive man. Perhaps that rejection was enough to cause him to kill. Victoria wrote Bruce Duncan's name on her list and put an asterisk next to it.

Not Gerard Cohen. True, he lived close to Peg, but that didn't mean anything. He was elderly, probably in his mid-seventies, not likely to dash around strangling people. In addition, he was struggling to rebuild his own life after his wife's death, concentrating on routine and normality.

Dawn Haines? She had been at the theater in view for the entire dress rehearsal.

This brought Victoria to Roderick again, and she reluctantly put an asterisk next to his name.

She made a note to find out more about Leonard Vincent, Peg's ex-husband. More often than not, killers were members of the victim's family, so she put an asterisk next to Leonard Vincent's name. She'd never met him, as far as she knew. She would have to think of some way to cross paths with him accidentally.

She paused over Teddy's father, Jefferson Vanderhoop. Then she put a small, faint check mark next to his name, just to be fair. She would have to find out what his alibi had been. But Jefferson Vanderhoop was a poet. Rough, but powerful. Someday, if he kept writing, he'd be quite good. She erased her check mark.

She crossed Teddy's mother's name off her list, then had second thoughts and wrote "stet", the printers' term for "let it stand," next to Amanda Vanderhoop. Had Amanda's call to the police really been from Los Angeles? With a cellular phone, she might easily have been calling from right here. Amanda claimed she had arrived by boat after the storm and had called Casey from the ferry terminal, but neither Victoria nor Casey had seen her disembark from the ferry. Victoria couldn't imagine Amanda as a killer, though she had an uneasy feeling about her. Part of that feeling was because of Teddy's reaction to his mother's boyfriend. Could the boyfriend be the killer with some motive Victoria couldn't now imagine? Even though rehearsals had been going on for almost two months, Victoria had never seen the boyfriend. He'd never picked up Teddy and Amanda, never sat in on rehearsals.

Who was he, anyway? An Islander? She wrote "Amanda's b.f." and put a large asterisk next to his name. She would have to ask Teddy more about him.

She hated to think that Ruth Byron or her son, George, had any part in the killings, but in fairness, she put a small check mark next to each of their names.

Then, of course, there was Rebecca, Dearborn's wife and Ruth Byron's sister. Victoria could imagine Becca without compunction killing off anyone who annoyed her, simply to get herself cast in a starring role. Had she been on Island at the right time? Victoria punched a hole in her paper by putting a large firm asterisk next to Becca's name. Rebecca, even more than

Dearborn, had ravaged Victoria's play.

Victoria put her notes in her cloth bag and was easing herself off the stone wall again when Howland's old white station wagon pulled up the hill and stopped in front of her.

"Sorry, Victoria. It took longer than I expected. Summer traffic." He escorted her to the passenger side and opened the door. "What's going on?"

"Too much." Victoria explained about Roderick picking her up at the coffeehouse because the audience was howling for the author. "He confessed to killing both Peg Storm and Robert Scott."

"Really?"

"Then he tried, according to him, to commit suicide, and obviously failed. Someone had substituted a toy gun with a red flag for the stage gun with which he'd intended to kill himself."

Howland laughed.

"It's not amusing. From what I can gather," Victoria went on, "Nora had loaded the stage gun with blanks. An unknown someone apparently took out the blanks and loaded the gun with real bullets."

"Roderick."

"No, not Roderick. He unloaded the real bullets, thinking they were blanks, and reloaded the gun with his own real bullets."

"And after that, someone unknown substituted the toy gun with the gag flag? That's hardly plausible, Victoria."

Victoria shrugged. "That's what happened."

"Where would someone buy a gun with a flag that can be shot out of it?"

"Shirley's Hardware, of course. We can ask Mary." Victoria scribbled a note to herself. After a pause, she cleared her throat. "I suppose I need to tell you something else, too," Victoria glanced at Howland. "You'll find out when we get to my house."

"Now what?"

"Teddy's been hiding in my attic."

Howland erupted. "For God's sake, Victoria."

An in-line skater suddenly appeared in front of them and Howland jammed his foot on the brake and swerved to miss him. The Rollerblader looked over his shoulder and continued skating, gliding from one side of the lane to the other.

"Taking up the entire right lane," Howland muttered. "At six miles an hour, or whatever his top speed is. On the main road."

Victoria had braced herself, with a hand on the dashboard.

Howland picked up speed again. "The police have been out in force, day and night, and the boy's mother is understandably upset."

"I suggested to Sergeant Smalley that he call off the search as soon as I discovered Teddy. He didn't want his mother to know where he was."

"Victoria, you can't ignore his mother's rights." Howland turned abruptly onto Old County Road. A car coming toward him honked. Howland jerked his head at the driver.

"His mother's boyfriend seems to be a problem for Teddy," Victoria continued, once Howland was on the smooth stretch of Old County Road.

"His mother has rights, Victoria." Howland emphasized each word. "You simply can't hide her child from her."

"Well, I did." Victoria faced forward, her mouth set in a straight line. "I promised Teddy I wouldn't tell anyone where he was."

CHAPTER 27

The cook, Red Callaghan, and his two colleagues got into the back of the county van. Gus Ferreira drove them as far as the airport entrance on the Edgartown-West Tisbury Road and dropped them off with a warning about how he'd be right behind them and don't try any tricks.

The three wore their own jeans and T-shirts and the county's fluorescent orange vests. They carried pointed sticks with which they were to spear papers and plastic roadside litter. Litter and things they had to bend down to pick up, like cans and bottles, they would deposit into burlap bags slung over their shoulders.

They walked steadily. The vehicle, on the other hand, lurched up behind them, waited until they got pretty far ahead, then lurched again at five or six miles an hour. It would catch up and wait. Boring.

The work crew was not bored, however.

The two young trusties, one a white guy named Adam, one a black guy named Everet, called back and forth to one another, making jokes about items they found along the road. Chef Callaghan ignored the jokes as puerile. Occasionally, he'd pull up a stalk of tall grass and chew on the end until he got to the tough stringy part. Then he'd fling the spent grass off to the side and pull up another, spearing litter as he chewed. Not a bad way to spend an afternoon.

The afternoon was what Victoria Trumbull would call "typical Vineyard weather," the kind of day that occurred once or twice a summer. Dry and cool, with a brilliant blue sky that went on forever.

Chewinks rustled in the dead leaves beyond the bicycle path. Crows cawed messages to one another, giving the location of fresh roadkill. The air smelled of sun-baked pine, scrub oak, and the salt sea. The surf rumbled on the south shore.

Occasionally, Chef Callaghan would glance over his shoulder at Gus in the county van, and Gus would raise a hand in acknowledgment. The chef would wave back and continue spearing and chewing and bending over to pick up something or other.

They'd gotten as far as the place called Jimmy Green's, where the last heath hen in the world had lived and had died its lonely death in the 1930s. Red Callaghan glanced over his shoulder. The county vehicle seemed farther away than usual, and Gus seemed to be resting his head on the half-opened window.

The cook pulled up another stalk of grass and continued to walk and spear and chew. The next time he glanced up, the vehicle was in the same place, and he could just make out, in the distance, Gus's closed eyes and open mouth.

Callaghan waited until a car passed, then with a burst of energy, shucked off his vest and tossed it into the woods that had grown up since the heath hen died, tossed the pointed stick after the vest and the half-full burlap sack on top of the vest and the stick.

"I don't know about you guys," he called out to his fellow workers, "but I'm outta here," and he took off through the woods on the north side of the road.

At the police barracks, Sergeant Smalley was dealing with more problems than he wanted. He had summarily dismissed both Bruce Duncan and Roderick Hill after the call from the sheriff. The sheriff hadn't been able to reach Gus Ferreira, who was driving the county vehicle for the roadside detail.

"His radio okay?" Smalley had asked.

"Should be," the sheriff replied. "We check them before use, and besides, Gus has a backup cell phone."

"Could be in a dead reception area."

"Possibly. The crew was working east from the airport along the Edgartown-West Tisbury Road. *State road*," he added, with emphasis.

"Okay, you made your point."

"Appreciate it if you'd locate the van, see what Gus is up to," said the sheriff. "Stop by the jail first and I'll give you details."

Smalley stowed papers in his briefcase to work on at home. He felt sorry for himself. He'd have to cancel his dinner date with Alison. Damn. All because Gus was probably taking a leak in the bushes beside the road.

Roderick and Bruce Duncan left their names, addresses, and phone numbers with Tim Eldredge, downstairs at the front desk of the police barracks.

"I don't suppose I can get a ride with you?" Duncan asked, outside.

"You suppose right," said Roderick. "You wouldn't let me get in a word edgewise."

"You heading for the theater?"

Roderick pulled an enormous watch out

of the depths of his costume. "The evening performance is scheduled in less than three hours."

"I'm heading that way."

"Thought you were avoiding the theater. You got something against my uncle and aunt? You think a serial killer is on the loose? Think you're next? Wouldn't surprise me one bit."

"Just a minute," said Duncan, holding up a hand. "I only said I was *heading* that way. I don't expect you to go out of your way for me."

"Give me one good reason why I should give you a ride."

"Save energy," said Duncan.

"Oh, hell. Get in."

"You can let me off in front of the theater."

"Right."

Once he had picked her up, Howland drove from the playhouse to Victoria's. The news that Teddy had been hiding out at Victoria's all along had put him in an evil temper. "Everybody has to be notified about Teddy being found, Victoria. The authorities, the parents, everybody."

"Alison contacted everyone except his mother. She can't seem to find her," Victoria replied.

Howland braked for a string of mopeds. "Goddamned road hazards." He blasted his horn and steered into the left lane. An approaching car pulled off onto the shoulder until Howland was safely past.

"Watch it, buddy!" the driver shouted.

"They're all out of shape. Saving money by riding pillion."

" 'Riding pillion'," Victoria repeated. "How quaint."

"Shorts and sandals and bare arms. Think they're in an amusement park ride. Draining the resources of the hospital."

Victoria cleared her throat again. "He's got chicken pox."

"Jeezus Christ, Victoria." Howland slammed his hand on the steering wheel.

"I had nothing to do with the chicken pox."

"I wouldn't put it past you."

They approached Whippoorwill Farm, and Howland slowed to let a truck turn out. The driver waved. Howland ignored him.

"Who was that?" Victoria asked, turning to see who was driving.

"Who knows. Who's with Teddy?"

"Dr. McAlistair is with him."

"Alison, yes. We have to find his mother. And his father."

"His father is on the way. He was reading

poetry at the coffeehouse."

Howland braked to avoid three crows dining on fresh-killed skunk. Victoria wound up her window. The car behind him honked.

"Following too close," muttered Howland.

"Teddy's father is a poet, too. Like Roderick." Victoria glanced over at Howland. His face was flushed.

"So you, Madame Detective, have eliminated him from the list of suspects because he's a poet?"

"Not entirely. I'm open-minded."

Callaghan made his way to the bicycle path and hiked along it briskly, whistling a merry tune, hands in his pockets. He slowed briefly to check his watch, and continued. A half-dozen helmeted bicyclists came up from behind him.

"Nice day!" the leader called out.

"Got that right," he called back to the waving orange pennant on the last bike.

After he'd walked a half-mile or so, he checked his watch again, and then cut through the huckleberry brush that separated the bicycle path from the road, waited a few minutes until a dark blue Toyota approached from Edgartown, and stuck out his thumb.

The car stopped. He opened the passenger

door, and the driver, a young woman wearing sunglasses, leaned over the passenger seat. "Where are you heading?" she asked. Besides her sunglasses, she had on a skimpy bright orange bathing suit top and a towel knotted so her belly button showed.

"Vineyard Haven," he answered. "Thanks for picking me up."

"No problem. I'm going that way. You work there?" She glanced in the rearview mirror and took off with a squeal of tires.

He fastened his seat belt hurriedly. "Meeting a friend."

"Girlfriend?"

He shrugged. He did not want to converse. He decided he'd better not call attention to himself by being surly. "Nice day," he mumbled.

"Gorgeous."

"Going to the beach?"

"I've just been. The water's perfect."

So they talked about the weather, swimming, beaches, the summer crowds, and she turned right onto Old County Road.

Callaghan saw, a moment too late, an old white Renault station wagon approaching, and turned his head away.

"You see something?" his driver asked.

"I thought I saw a wood lily."

She slowed. "Want me to stop so you can

take a look?"

"No! No thanks. I need to get to Vineyard Haven. Thanks for asking, though." He could feel sweat trickling down his forehead and back.

CHAPTER 28

"What the hell . . . ?" Howland swiveled around to get a better look at the Toyota that had slowed after it passed them. "That looks like Red Callaghan, the jailhouse chef."

"Be careful," said Victoria, bracing her hand against the dashboard again.

Howland moved back into the right lane. "Looked just like him."

Victoria sat up straight. "Don't you think we should follow that car?"

"We've got to find out what's happening at your house."

"But if it is the chef, shouldn't we go after him?"

"No."

Neither of them spoke again until they turned into Victoria's drive.

The police car Alison had borrowed from Sergeant Smalley was parked under the Norway maple next to a blue pickup that smelled of fish.

Alison came to the kitchen door and greeted them. "Father and son are re-united."

"How is he?" Howland asked.

"He's on the couch in the library, sleeping now," said Alison. "He feels awful, hot and achy. His father is sitting with him, reading the paper."

"Do we need to call the doctor?" Howland asked.

Alison drew herself up to her full height. "I *am* a doctor, after all, Mr. Atherton. More than qualified to deal with chicken pox, thank you. Everything is under control."

"What the hell's the matter with everyone?" Howland snapped. "Someone call Smalley."

"I've notified Sergeant Smalley. He should be here any minute." Alison gave Howland a tight smile. "He's taking me to dinner at Le Grenier, then to the boat."

"On his expense account, I suppose," Howland said. He suddenly seemed to take in what she'd said. "You're leaving?"

"I'm sure Mrs. Trumbull has dealt with chicken pox patients in the past."

"Is that the phone?" Victoria brushed past Howland to answer.

"I'll get it," said Alison. She came out a few minutes later, looking annoyed. "John's had to cancel our dinner date. A problem's come up at the police barracks."

"May I take you to dinner in his place?" asked Howland.

Alison looked at her watch.

"Go ahead," said Victoria. "I'll tend the patient. Besides, Tim Eldredge and Junior Norton plan to play an all-night poker game here tonight."

"Oh?" said Howland. "*Two* cops?"

"Tim has invited Dawn Haines," said Victoria. "I think he's finally noticed her."

"Maybe I'll join them after I take Alison to the ferry. But I'd like to see Teddy first."

"You know where the library is," said Victoria.

Teddy was sleeping on the sofa, a Victorian concoction with a carved wooden back depicting roses. Tucked among the rose leaves was a perfectly carved insect that looked remarkably like a Japanese beetle.

Jefferson Vanderhoop sat next to Teddy's bed, reading the sports section of *The Boston Globe.* He looked up and grinned as Howland entered the room.

"How about those Sox, hey?" Vanderhoop said.

"I don't follow football," said Howland.

Vanderhoop stared at him and stopped chewing whatever he had in his mouth.

"Your son okay?" asked Howland.

"Red Sox," said Vanderhoop, starting to chew again.

"He okay?"

"I guess. You ever have chicken pox?"

"I have no idea."

"If you haven't had chicken pox, you better stay away from my kid. You don't want to catch it. Complications like scars, shingles, arthritis, joint disease. Can sterilize you."

Vanderhoop returned to the sports pages, and Howland backed out of the room and headed for the kitchen.

"Would you like some wine to take with you?" asked Victoria, reaching into the refrigerator. She held up a three-quarters-full bottle.

Howland didn't respond. Instead, he asked Alison, "Will contracting chicken pox as an adult cause sterility?"

"Rarely," said Alison. "The disease is worse for adults, though. More adults than children die of chicken pox."

"Wine?" asked Victoria still holding the bottle.

"Thanks, Victoria," said Howland. "I'll replace it." He took the bottle from her.

Alison looked puzzled. "To a French restaurant?"

Howland checked the label. "Australian wine at that. Le Grenier is in Vineyard Haven."

"And . . . ?"

"Vineyard Haven is dry," Howland explained. "Don't try to make sense out of Island regulations. You can buy wine in Oak Bluffs or Edgartown, and restaurants in the four dry towns will serve you." He shrugged. "They just can't sell it to you."

"Is Teddy still asleep?" Victoria asked.

Howland nodded. "Have you had chicken pox, Victoria?"

"Of course. Everyone's had it. Haven't you?"

"I was coddled as a kid. I didn't catch anything."

"Highly contagious," said Alison. "Ten-day incubation."

After Howland and Alison left for the restaurant, Victoria checked on Teddy, who was sleeping. His father looked up and grinned. "So the kid asked for me, eh?"

"According to Dr. McAlistair. How do you feel about dogs?"

"Teddy's always wanted one, but the wife wouldn't hear of it. Too messy."

"Is Teddy responsible enough to take care

of a dog?"

"Teddy's got more sense than me. You got some dog in mind?"

"I don't know," said Victoria, and left the library.

"Sure, I'll be happy to release Sandy to you, Victoria," said Doc Atkins when Victoria reached him at the animal clinic. "He's as good as new. Misses the boss, of course. You'd expect that. Want me to deliver him?"

"Would you bring some dog food with you?"

"Dog food, a couple of toys, and a bed. How's the boy?"

"He's come down with chicken pox."

The vet laughed. "Sandy's what the doctor ordered, then. I'll be there in a half-hour. You still got some of that Australian wine around?"

While she waited, Victoria rummaged around in the closet, found an unopened bottle of the same wine she'd sent off with Howland and Alison, and put it in the refrigerator.

As she was setting wine glasses and crackers and cheese on a tray, an ambulance pulled up in front of the kitchen door, red lights rotating. The siren whooped a couple of times. Victoria hustled out to see what had happened. Doc Atkins emerged from the driver's side, grinning.

"Don't get to use the siren and lights often." He opened the back door of the ambulance and lifted out a dog that in no way resembled the filthy creature Victoria and Joanie had taken to the clinic. He was a pale golden tan with fluffy fur. His tongue hung out as though he was smiling. His eyes were bright.

"Sandy?" asked Victoria.

"A couple of days can make a difference. Let's see the patient." Doc Atkins carried the dog into the library.

Jefferson Vanderhoop stood up and set the newspaper on the chair. "That was quick."

Sandy barked. Teddy opened his eyes. Doc Atkins set the dog down, and Sandy bounced over to Teddy and started licking his face. Teddy grinned. "Sandy, hey Sandy, old buddy."

Vanderhoop looked from the doc to Victoria to his son and back at the doc.

"Can I keep him, Dad? Please, Dad?"

Vanderhoop glanced at Victoria's face before he said, "Damn right, kid."

"Care to join us in a glass of wine, Mr. Vanderhoop?"

"Don't mind if I do. Name's Jefferson."

■ ■ ■ ■

Le Grenier was on the second floor of a building only a short walk from the ferry. Chef-owner Jean Dupon escorted Alison and Howland to a table by the window, where they could look out through green leaves to the street below. He examined the wine label, shrugged, and took the partially full bottle to chill. Looking down on Main Street, it was as though they were in a tree house, a secret hideaway. Alison ordered tuna. Howland ordered swordfish.

"Did Smalley say what the problem was at the police barracks?" Howland asked, while they were waiting to be served.

"He said something fishy was going on."

While they were eating, they talked about the theater, their jobs, life on the Island, Alison's work in Washington.

Chef Dupon returned to their table. "Monsieur Atherton, you naughty man." He shook a finger at Howland, and Alison looked up with concern. "Since you jail my sous-chef, business is off."

"Chef Callaghan?" Alison asked. "The chef at the county jail? *French* chef?"

"The cooking is French. The chef is not." Chef Dupon bowed and left.

Alison talked to Howland about her lost son, Douglas, for the first time in years. Teddy's sudden appearance had opened some door she'd slammed shut a long time ago. She thought of Teddy's swollen eyes and the spots that weren't itching, yet.

"Teddy cried for his dad," she said. "Not his mother."

"I got the impression that his father was kind of rough."

"He's the one Teddy called for. He's certainly not afraid of his father. Have you any idea who the mother's boyfriend is? Teddy's afraid of him."

Smalley was driving toward the county jail along the stretch of beach between Oak Bluffs and Edgartown when his cell phone rang. He pulled over to the side of the road.

"Smalley, here."

"A shooting at the playhouse," said the nine-one-one operator.

"Goddamned shit," said Smalley, and made a U-turn across summer traffic on Beach Road.

CHAPTER 29

Alison and Howland had almost finished their main course when they heard sirens — first one, then another — coming toward them on Main Street. The vehicles turned off a block or two before reaching the restaurant.

"Police?" asked Alison.

"Police, fire, or the town ambulance. Can't tell. We don't hear many sirens on the Island."

They were still speculating on what the sirens meant when Alison said, "There goes my cell phone."

"No symphonic phrase or catchy tune?"

"Vibration mode." She smiled, took the phone from her jacket pocket, and looked at the display. "I've got to call back." She rose from her chair. "I'll take the phone outside."

When she returned, Howland said, "Serious?"

"It was John Smalley."

"What's the trouble?"

"The bride of Frankenstein has been shot."

"Dead?"

"She's at the hospital, waiting to be airlifted to Boston."

"Dearborn's wife?"

"I assume that's who it is."

Howland raised his hand, and the waitress came over. "We'll skip dessert. My check, please."

"Was everything all right?"

Alison kissed her fingers. *"C'est magnifique,"* she said.

Tim Eldredge had just walked into Victoria's kitchen, following Dawn Haines. He was freshly showered and shaved and was wearing a clean uniform.

"You look trim," Victoria told him.

"Thank you, ma'am," said Eldredge. "Sergeant Smalley gave me a couple hours off this afternoon."

"You clean up pretty good," observed Vanderhoop. "You were a mess when I saw you on my boat."

Jefferson Vanderhoop, Victoria, and Doc Atkins were sitting at the kitchen table with what was left of the bottle of wine and a plate with a few cracker crumbs. Teddy was sleeping, his dog curled up next to him on the library sofa.

The phone rang and Victoria stepped into the cookroom to answer.

"Sergeant Smalley, here, Mrs. Trumbull. Let me talk to Tim Eldredge."

Tim set down his jug of cranberry juice and a six-pack of microwave popcorn on Victoria's countertop.

"No beer?" Victoria asked as she handed him the phone.

"On duty." Tim took the phone. "Eldredge." He suddenly tensed. "Yes, sir. Right away, sir."

"Now what?" said Victoria.

"Mrs. Hill's been shot."

"The next in order of appearance," said Dawn. Her face paled. "Rebecca Hill. The bride of Frankenstein."

"Shot dead?" asked Teddy's father.

"She was taken to the hospital, sir," answered Tim. "Sergeant Smalley's ordered me to get to the theater, right away. Sorry, Dawn. I'll call a cab for you."

"I can give Dawn a lift in the ambulance," said Doc Atkins.

"If you don't mind a little fish smell, how about a ride in my truck," countered Teddy's father.

"I think I'd rather stay with Mrs. Trumbull, if that's okay, Mrs. T?"

"There's plenty of room," said Victoria. "I hope you've had chicken pox."

"The theater's around the corner and up a couple of blocks," said Howland. "We'll get there faster by walking than by driving."

Alison kept up with Howland's long strides. "What on earth is going on?"

"Hate to think Bruce Duncan might be right about the characters being killed off in order of appearance."

"If true, Howland, we're dealing with a psycho. Two murders, a third attempt, and a frightened boy. This is starting to fit the profile of a serial killer. As soon as he learns that Teddy is at Victoria's . . ."

"I'm thinking the same thing. Come on." They walked faster.

"You'd better go directly to Victoria's," Alison said.

"Smalley asked me to check ever some paperwork at the theater," said Howland. "Tim Eldredge and Junior Norton are with Victoria. I'll talk to Smalley. Find out what the hell happened, then go on to Victoria's. Join me there later."

They turned right onto Church Street. Alison checked her watch.

"Did Smalley say who did the shooting?" Howland asked.

"He didn't give me any information at all, beyond the fact that they're flying Becca to Boston."

A crowd had gathered in front of the theater. The West Tisbury police Bronco was there and so was a Tisbury police cruiser. Blue and red lights flashed on spectators' faces. Katie Bowen, a reporter for *The Island Enquirer,* was talking to Junior Norton.

Howland stopped. "What in hell is Junior doing here?" He dashed across the street.

Alison followed. "At least Tim Eldredge is still at Victoria's."

"No, he's not!" Howland pointed to a state police car pulling up behind the Bronco, blue lights rotating, the same vehicle that had been parked under Victoria's maple tree earlier. Tim Eldredge got out of the driver's side and hitched up his belt.

"What in hell are you doing here?" Howland shouted.

"Sergeant Smalley ordered me to haul ass here, sir."

Howland caught up with him and grabbed the front of Tim's clean uniform shirt. "Who's with Victoria and the boy?"

"Dawn is. And the boy's father. Sir." Tim

lifted his chin from the collar that was getting tighter in Howland's grip.

"Where's Teddy's mother?"

"Nobody knows, sir."

"Damn!" Howland released his hold.

Tim stood up straight and smoothed his shirtfront. "Sir, I've got to report to Sergeant Smalley immediately."

Alison said, "Howland, you'd better haul ass to Victoria's. You have your cell phone?"

They exchanged numbers, and Howland took off at a run to get back to his car, parked on Main Street.

Smalley climbed onto the stage and faced the audience, the cast, and the crew. He'd closed the doors as soon as he got there, and now Tim Eldredge and Junior Norton were keeping people from leaving. Who knew how many people had left before he'd arrived.

"Sorry to detain you, folks, but as I'm sure you know by now, there's been an accident," he said, when the audience had stilled. "Becca Hill, who was playing the part of the bride of Frankenstein, was injured and is being airlifted to Boston." Smalley was explaining that he would need to talk to each one of them, when his cell phone rang. "Excuse me, folks." He turned his back to the gathering. "Smalley, here."

"Sergeant, we've been waiting for you at the jail for almost an hour."

The murmuring of voices behind him started up again.

"Sorry, sheriff. Got sidetracked. There's been a shooting at the theater. Totally slipped my mind to call you."

"Fatality?"

"Not yet. They airlifted her to Boston."

"Further development about the county vehicle, Sergeant. Ira Bodman called from his tractor to report the van is stopped by the side of the road, engine running, driver asleep."

"*Asleep?* What about the cleanup crew?"

"Missing."

"All three?"

"Roger."

"Shit," said Smalley.

"Ira's low on fuel and can't stay with the van."

"Tell him to shut the goddamned engine down and wait."

"He's headed for Morning Glory Farm on his tractor. Says he can't shut the tractor down because he won't be able to start it up again."

"For Christ's sake, send someone from your end. I'm dealing with a hundred-fifty restless people."

"Sorry, Sergeant. I'm dealing with three prison escapees, four restless inmates, and what looks like a drugged driver. On the *state road*."

Smalley sighed. "Okay. I'll put Eldredge in charge, and get there as soon as I can. What's the location of the vehicle?"

"At the top of the swale right around Jimmy Green's, you know, where the heath hen . . ."

"I know where it is."

Alison was starting up the theater's steep stairs when she encountered Smalley, coming down.

"You're not leaving?"

"Three prisoners escaped from a work detail on the West Tisbury-Edgartown Road. Don't know when I'll be back."

"What can I do to help?" Alison looked up at him.

"I've put Tim Eldredge in charge. He and Junior Norton will be taking statements from the cast. Mind helping out with that?"

"You realize that leaves Victoria Trumbull and the boy unguarded, don't you?"

"I have no choice." He was halfway down the stairs and shifted uneasily. "Explain to the audience what the procedure is, what they can expect. You know the drill."

"And the shooting?" asked Alison.

"Dearborn Hill went to the hospital in the ambulance with his wife."

"How is she?"

"No one's said, at this point." He shrugged.

"John, shut down the play immediately."

"I've already done so." Smalley rubbed his palm against his chin, and Alison heard the slight scratch of evening whiskers.

"Sorry about the canceled dinner date."

Alison clutched the stair railing. "Not a problem. Howland filled in for you."

Smalley grunted. "I hate to leave you with this mess."

"It's okay, John. If I can cope with chicken pox, I can cope with this."

Chapter 30

After he'd driven through town and was on a clear stretch of road, Howland dialed Alison's cell phone.

"Can't talk now," she said. "I'm with John."

"What's his problem?"

"The roadside cleanup crew escaped."

"Damn," said Howland. "That *was* Callaghan, the cook, I saw in the Toyota. I should have listened to Victoria."

"I can't talk now," she repeated. "I'll call back later."

"Smalley got his cell phone with him?"

"Yes," she said, and disconnected.

Smalley explained what he wanted Alison to do and left the theater. Alison took his place on stage. Spread out below her was a vast field of bobbing faces. She was terrified of public speaking. The murmur of voices stopped. She felt as though she were about to perform, to sing an operatic role she didn't know, when she'd never been trained to sing, something like that.

She spotted Roderick on the set, reassuringly familiar. He had pulled off most of his gummy makeup and had dropped the mess onto a copy of *The Island Enquirer*. He was scrubbing his face with a colorful beach towel.

George Byron, still wearing the Arctic explorer's costume, was on the end of the front row, as far away from his cousin Roderick as it was possible to get.

The stage manager, Nora Epstein, dressed in an all-purpose costume that apparently served for the several roles she was reading, strode up to the stage apron.

"He can't expect me to be in four places at once."

"I beg your pardon?" said Alison, leaning down to hear the woman above the growing murmur of the audience.

"Dearborn Hill has me reading three parts. I can't watch the prop table and be on stage at the same time."

"Please sit down, Ms. . . . ?"

"Epstein," called out George from the side. "Nora Epstein."

"Thank you," said Alison. "Sit down, Ms. Epstein. No one's blamed anyone yet."

The murmur of the crowd grew louder.

Roderick, in the front row, tossed aside the towel. "It's all my fault."

Nora whipped around. "Trying to get attention as usual, are you?" she snarled.

"Return to your seat, please, immediately," Alison ordered. After Nora was seated, Alison stood tall and raised both hands as if she were holding back traffic. The murmuring stopped. That was satisfying.

"We'll be taking statements from all of you." She looked down at the front row. George Byron grinned at her. "To expedite the process, count off, from one to three. All ones up on stage with Sergeant Norton, twos in the back of the auditorium with Trooper Eldredge, and threes downstairs in the café with me."

While the audience was shouting out "one," "two," "three," one by one from the first row all the way to the back of the theater, she moved from the stage apron and dialed Howland's cell phone.

"Where are you now?" she asked.

"Almost at the town line."

"Any thoughts?" she asked.

"I believe we're dealing with one killer."

"I agree," she said.

"He's either a lousy shot, or didn't have a clear view of the bride. She was on the bed in that scene. Damn these mopeds," Howland grunted. "Four of them strung out, so I can't pass. Was it Becca for sure?"

"Yes."

"As soon as the killer learns Teddy's at Victoria's, he's going after him. Victoria can't keep him safe all by herself."

"His father's there," said Alison. "So is Dawn."

"The killer missed Teddy the first go round. He'll try again. Bruce Duncan is right."

"Fits the profile of a serial killer."

"I've got to pass these mopeds," said Howland. "No sense of self-preservation." After a moment, he continued. "Besides you, me, Victoria, and his father, who knows where Teddy is?"

"I called his dad, and Victoria called Sergeant Smalley. I'm sure John's informed all the other Island police departments. With the good news that Teddy's safe, he probably announced it over the scanner."

"Everyone on this Island has a scanner."

"What about Teddy's father?"

"I don't know," said Howland. "Wait a sec. I have to turn onto Old County Road." Moments later he came back on. "I don't know about Dawn Haines, either. Or Roderick. Or Bruce Duncan. Or that smart-ass

George Byron."

"His mother owns the playhouse. She wouldn't want her son acting in this particular play, would she?"

"No love lost between Ruth Byron and her sister. Wonder if anyone's thought to inform Ruth that her sister's been shot?"

"I've got to get back to my audience. They've finished counting off."

"What?" said Howland, but she hung up without answering.

The woman driving the blue Toyota dropped Red Callaghan off at Cronig's State Road Market. Atherton had seen him, he knew, and he wanted to distance himself from the blue Toyota as soon as possible. He waited until the car was out of sight, then hitchhiked past Vineyard Haven and into Oak Bluffs. At the crowded steamship authority ticket office, he picked up a boat schedule and sauntered past the restrooms to the seawall beyond, where he leaned against the railing, studying the schedule and gazing out at Nantucket Sound.

"Darling!"

He turned, smiled, and held out his arms to the small woman with dark hair who rushed up to him and snuggled against him.

"God, it's good to see you, Amanda. Two

months in that crummy lockup . . ."

"You got all the stuff I sent you?"

He opened his arms. "I'm here, thanks to you."

"No trouble?"

"Like a charm. Assigned to roadside cleanup duty, prepared snacks, coffee, and lemonade for the driver, driver dozed off, and I left. Easy as that. You bring a shaving kit and money?"

"And a wig and a clean shirt."

"You doll. Let me have it. I'll hit the john and shave off my mustache before we get the tickets."

"Not your gorgeous mustache?"

He stroked the lush auburn growth. "Afraid so."

When he returned, he was clean-shaven and no longer bald. Amanda was leaning against the railing, her back to the water.

She laughed. "Hello, stranger. I wouldn't have recognized you. You look so . . . so dignified."

Callaghan ran his hand over his smooth upper lip. "What do you hear about your kid?" he asked as they sauntered toward the ticket office.

"The police called off the search for him."

"Meaning?"

"I don't know what it means. They haven't

told me."

They bought two round-trip tickets and stood where they could watch traffic on the roads that led to the wharf.

"They're not going to call off a search for a missing kid." Callaghan leaned against the railing next to her and scanned the roads. "Cops don't give up when it comes to kids."

"If they've found him, they'd call me right away, wouldn't they? His mother?" Her eyes were moist.

"They know where to reach you?"

She pulled her phone out of her pocketbook. "Damn! I forgot to recharge it. They've got my number at Mrs. Trumbull's. I'll check when I get back."

"Since the kid isn't that keen on California, you think he ran away?"

"He wouldn't do that. He's a good boy. I hope his blankety-blank father didn't snatch him."

"That likely?"

"Wouldn't put it past him."

"About California . . . ?"

Amanda sighed. "The TV deal fell through."

"What?" Callaghan opened his eyes wide. "I thought the contract was signed and sealed?"

"I thought so, too. But they wouldn't close

346

the deal without Teddy's father's signature, since we're not divorced yet."

"And the old man wouldn't sign?"

She shook her head. "He refused. Point blank. I told you what they offered me, didn't I?"

"Offered *you?* Thought it was Teddy who got the offer."

"The contract was made out to me. Close to a million dollars. Nobody hands out that kind of money to an eight-year-old boy. I'm his mother." She patted her chest. "His legal guardian. But the lawyers at the studio insisted on both parents signing. Sexist. If I were Teddy's father, you can bet the lawyers wouldn't insist on the mother's signature, too."

Callaghan looked thoughtful. "So you won't be sharing the million with his old man."

"Looks like I won't be sharing the million with you, either. We're wasting time." Amanda moved away from the railing and started to walk toward the dock. "We've got to get you off the Island."

"Damn right. Atherton spotted me."

"What!" She turned and stared at him.

"The two round-trip passenger tickets will throw them off temporarily. The cops will look for a single guy, bald with a mustache,

347

not a couple with a distinguished, clean-shaven, gray-haired gentleman." He patted the silver wig. "Return to the Island on the next boat, and I'll get myself lost."

"What about us?"

"Recharge your phone. I'll give you a call when I'm somewhere safe. In the meantime, we've gotta get on that boat," he nodded at the boarding ferry. *"Now."*

People and cars were moving down the long dock.

"Walk," said Callaghan. "Don't run."

They boarded. Callaghan and Amanda went up the stairs to the upper deck.

As the ferry pulled away from its slip, they looked back at the town. A police car, blue lights flashing, was driving the wrong way up the one-way street that led to the dock.

Leonard Vincent, Peg's ex-husband, was working on his new house in Chilmark, listening to WMVY's album sound and halfway listening to the scanner, when he heard the announcement that a missing boy had been located and was safe.

He set down the nail gun, turned WMVY down, and the scanner up. Had to be the Vanderhoop kid. Guarded conversation on the scanner went back and forth, and pretty soon Lennie Vincent guessed that Teddy

Vanderhoop, age eight, definitely was the found boy. Where had the kid been hiding? Quite possibly with Victoria Trumbull, he thought. The kid had seen something the night Peg was killed. But what?

Lennie laughed. He cleared up the loose tools on his construction site, packed everything in the toolbox that lay athwart the pickup bed, and headed down Island.

"Idiot cops," he mumbled to himself, grinning hugely. "So they think he's safe, do they? Assholes."

Ruth Byron discovered the hideaway in the costume barn when she went there with a pillow in a clean pillowcase for George, who'd forgotten it.

The first thing she saw was a padlock on the door, hanging open from the old rusty hasp that had always been held shut with a wooden peg. A padlock? Surely, George hadn't decided to lock himself in. Or out? There was a key in the padlock with a brown and white ribbon looped through it. Strange.

She pushed open the barn door and stopped in astonishment at what she saw inside. The setup was certainly not George's doing. His bed, stored in the barn while his room was being papered, was made up with a blanket, sheets, and a shabby pillow she didn't recognize. The bookcase had been pushed close to the bed and was stocked with canned and packaged food and boxes of crackers. The kind of food George didn't normally eat. A pile of comic books was set next to a reading lamp on an end table beside the bed. What in the world was this all about?

She hurried back to the house and called George's cell phone. A robotic voice announced that George was unavailable, she could leave a message or press "one" for other options. She told the recording to have George call her, right away.

She dialed Victoria Trumbull's number. An unfamiliar sounding man answered and said Victoria was busy and would have to call back. Who was he?

She called the West Tisbury police station and got Chief Casey O'Neill. . ◦

"I have no idea what's going on," said Casey. "I ordered Victoria to stay out of this murder investigation, and she hasn't spoken to me since."

"Would you check her house, please? Some man answered the phone and refused to put her on."

"Sure," said Casey. "But all hell has broken loose in town, and I'm here late coordinating stuff. It'll take me at least a half-hour to check on her. Don't worry about Victoria."

Ruth, against her better instincts, called the theater, and Junior Norton answered.

"What's going on?" she asked.

"There's been an accident," Junior reported.

"An accident?" Ruth was alarmed. Her theater building on fire? She'd put off fixing the electricity until she had some money. She should never have waited.

"Mrs. Hill got hurt," said Junior. "They're flying her to Boston."

Ruth felt a surge of relief. "What happened?"

"She got hurt," Junior repeated, and Ruth could imagine him half-closing his eyes, not able to give out information. "Mr. Hill is with her."

"Becca is my sister. Why didn't someone notify me?"

"Sorry, Mrs. Byron. The Tisbury police tried to reach you, but your phone's been busy."

CHAPTER 31

At the theater, the three law enforcement officers systematically questioned every one of the one hundred fifty members of the audience, cast, and crew. No one had seen anything. The bride of Frankenstein had sat up in her nuptial bed when the monster crashed through the window, screamed once, and fell back onto the bed. The audience had been delighted.

The monster had shouted, "I didn't do it this time!" which caused more laughter, catcalls, and whistles.

Several minutes had gone by before Frankenstein or Dearborn Hill or whoever he was, realized that his bride wasn't acting, that she really was lying there bleeding for real. Several more minutes went by as the audience segued from hilarity into sobriety. Still more minutes went by before the ambulance arrived, then the police. The police had shut the doors.

From what Alison, Junior Norton, and Tim Eldredge could determine, close to fifteen minutes had passed before the theater had been closed down and people prevented from leaving.

Had anyone seen people leaving? No, they were too interested in what was happening on stage. No one had been down in the café. No one had been in the ticket booth. No one had been watching the doors.

"Didn't you think someone would sneak in without paying?" Alison had asked the crew and cast members who were not actually on stage.

The answer had been, "It was a full house. No one could have squeezed in. Even standing room was sold out."

And no one had seen anyone sneak out of the theater.

Teddy had fallen asleep again, under the weight of a fluffy, clean, warm dog. His very own.

Doc Atkins, Victoria, and Teddy's father finished off the Australian wine, and the vet, seeing the boy and the dog settled in, left, with a satisfied smile. Jefferson Vanderhoop went off to Cumberland Farms to get some ice cream for his kid and his kid's dog. Not chocolate, the vet had warned. Bad for dogs.

Victoria settled an exhausted Dawn Haines in the West Room, where the breeze whispered through the screen, gently lifting the sheer curtains. How had Dawn imagined she could stay up all night playing poker with those two policemen?

Then Victoria realized that she, too, would rise to an occasion such as having two attractive men competing for her attention, and she smiled. How ridiculous to think she needed a police guard. Totally unnecessary. Nice, though.

Karen and Tracy, her two lodgers, would be home by midnight, after they finished their shift at the motel. Elizabeth would probably get home from the harbor around the same time. Only a couple of hours from now. Teddy's father would be back soon. Fifteen minutes to Cumberland Farms, five minutes to purchase the ice cream, fifteen minutes back again.

Victoria tiptoed into the library to see her patient. Sound asleep. Sandy looked up at her, and laid his head back on Teddy's chest, eyes closed. Teddy must be hot with that dog enveloping him like that, but she left them alone and softly shut the door.

She looked at her watch. Jefferson had been gone for only ten minutes. He'd be back in a half-hour, maybe less.

A vehicle turned off the Edgartown Road into her drive, and she went to the door. A man she'd never seen before, a tall slender man with slicked-back hair who she could just make out in the light from the entry, got out of a battered pickup truck he'd parked right in front of the steps.

"Please park under the maple tree," she called out to him and added, "People need to get past."

"Okay." The man got back into the truck, drove around the circle, parked, and sauntered back to where she was still waiting on the steps.

"And who are you?" Victoria asked, blocking his way.

"Name's Vincent," he replied. "Leonard Vincent."

"Peg Storm's husband?" Victoria still blocked his way.

"Ex-husband," he said.

"I believe the police are looking for you."

"So I hear. You going to ask me in?"

"Would you mind telling me why you're here? At my house?"

"Sure. You can ask." He grinned. His teeth were badly stained.

She cleared her throat. "Well?"

"I figured the boy is staying here."

"The boy?" said Victoria.

"You know, *the boy.*"

"Where did you hear that?"

"Figured it out from the police scanner, lady."

"May I ask what your business is with the boy?"

He chortled. "Sure. You can ask."

Victoria took in a deep breath and let it out. "This conversation is unsatisfactory. I was hoping to meet you, and now I have." She continued to block the doorway. "Thank you for dropping by, Mr. Vincent . . ."

"Name's Lennie. How about asking me in?"

"I don't think so."

Lennie grinned again, set one hand on the door frame and leaned against it. "Okay, lady, you win. Kid was my neighbor. Heard he was here and wanted to see how's he doing."

Victoria, torn between wanting to guard her patient and curiosity about Peg's ex-husband, finally stepped aside and led him into the kitchen.

"Won't you sit down?" She nodded to one of the gray-painted kitchen chairs.

"Don't mind if I do." He swung the chair around and straddled it, arms crossed over the back. He looked around. "You alone here?"

"No." Victoria decided she'd better take control of the conversation. "I've wanted to meet you, Mr. Vincent."

"Lennie."

"I understand you're a sailor."

"Who says?"

"Have I seen you sailing a catboat on Lagoon Pond?" She hadn't, but Peg had talked to her about the catboat. "And you have an outboard motor boat, I believe."

"Yeah, I do."

Howland's old white station wagon coughed, shuddered, and coasted to a stop. He turned the key in the ignition. The engine started briefly, sputtered, and died. He checked the gas gauge. The needle rested below empty.

"Damnation!"

Tiasquam Repairs would be closed at this time of night. He'd have to hitchhike to Victoria's. Fortunately, her house was only about two miles away. Howland gathered up papers he thought he might need, tucked the car key under the floor mat, and was about to step out of the driver's side when Bruce Duncan's van went past. He caught sight of the "GOODDOG" license plate and the bumper stickers plastered on the van that read "VETA". If only he'd been a few seconds earlier, he could have hitched a ride with Duncan.

He decided it would make sense to stay with his car rather than start walking, so passing motorists would see that he was having car troubles. He stood where he was visible, saw the headlights of an approaching car, and stuck out his thumb. The car slowed and stopped.

Howland opened the passenger-side door, the dome light went on, and Roderick, still in some of his costume, leaned over his cousin, George Byron, who sat in the passenger seat. "Where are you heading?" asked Roderick.

"Victoria Trumbull's," said Howland, feeling a sense of déjà vu.

"So are we. Hop in the back seat," said Roderick. "You can shove that stuff to one side."

The stuff consisted of the rest of Roderick's blood-soaked costume, a clear plastic bag containing fangs and hairy fingers, and a gun.

Howland pulled a pen out of his pocket and picked up the gun by its trigger guard. "What are you doing with this?"

Roderick looked over his shoulder. "That?

It's the stage gun."

"What are you doing with it?"

"Cousin George was supposed to shoot me in the last act, but he never got a chance."

Howland hefted the gun on his pen. "Loaded?"

"With blanks," said Roderick.

Howland took a handkerchief out of his pocket and opened the chamber. Not blanks, real bullets. He shook the fangs and fingers out of the plastic bag and put the gun in the bag instead, then tucked the plastic bag containing the loaded gun into his jacket pocket.

"What are you doing?" asked Roderick

"Evidence," replied Howland. "Precautionary."

"Where are you staying?" George asked Roderick.

"In my car," answered Roderick.

Howland said, "I thought you were living with Dearborn?"

"They locked me out. You're staying with Aunt Ruth, aren't you, George?"

"My mother's redecorating my room. I'm sleeping in the costume barn."

The car swerved and Howland grasped the seat in front of him. "The costume barn?" asked Roderick. "You mean, behind your house?"

"Yeah, my mother's house," said George. "Where we used to play when we were kids. Why?"

"Oh my God," said Roderick.

"Were you thinking of staying there?" said George, and Howland saw him sit up straight. "You were the one who fixed up the place in the barn, weren't you? Why didn't you say something to my mother?"

Roderick made puffing sounds, his lips going in and out like his Uncle Dearborn's sometimes did. Howland watched with fascination from the back seat.

George laughed. "That explains everything. I didn't know you were into comic books. *Batman? Daredevil? Tomb Raider?* Jeez, Roderick." He laughed some more.

Roderick continued to make puffing sounds, and Howland realized the guy was hyperventilating and just possibly might black out.

"Watch him, George," Howland warned.

CHAPTER 32

Victoria watched Leonard Vincent, who continued to watch her in return. He'd said he wanted to see Teddy, but did he have something else in mind?

"I'll take you to visit Teddy, if you'd like, Mr. Vincent."

"Lennie," he said again. "Why not?" He got to his feet and swung the chair around, then followed Victoria to the library. She opened the door gently. Teddy, face flushed and liberally spotted, slumbered peacefully under the weight of Sandy. He slept on. Sandy looked up, curled his lips back in a snarl, bared his teeth, and growled.

"Have you had chicken pox, Mr. Vincent?" Victoria asked.

Lennie backed out of the room. Sandy continued to growl. Teddy, in his sleep, wrapped an arm around his very own dog, who put his head down with his eyes still open and a low rumble of a growl directed at Lennie Vincent.

"What's Peg's dog doing here?" Lennie demanded.

"Guarding Teddy."

"Never did like that mutt. The kid gonna keep him?"

"Yes."

"Good riddance. One of her possessions I sure as hell don't want."

Victoria closed the library door and kept herself between Lennie and the closed door. As they walked back to the kitchen, Victoria wondered what to do with the information she now had: that Sandy didn't like Peg's husband. Had Lennie killed Peg? Possibly, but why kill Bob Scott? That didn't seem likely.

She mused on the possibility of Lennie as a killer, when she saw the lights of a vehicle turn into the drive. A light-colored van pulled up under the maple tree next to Lennie's truck. The driver got out. In the light from the entry, she could see him limp toward the kitchen door. Bruce Duncan.

Her skin prickled. Teddy had recognized a van that drove away from Job's Neck. She couldn't see the license plate, which Teddy said spelled out something he couldn't read. At the pet store, she'd asked Bruce about his limp, and he'd told her he'd barked his shin. Had the barked shin come from banging into Teddy's Lego box? Bruce had insisted from the beginning that people were being killed in order of appearance. That was what he'd said, even though Peg had been the only victim at the time. Even before Bob Scott was killed.

She had two suspects in the house now. If one of them was the killer, would he go after Teddy with the other present? Before Duncan reached the kitchen door, Victoria slipped into the parlor and found her grandfather's heavy, gold-headed, ebony cane leaning next to the bookcase. She propped herself on it as though she needed its support.

Lennie had turned the chair around and sat again. He watched her with an amused expression. "You gonna go after someone? Pretty lethal, that stick."

His over-familiarity unnerved her, and she didn't reply. She waited by the door until Bruce Duncan limped up the steps, and then ushered him into the kitchen.

"Bruce," she said. "What brings you here?"

Lennie chuckled. "Hey, asshole. Having fun with your animals?"

Bruce flushed. "Don't be disgusting."

"Couldn't make it with my wife, could you?"

Bruce stepped toward Lennie, fists clenched.

"Stop it," said Victoria, and thumped her grandfather's stick on the floor. "How can I help you, Bruce?"

Bruce turned away from Lennie. "I heard they found Teddy."

Victoria did a quick calculation. Teddy's father should be back soon. She checked her watch. Perhaps fifteen more minutes. That seemed forever. Would she be able to stall for that long?

The two police officers, Tim Eldredge and Junior Norton, wouldn't be able to help. They had responded to Sergeant Smalley's call to get to the theater. Where was Howland? She could awaken Dawn, who was probably asleep by now, but that would put Dawn in danger, and what could Dawn do to help?

McCavity stalked in from some hideaway, paused at the door of the library and sniffed. His fur rose in a ridge along his back, his tail fluffed up.

"What's your cat's problem?" asked Duncan. He knelt and offered a hand to McCavity, who twitched his tail and glanced over his shoulder. Bruce pulled a catnip mouse out of his pocket and held it by its tail in front of McCavity. With great dignity, McCavity ignored the mouse, then, turned in a flash and pounced. "Works every time," said Duncan. McCavity had rolled over on his back, and his hind claws tore at the mouse. "What's behind the door?"

Victoria clutched the cane in both hands. "Teddy's here."

"I gathered as much."

"He's asleep. He came down with chicken pox."

"Better to have it now than when he's older," said Duncan. "As I well know. Okay if I peek in at him?"

Victoria watched his hands. One had extracted the mouse, the other might reach into his pocket for a weapon of some kind. Lennie slouched in the kitchen chair, watching. Victoria opened the door a crack, and tensed.

Teddy slept on. Sandy lifted his head, opened his mouth in a sort of doggy grin, tongue out, and wagged his tail.

"The boy's dog?" Duncan whispered.

"He is now."

"Looks a lot like Peg Storm's dog, Sandy."

"Ummm," said Victoria. She shut the door again, kept her back to it, and relaxed her grip on the cane.

"Someone ought to be here with you, Mrs. Trumbull," said Duncan. "I mean, the boy's life may be in danger."

Victoria had been intent on watching Bruce Duncan and hadn't kept her eyes on Leonard Vincent. He no longer sat in the gray-painted chair. He was prowling around the kitchen, opening cupboard doors. He'd found the bottle of rum that she and Elizabeth mixed with cranberry juice. He'd also found a glass and poured himself a generous drink. He leered at her and held up the glass.

Victoria was outraged. She started to say something, but stopped herself, and checked her watch instead. Where was Teddy's father?

She heard the rattle of an out-of-shape car as it ground to a stop in front of the stone steps. She remained standing, halfway between the kitchen and the library.

Leonard Vincent leaned against the counter and guffawed. "Aren't you going to order *them* to park under the maple tree?"

Bruce Duncan, with a look of disgust, turned his back on Lennie.

Footsteps approached, voices, then Howland entered. Victoria dropped the cane with a clatter. She hadn't realized how tense she'd been. Duncan picked up the stick and handed it to her.

"Thank you," said Victoria.

Howland was followed by George Byron and Roderick, who was also limping.

"Company!" said Lennie. "Pour a drink for anyone?" He brandished the rum bottle.

"Who the hell are you?" said Howland.

Lennie grinned. "Don't you wish you knew."

"Leonard Vincent," said Victoria.

"What'd you do to yourself, sonny?" Lennie pointed at Roderick's leg.

"Tripped over a rock," Roderick said. He turned to Victoria. "Howland was hitchhiking on Old County Road."

"Ran out of gas," said Howland.

Lennie hooted.

"So I picked him up . . ."

Victoria heard a low growl. She opened the library door, and a fluffy, tan beast, fangs bared, saliva dripping from its jaws, eyes red coals, flung itself on Roderick and sank its teeth into his good leg.

Roderick screamed.

"Sandy?" called a weak voice from the library.

Before anyone could react, there was a second screech. McCavity streaked into the room puffed up to twice his normal size, eyes narrow slits. He headed directly for the dog, but Roderick, attempting to detach Sandy, kicked out his leg with the dog still attached, and McCavity's unsheathed claws sank, instead, into Roderick's sore leg.

Victoria, not sure at first which animal to go after, finally seized Sandy around his middle and pulled him away from Roderick. A swatch of Roderick's monster costume came away in Sandy's clenched teeth. Victoria handed the still-growling dog to Howland.

Roderick dropped onto the floor, moaning, holding first one leg then the other.

McCavity went after the dog in Howland's arms. Victoria plucked the cat off Howland's trouser leg.

Roderick moaned, "I didn't mean to kill her. I didn't mean to kill Bob Scott, either."

"Mr. Vincent, make yourself useful. Get the witch hazel from the bathroom," Victoria ordered. "And a clean rag from the shelf above the washing machine."

"I'm no use to anyone. Everything I do is a failure." Roderick put his head down on his knees.

Lennie came back with the witch hazel and a rag. Victoria handed them to Bruce Duncan, who got down on his knees, rolled up Roderick's pants legs, and swabbed the deep, angry scratches and barely healed scrape on one leg and the puncture wounds on the other.

"Animals understand people," said Bruce Duncan, with some satisfaction.

Howland tucked Sandy against his shoulder. With one hand he opened up his cell phone and Victoria heard him ask for Smalley.

Jefferson Vanderhoop came in through the kitchen door and looked around with interest. Victoria hadn't heard his truck drive up. "Butter pecan and vanilla. Excuse me." He brushed his way past Howland, who was still talking on his cell phone, and unloaded two half-gallons of ice cream from a plastic bag into the freezer. "What've we got, a party?" Vanderhoop said, before he'd fully taken in the scene: Roderick sitting on the floor, moaning, Bruce Duncan kneeling next to him applying something to ugly-looking wounds on Roderick's legs, Victoria holding a resentful cat still puffed up in fight mode. And then he saw Lennie.

"Hey, old buddy," said Vanderhoop. "What are you doing here?"

Lennie smirked. "Looking for some peace and quiet."

CHAPTER 33

As George Byron and Roderick talked
quietly near the door, Victoria overheard
George say, "Planning to read comic books
in the costume barn, Cuz?" He put his
fingertips to his lips, his head to one side,
and lisped, *"Powerpuff Girls?"*

"Costume barn?" Victoria interrupted.

George turned to her. "You know, the
barn behind my mother's house where she
stores theater costumes?" George grinned.
"I was planning to stay in the barn, but
there was this hideout all set up, padlock on
the door, a stock of junk food, bed made,
reading light, and *comic books.* Turns out it
was *his* idea." He gestured to Roderick.
"Hiding from Aunt Becca?"

Roderick groaned. "Another failure."

Howland, holding Sandy in one arm,
closed his cell phone with his unoccupied
hand. Sandy peered over Howland's shoulder at Roderick and growled. Howland

murmured something to the dog, who reached up and licked his ear.

Teddy called out from the library, "Sandy?" and the dog wriggled out of Howland's arm, gave a last growl at Roderick, and raced to his new master.

Victoria suddenly put everything together. "Roderick, you went to Peg's house the night of dress rehearsal. Why?"

"Stupid." He shook his head. "A stupid, stupid idea."

"What *was* the idea?" Victoria asked gently.

Bruce Duncan slopped more witch hazel on Roderick's wounds and handed the almost empty bottle and rag to Lennie. "Put this back where you found it."

"Whatever you say, asshole."

Howland crossed his arms and leaned against the wall next to the clock.

Jefferson Vanderhoop, who'd been tending his boy, said, "Mind if I feed the kid some juice, Mrs. Trumbull?"

"Help yourself."

He opened the refrigerator, poured orange juice into a glass, and took it into the library, where Teddy was sitting up, arms around his dog.

Another car pulled up under the maple tree next to Bruce Duncan's van. Lennie, on his way back from the bathroom, peered out of the window. "You sure know how to throw a party, Mrs. T."

Victoria looked up as footsteps pattered up the stone steps of the entry, and Teddy's mother appeared at the door. Amanda's dark hair was windblown and her usually pressed slacks were wrinkled.

"Teddy?" she said. "Have they found him?"

"Mommy!" Teddy called out.

"Darling!" Without acknowledging the six people present, one cringing on the floor, another kneeling next to him, Amanda rushed into the library. Sandy growled.

Victoria heard loud voices from the library.

Teddy's father asked, "Where's the boyfriend?"

Teddy's mother answered, "Gone."

"I've got a dog, Mommy!"

"Honey, you're covered with spots!"

"I've got chicken pox, Mommy!"

Teddy's mother said, "You know you can't have a dog, honey."

Teddy's father said, "The hell he can't."

Victoria smiled to herself and turned back to Roderick. "What *was* your idea?" she said again. "Did you intend to kidnap Teddy for some reason? Hide him in the costume barn? Was that it?"

Roderick nodded miserably.

"Why, Roderick? Why?"

"Stupid idea," Roderick mumbled again.

"Yes it was, but what were you thinking?"

He winced as Bruce Duncan rolled his pant legs back down over his wounds.

"Roderick?" prompted Victoria.

"Howland got the role of the monster, the part I wanted."

"You were welcome to it from the first," said Howland.

"What does kidnapping Teddy have to do with playing the monster?" Victoria asked.

Roderick put his head down on his knees. "Everyone would be worried about Teddy, and then I'd find him, and be a hero, and they'd let me play the monster."

"Jeezus Christ." Howland straightened and bumped his head on the wall clock.

"Exactly what happened that night?" Victoria asked.

Bruce Duncan got to his feet, glanced at the clock, and said, "I don't need to hear any more. Good job, trapping the killer, Mrs. Trumbull. Congratulations."

"I think you need to hear the rest," said Victoria, holding up her hand. "Howland, make sure no one leaves."

"Here comes a police car," said George, looking out of the kitchen window. "Bronco." Blue and white lights flashed across the kitchen walls.

Lennie peered out at the flashing lights and said to Roderick, "Now your car's blocking two cars, sonny. One's the cops."

"Never mind," said Victoria. "Roderick?"

"I fixed up the costume barn for Teddy. Nice snacks, my own comic books . . ."

Tomb Raider?" said George. "*Daredevil?* I believe I mentioned *Powerpuff Girls?* Hee hee!"

Roderick ignored his cousin George. ". . . a good reading light. Teddy wasn't going to be there long."

"He'd certainly recognize you," Victoria said.

"No, no. I was going to blindfold him. Anyway, he didn't know me. I was just the understudy."

"And?" Victoria sighed. She'd been standing long enough. She pulled out one of the gray chairs and sat, still holding her grandfather's cane.

"I knew all his lines." He nodded at Howland. "I looked more like the monster than Howland Atherton did."

"That's for sure," muttered Howland.

Roderick continued. "Before Peg and

374

Teddy left the theater at the end of Act One, I disguised myself."

"Can't imagine how," said Bruce Duncan.

"Be quiet, Bruce," said Victoria.

"I disguised myself and went into her house and took out all the fuses in the fuse box in her cellar and hid them."

"Why?"

"I figured she would have to go down to the cellar, and it would take her a lot of time to find and replace the fuses. That would give me time to capture Teddy. I didn't know he was going to stop at his own house first. Stupid, stupid."

"Right," said Bruce Duncan.

"Then Peg came home," Victoria continued, "the lights didn't work, and what happened next?"

"I asked her where Teddy was. She started to scream, and I put my hand over her mouth. I didn't mean to kill her."

Bruce Duncan was about to say something, but Victoria held up her hand. "Let him talk, Bruce." She turned back to Roderick. "Then what?"

"I panicked. I ran out of the house to my car. It was parked at the end of the Job's Neck Road."

"How did you hurt your leg?"

"I tripped over a rock in the dark."

"When did you run into Sandy?"

"When I first got to Peg's. Sandy came out to greet me, tail wagging and all . . ." He paused.

"Yes?" said Victoria.

"I didn't mean to hurt the dog. I tripped over him, and then when I tried to pat him, tell him I was sorry, I fell over my feet and landed on him by mistake. I guess I hurt him bad. He ran off, yelping."

"Monster!" hissed Bruce Duncan.

The blue and white lights of the police vehicle continued to flash across Victoria's kitchen walls, and Casey, in her summer uniform, white shirt with a gold and blue patch on the sleeve, marched up to the door. Howland stepped aside. Casey glanced at the scene before her, one hand on the butt of her gun, and waited.

Victoria nodded to the chief, and continued to question Roderick. "You left Peg lying on the floor? You didn't check her pulse or breathing?"

"I panicked," said Roderick.

"You didn't call nine-one-one?"

"I didn't think of it. I drove to Island Java and drank a couple of cups of coffee."

"Exactly what you needed," said Lennie, pouring himself another glass of Victoria's rum. "Coffee nerves."

Casey glanced around the room at the assemblage, then back at Victoria with a glint of admiration.

"Now then, what about Bob Scott?" Victoria asked. "You didn't know your own strength, did you?"

He shook his head. "I didn't mean to kill him, either."

"The stage crew carried him off, but you knew he'd recovered enough to sit on the couch, didn't you?"

"And died," said Roderick, looking with dismay at his great hands.

Victoria folded her own hands over the gold knob of the cane. "I understand your aunt was a target tonight."

"I didn't shoot Aunt Becca. I know I didn't. I was angry with her, but I would never have killed her. I wouldn't have killed anyone. I didn't mean to kill anyone. If I weren't so, so . . ."

"Atta boy!" said Lennie. "Cheers!" He held up his glass.

"Is there anything else you can tell us, Roderick?"

He put his head down on his knees. "I'm sorry."

Victoria turned to Bruce Duncan. "Where did you get the hemlock that killed Bob Scott?"

Bruce scrambled to his feet. "What? What?"

"The toxicology lab in Boston found hemlock in Robert Scott's stomach, and hemlock in the cup you offered him, a refreshing drink after he'd been almost strangled to death in his scene."

"Don't look at *me* like that." Duncan pointed to Roderick, who was cowering on the floor. "There's your killer. Thought nothing of snuffing out the lives of five hundred . . ."

"Goldfish," said Howland. "We know all about that. Go on, Victoria."

"Hemlock was the poison the Greeks used to kill Socrates. They considered hemlock a humane death. It grows almost everywhere on the Island. Where did you find it, Bruce?"

"You're wrong, totally wrong. I didn't offer him any drink."

"How did your fingerprints get on the plastic cup?"

"The cleaning woman was supposed to throw that away," said Bruce Duncan. "She's supposed to pick up trash. She did. I'm sure she did. Scott would never have taken that drink from me if I'd been wearing gloves."

Bruce Duncan stared at Victoria in horror, as though he'd suddenly realized what he'd confessed, and then darted towards the door. Casey blocked it.

"Cuff him!" said Victoria.

CHAPTER 34

Howland closed up his cell phone and headed toward one of the kitchen chairs. "Smalley's on his way here, Casey. Two of the escaped convicts gave themselves up. The third got away."

"Which one?" Casey asked.

"Chef Red Callaghan." Howland sat down with a sigh. "The chef apparently spiked the driver's lemonade, and after the driver passed out, hitched a ride with a woman in a blue Toyota. I spotted him, and Victoria tried to get me to follow the car." He winced. "I refused. A mistake."

Victoria, from her seat at the table, opened and closed her hands over the knob of her grandfather's cane and said nothing.

"What was the chef in for, Howland? Drugs?" Casey asked.

"Yes."

"You think he got off Island?"

"Seems certain," said Howland. "The

state police picked up his trail to the Oak Bluffs ferry terminal. The ticket seller recalled seeing a bald man with big mustache pick up a schedule, but she didn't remember his buying a ticket."

Casey moved her hand off the gun butt. "They didn't apprehend him when the ferry docked?"

"No one answering that description got off at Woods Hole. No single man, bald, with mustache. Families, couples, kids."

Victoria tapped the floor with the cane. Everyone turned to her. "He had an accomplice," she said. "Someone helped him with the disguise. A girlfriend . . ." she stopped. "I never thought to ask Teddy what his mother's boyfriend looks like."

"His mother's in the library now with Teddy," said Casey.

"Let the state police handle her." Victoria glanced at Casey, who ignored her, and went to the library where Teddy's mother was with her son.

Bruce Duncan, his hands cuffed behind him, continued to protest. "You've got the wrong man! This is a horrible mistake! I'll sue!"

Lennie cackled.

Casey returned. "Teddy says his mother's boyfriend is bald with a big red mustache.

His mother doesn't say anything."

"Go on, Victoria," said Howland. "Back to how you fingered Bruce Duncan."

"All the actors knew that Peg was trying to discourage Bruce tactfully. Apparently, he was obsessed with her."

"That's simply not true," shouted Bruce. "She led me on, making me think she cared for me."

"Oh, shut up," said Lennie, lifting his glass to Victoria.

"I can only surmise what happened. Bruce followed her the night of dress rehearsal, hoping to glimpse her, but the lights in her house were out."

Roderick, still huddled on the floor, groaned.

Bruce turned away from him with a look of disgust. "I went there to help her," he said. "She did need help. My help, after that . . ." he turned on Roderick and didn't finish.

Victoria watched him for a moment before she continued. "We know, according to Teddy, that Peg screamed. I can only guess that you, Bruce, perhaps going to her help, as you said, saw a man leave the house. Am I right?"

"Yes," said Bruce.

"A large man you thought was Roderick

because of his size. You rushed to Peg's aid
. . ."

Duncan nodded. "That much is true. But she was already dead." He nodded at Roderick.

Roderick groaned.

Victoria went on. "Peg was on the floor, wasn't she? Alive, but incoherent. Did she whisper something to you?"

" 'Roderick.' She whispered, 'Roderick tried to kill me.' "

Roderick nodded miserably.

Howland and Casey exchanged glances.

"I can understand how upset the scene must have made you," Victoria said. "Did you think Roderick had molested her?"

"Yes. That was it."

"Perhaps you thought she had cooperated with Roderick? That had to have hurt your feelings."

"You understand, Mrs. Trumbull, don't you. She teased me, sneered at me behind my back, then made out with that clown."

"No, no, no," said Roderick, shaking his head. "No, no!"

Lennie chortled. George turned his back on the others, went into the cookroom, and sat down. The rest stood silently.

Victoria waited a moment, then continued. "You put your hands around Peg's neck and shook her, tried to get her to confess to you, was that it? Had she recovered enough so she could talk?"

"She told me Roderick tried to kill her."

Howland shifted position slightly.

"You must have thought she was lying to you, that Roderick was having an affair with her?"

"No!" shouted Roderick.

"It was obvious," said Duncan, glaring at the people standing and sitting around him. "Mrs. Trumbull seems to be the only one here who understands my situation."

"Roderick pressed his gloved hand against Peg's mouth and nose. We know that. But it was you who put your hands around her neck and squeezed life out of her."

"I was trying to get her to talk to me," said Duncan.

"Why did you throw her down the cellar stairs?"

Duncan turned. "I didn't want them to find her right away."

"And Roderick, foolish Roderick, played right into your hands, didn't he?"

"He *is* foolish." Duncan looked down at the floor.

"Why were you after Teddy?" Victoria asked.

"I heard Peg scream, 'Run, Teddy, run!' I

thought Teddy had seen me."

"Before you even went into Peg's house? I would guess that Roderick put his hand over her mouth, then lifted it enough so she could tell him where Teddy was, and that's when she screamed. Teddy never saw you. But you went into his house looking for him?"

"I wasn't thinking clearly," Bruce said. "When I didn't find him in his house, I started going through the desk looking for people he might have run to."

"Teddy did see you, when he climbed the tree. But from where he was sitting, he could see you only from the waist down." Victoria tapped the cane on the floor. "When he broke the branch, you ran out the back door and tripped over his toy box."

"Wonder I didn't break a leg, falling down the stairs. Kid shouldn't have left it there."

Victoria smiled for the first time. "That's what his mother kept telling him. Teddy hid because he was frightened and didn't feel well," Victoria continued. "He thought the intruder was his mother's boyfriend. Teddy didn't want the boyfriend to find him. He had no idea Chef Callaghan was locked up in jail."

"Not securely enough, apparently," said Howland. "I recommended him for the road-work detail."

"Teddy was coming down with chicken pox and he wanted a safe place to rest." Victoria smiled again. "Here."

"Peace and quiet," said Lennie, finishing the last of his rum and holding the glass up the the light as if more might miraculously appear.

"What about Bob Scott's death?" Casey asked. "That exchange of bullets in the stage gun? The attempt on Becca's life?"

Roderick was still on the floor, head on his knees.

Victoria said, "Roderick removed what he thought were blanks and substituted bullets in the stage gun. Right, Roderick? The blanks actually were real bullets."

He grunted.

"We don't know who substituted the toy gun with the gag flag for the stage gun."

George, in the cookroom, raised a hand. "Guilty."

"Fortunate that you did," said Victoria. "I'm curious to know where you found a joke item like that."

"Mary at Shirley's Hardware."

"That explains it." Victoria turned back to Duncan, who was rubbing one foot on the leg of his jeans, having trouble balancing himself with his hands shackled. "Bruce, you took out the blanks and substituted real bullets, didn't you?"

Duncan said nothing.

"You hoped we'd think a serial killer was at work, that we'd never suspect you because you were the one who alluded to a serial killer. That's why you killed Bob Scott, isn't it?"

Duncan was silent.

"You were willing to let Roderick take the blame?"

Bruce Duncan stood up straight. "He deserved it."

"What about Becca's shooting? Where were you? In the wings?"

"I bought a ticket, bought it from that girl who didn't even recognize me."

"Didn't anyone in the audience see you with the gun?"

Duncan smirked. "I had it in my pocket. When I pulled it out, they were busy feeding cute lines to the freaks up on the stage. They wouldn't have noticed a rocket launcher in their midst." He laughed. "I had a seat on the aisle, and I slipped out at the beginning of Becca's scene and stood by the door. The only reason I failed to kill the bride of Frankenstein was because some guy standing near me jostled my arm when he started cheering."

"Does anyone have questions?" Victoria looked around.

Lennie peered out the window and addressed Roderick's back. "Now you're blocking three cars, sonny. *Two* of them are cops."

Roderick started to get up, but his legs gave way and he fell back on the floor.

Smalley entered the kitchen along with Junior Norton and Tim Eldredge. All three carried drawn guns.

"You can put your weapons away," said Victoria. "We've identified the perpetrator. Sergeant Smalley, you might want to read Bruce Duncan his Miranda warnings."

"You've got to stop taking the law into your own hands," said Casey, when she came to Victoria's for coffee the next morning.

"Would you like my resignation?" said Victoria, pulling off her baseball cap. She'd been wearing it all morning.

Casey sighed. "Forget I said anything. That nut might have killed you."

"I wasn't on his list."

"Telephone for you, Gram," called Elizabeth from upstairs. "You can pick it up in the cookroom."

Casey handed her the phone.

"Mrs. Trumbull, I presume." A sonorous

388

voice. Mellow, plummy, theatrical.

"Yes?"

"I am Nicholas Wright, artistic director of the Provincetown Players."

"I've heard of you," said Victoria.

"I should hope so," said Nicholas Wright. "I am putting together next season's schedule of plays, and would like to discuss with you the purchase of performance rights to *Frankenstein Unbound*."

"Oh?"

"I understand it's an extraordinarily fine play. Demanding."

"Thank you," said Victoria, smoothing her hair. "I'm glad to hear that a reputable theater appreciates the seriousness of the subject and the gravity of the . . ."

"Serious? Grave? No, no, no, Mrs. Trumbull. *Frankenstein Unbound* is one of the finest farces to strut across the boards in decades. Comical. Witty. Slapstick."

There was a long pause before Victoria told him, "I'll have to call you back." She turned the phone off and held it against her chest. McCavity strolled in, glanced around, and leaped into her lap.

"A failure, Casey," Victoria said, and handed the phone to the chief. "A total failure. My serious work was misunderstood. A farce. Slapstick, he called it. That's success. Now the playhouse will turn Equity. Nothing can be done about it."

Casey set the phone back in its cradle on the wall. "You solved two murders and two attempted murders, Victoria. Hardly a failure. You can write another play any old time."

The phone rang again and Casey handed it to Victoria.

"Victoria? It's Ruth Byron. Got a minute?"

"I do," said Victoria. "Several, in fact."

"Wait until you hear what's happened."

"You sound a great deal more cheerful than I feel."

"I fired Dearborn and got rid of my sister, both at once."

"How is Becca?" Victoria asked.

"She's fine. She'll live. She's making the most of her injury, of course."

"You can't blame her."

"That's not what I called you about. The Provincetown Players have hired both Dearborn and Becca, contingent on their performing your play."

Victoria looked up at Casey, her eyes hooded, her wrinkles sagging. "I suppose that means there's no way my play will ever be taken seriously," she said to Ruth Byron.

"But it is being taken seriously! Farces are

difficult plays to stage, probably the most difficult. Timing is critical. Please sell them performance rights, Victoria, will you?"

"I don't want my name on the play."

"And furthermore," Ruth went on, "my board is thrilled with the receipts from those few performances of *Frankenstein Unbound*. We made enough to support the theater for two years. The board declared that this was amateur theater at its best."

"Amateur? Dearborn and Becca? Roderick?"

"Yes, Victoria. Don't you see? You've infused new life into community theater."

Victoria handed the phone back to Casey who again returned it to the wall cradle. She looked out the window at the view of the village beyond her overgrown meadow, at the church spire, the library, and the store.

Casey waited.

Victoria patted McCavity absently. "I suppose they'll want *Dracula* next."

McCavity turned in her lap, faced away from her, lifted a hind leg, and began to clean himself.

ABOUT THE AUTHOR

Cynthia Riggs, a thirteenth-generation Islander, lives on Martha's Vineyard in her family homestead, which she runs as a bed-and-breakfast catering to poets and writers. She has a degree in geology from Antioch College and an MFA in creative writing from Vermont College, and she holds a U.S. Coast Guard Masters License (100-ton). Visit her Web site at www.cynthiariggs.com.